THE WIND BLASTED.

The towns and people began to smear. Like riding the merry-go-round, everything out of control, blurred and spinning. Like making love—the handlebars that feel like her hands as they lock in yours, unlock, and lock again as you speed up. And when you're through the stoplights and back in the fields you slow some, you hear the quiet again, your own breath, your beating heart. Weeds rattle in the ditch, unlatched barn doors bang far away. In the headwind you never hear these. With the wind, they are music.

A CROSSING

A CROSSING

A Cyclist's
Journey Home

BRIAN NEWHOUSE

POCKET BOOKS

New York   London   Toronto   Sydney   Tokyo   Singapore

POCKET BOOKS, a division of Simon & Schuster Inc.
1230 Avenue of the Americas, New York, NY 10020

Copyright © 1998 by Brian Newhouse

Library of Congress Cataloging-in-Publication Data

Newhouse, Brian.
    A crossing : a cyclist's journey home / Brian Newhouse.
      p. cm.
    ISBN: 0-671-56898-1
    1. United States—Description and travel.   2. Bicycle touring—
United States.   3. Newhouse, Brian—Journeys—United States.
I. Title.
E169.04.N49   1998
917.304'929—dc21   98–16184
                                           CIP

First Pocket Books trade paperback printing August 1998

10 9 8 7 6 5 4 3 2 1

Cover design by Brigid Pearson
Cover photo © Ryuichi Sato/Photonica

Text design by Stanley S. Drate/Folio Graphics Co. Inc.

Printed in the U.S.A.

SOME CHILDREN SEE HIM
Lyrics by Wihla Hutson; Music by Alfred Burtt
TRO copyright © 1954 (Renewed) 1957 (Renewed) Hollis Music, Inc.,
New York, NY

For Neal

ACKNOWLEDGMENTS

First thanks to Rochelle Rice and Jonathan Lazear, for green lights. Thanks also to Marge Barrett, Michael Dennis Browne, Brian Cabalka, David Cline, Marilyn Heltzer, Mary Kurcinka, Susie Moncur, Leandra Peak, Dan Slater, and Bonnie White. And because hell has frozen over—best thanks to Angela and Claire.

Some also have wished that the next way to their father's house were here, and that they may be troubled no more with either hills or mountains to go over, but the way is the way, and there is an end.

—JOHN BUNYAN (1628–88)

A
CROSSING

JULY 27

St. Paul

The four bike bags will each hang from their own racks, the two big red ones in the rear, the smaller black ones in front. Most of my evening was spent loading and unloading them, bobbing each one in my hand before test rides under the streetlights out front, until I could pedal no-handed straight as a train.

Left rear: four pairs of boxers, three T-shirts; socks, long underwear, mittens, rain pants, and windbreaker, a pair of street pants and a button-down shirt for church if I decide to go; grease and tools.

Right rear: rye crackers, a can of tuna, two water bottles, my jackknife, riding shorts, pens, and probably too many toiletries. The one-man tent, sleeping bag, and foam pad will ride the rack over the rear wheel.

The front panniers are lighter; the left one holds only a pair of street shoes, spokes, and a ground cloth for the tent, the right contains granola bars and maps triple wrapped in plastic.

In the handlebar bag are my camera and traveler's checks. It all fit with room to spare, so here and there I tucked my helmet, riding cleats, and riding gloves. With even a bit more room left, I laid a book in the right-front pannier down along the maps.

The rest of the evening was spent writing cards to my brother's and sister's families. Clustered within miles of the Illinois farm on which we grew up, they are all having one hard time with why I need to do this. I make sure the tone is pleasant, factual, surfacey. *The mail stopped for two months. . . . Seven o'clock flight to Seattle. . . . The boss at the radio station has hired another announcer temporarily to take my place. . . .* In a strange way they felt like a last will and testament. I reread the cards and thought about adding something profound, but only came up with, *Hope the corn has tasseled by now. Greet your kids from the city uncle.*

Then the phone rang and it was Dad.

"Brian, tell me why on earth you need to do this. What are you trying to prove anyway?"

"Dad, we've been through this."

He didn't say anything for a long minute. When I announced months ago that I was going to ride my bicycle alone from the Pacific to the Atlantic, this same empty silence filled the line. Since then Mother has done the worrying for all three of us, keeping our long-distance calls filled with fret while Dad on the shop extension phone says little or nothing. Each week she's asked why. Most of the time I simply say, I just want to. But now, it was Dad who was actually saying something, or trying to, anyway.

To tell you the honest to God truth, I *don't* know why I'm going. I mean, there are reasons, but they don't add up. If I were straight with him I could tell him that this is an escape; that after ten years together, Lili and I broke up this spring and I jumped right into Karen who wants a husband and says God told her I'm the one; that she prays every day I'll get saved. These would be reasons enough, wouldn't they? But he, too, prays I'll get saved, preferably before I leave on this trip and smack into some westbound Peterbilt.

But that's not it. And I don't know that there is an *it*. All I know is that at twenty-eight years nearly everything in my life feels like someone else's creation. I just want to, that's why. I just want out. And I've never wanted anything so bad.

Tonight, without Mother on the other line, Dad's silence stretched into the sound of frustration or worry or something he couldn't let out.

Then suddenly he blurted, "I wish I could come with you."

I looked across the living room at the bicycle, shined and oiled, at the airline shipping box and panniers stuffed and ready. I couldn't think what to say. He actually sounded serious.

"It's a long ways, Dad."

He took a breath, but said nothing. It seemed he was waiting. I bought another second by moving the phone to the other ear, and in that moment something hardened inside. I tried to joke.

"You'd need new tires for your Huffy."

He laughed that dry, easy chuckle of his to cover whatever emotion had almost risen to plain speech, then he said goodbye.

JULY 29

 30 MILES

Sedro Woolley, Washington

And so it was: the great adventure starts with a pie in the face.

The Greyhound dropped me off along the beach in Anacortes this morning. I pulled the bike from the hatch and put it back together. My hands shook with excitement. This pudgy bald guy came up all smiles.

"Nice bike," he said. "Where you heading?"

"Coast of Maine."

"No kidding. Where's your buddies? Which way you going?"

"I'm by myself," I said, pulling the bungee cord over the sleeping bag. "The northern tier, Idaho, Montana, North Dakota, Minnesota. Wisconsin, then I'll ferry across Lake Michigan and cut through Michigan, Canada, into upstate New York and through New England."

He sighed and squatted next to the bike.

"I did this ten years ago," he said. "But we had a whole group, ten, twelve of us. Wound up in D.C. We ate like horses."

He dragged a finger across the chain and looked at the oil trail on his skin. "Best damn thing I ever did." He shook his head and sighed again.

A tour bus parked behind us touched its horn. The guy wiped his finger on the asphalt, stood, and held out his hand.

"Don't know if I'd do it alone, though." He pumped my hand for probably ten seconds. After about seven or eight seconds I tried to withdraw my hand. He looked embarrassed, then walked to the bus.

By the time I swung my leg over the seat, he was on the bus, his face pressed like an anxious ten-year-old's against the window. I stepped into the pedals and shoved off. I pushed the handlebars left to avoid a parked car, but the bike went straight. I leaned left, right, wobbled, then toppled onto the car, feet still strapped in the toe clips. I was so excited to begin, I'd forgotten to tighten the bolt that secures the handlebars. I lay red-faced against the car. The bars flopped and swung in the sun. The bus drove by, the man's face frozen in laughter.

Bolt tightened, I coasted toward the beach. Tide was out. At a big puddle I got off, set the rear tire into the salty water, and knelt to put my hand in beside it. The sun was strong, and the water like a bath.

Months ago—when all I wanted was *out*, out of the winter-bound Midwest and the relationships I seem so proficient at screwing up—a picture like this formed in my head and some nights I fell asleep staring at it as if it were etched on the bedroom ceiling. The rear tire dipped in the Pacific, the front in the Atlantic. Now I watched my fingers wave up at me from this shining little Pacific pool. We're here. About to begin. Way out, a light west wind spangled the ocean surface into a billion tiny mirrors. As I got back on the bike, with the light and wind pressing me east, I don't know if I've ever felt such happiness.

Over the hill lay stands of lanky Douglas fir and long narrow fields of strawberries and broccoli. My intention was to keep it easy today. Break-in miles. I kept tabs on the right knee—both of the doctors I consulted said it could go fine, or blow anytime—and decided to stop after thirty miles. I spread my map on a picnic table in a Sedro Woolley park, and was checking it for the nearest place to camp when a guy rode up decked in silver panniers and a halogen lamp. Beautiful blond hair past his shoulders. His socks matched his bags.

"You ridin' the coast?" His voice was deep and smooth.

"To the Atlantic if that's what you mean. You?"

"South. Malibu." He flipped up his mirror shades. "You gonna camp here?"

"I wanted to." I nodded at the No Camping sign.

He craned his neck around. "Wow, guess I missed it."

OK—Rules of the Road. Now is as good a time as any to lay them down. First, no car rides. Second, no walking hills. Third, no hangers-on. That's what bugged me about the guy back at the bus. He wanted something. You could tell. If not to take a little piece from me or this trip, then to give it. I don't want either. Malibu here was going to pop the question about riding or camping together any second. This trip is about escaping connections and if you ride with somebody you always wind up splitting everything—food, toilet paper, tent oxygen. Malibu didn't seem like a compromise I wanted to consider. Especially on the first day.

"We're in the Skagit River Valley, see, here's the river." He spread his map over mine and traced a line of blue with his pinkie. He wore a little gold ring on it. "It's cut a pretty wide hole in these hills. I bet if we tool through town we'll find a flat spot, right down on the river to pitch tents. Might be mosquitoes, but it'd be free." He showed me his teeth. They were perfect.

I've always had trouble believing really good-looking people. They sell stuff. And this guy rode a silver Schwinn Paramount, about $2,400 worth of bicycle, *with matching panniers*, for crying out loud. I looked him up and down again, everything about him so fancy and tight, and then realized: camping with this guy would be more adventure than compromise.

Together we coasted out of the park and pedaled toward the Skagit River. His name is Lars. He is my age, twenty-eight. He dropped out two credits shy of a University of California engineering Ph.D.

"Now, bike touring's my life," he said. "That, and wind-surfing. I teach wind-surfing in Malibu when I need the money and when I'm not out here. Man, all I need's to feel the wind in my hair." The little breeze puffed his pretty blond mane over his back. The mirror shades were flipped down.

We stopped at a grocery and he cruised the aisles, shades still down. As we were loading our bikes outside, a rider on an old Schwinn coasted up to us. His whole face was a smile.

"Gentlemen," he said. "Duncan, from Canada. Where you two off to?"

I looked at Lars. Great. We were now "you two."

"We just met," I said, "and he's going south. I'm from Minnesota and I'm heading for the Atlantic. Just started today at the Pacific."

"Well, I'm honored to meet you!" He held out his hand and I shook it. It was wide, strong, sweaty. Lars glanced at his own after he shook hands, maybe wary of a little residue. Duncan was about five-four, and his thighs and arms were heavily muscled. He wore the old-style black wool riding shorts and rode a Schwinn Varsity, the tin lunch pail of bicycles.

"You men bedding down here for the night?" His voice had the strain of all-day dirt and wind.

"Lars here has a map that says we might be able to find a spot by the Skagit," I said.

"Join us if you want," Lars added.

We found a campsite near the Skagit outside town. I unrolled my one-man tent and smiled at the Minnesota air trapped in its wrinkles and folds.

Normally I wouldn't write about a bath, but this one will be with me until I die, I imagine. The Skagit is born miles overhead in the Cascades, the confluence of creeks named Thunder, Ruby, Lonetree, and Panther. Melted snow and rainy Pacific winds feed it until it roars off the mountains a frothy, freezing green. I peeled the sweaty cleats from my feet and stepped in. A herd of Holsteins muzzling clover on the other side of the river jerked when I screamed from the cold. Naked in the shallows, I soaped and rinsed, then baby-stepped into its middle, my nuts clinging high to my crotch. I lay back in the freezing water for just a second, and as I came up the sun edged out from behind a cloud. The Skagit turned into a blinding silver ribbon.

I heard laughter behind me, and quickly ducked back under to hide. A man and boy were canoeing the fast water near shore. The boy was in front, laughing for the speed. I stayed under as long as I could, but within seconds the cold was burning my skin. By the time they pulled even with me, I couldn't take it anymore.

I stood. What the hell. I waved.

The man smiled and lifted his paddle in a little wave back. The boy looked like he'd just seen Saskwatch.

"Dad, look!"

"Yes, I see," the man said reassuringly.

The kid couldn't stop staring. As they floated past he turned in his seat. Another few yards and the canoe slid into a fast riffle, and right then the boy stood for a better view of yours truly. The canoe heaved hard right.

"Sit down," the man barked. His voice echoed, pealing off the cow barn.

The boy plunked onto his seat and the canoe leaned even sharper to the right. The river caught the gunwale and slopped inside. The man countered hard left, nearly pitching his boy overboard. The river caught the other side and poured more water in on them. But they centered finally and began paddling again. They slid into the silver stretch of river.

"Don't freeze 'em off, now," the man called back to me.

They weren't frozen, but they were nearly up to my Adam's apple by the time I stepped onshore. My whole body felt raw. And clean.

I toweled and dressed, watching the father and son float downriver into the sunset. I sat on the bank to put my shoes on. The warmth of blood came back into my hands and feet. The peace of this whole scene, the cows, the river—I sat there, one shoe on, and watched the sterling water. A last riff of the boy's laughter came back on the breeze.

I remembered my own father and me in a canoe. It was just a nearby farm creek, nothing so grand as the Skagit. Most years it slithered unnoticed through northern Illinois and made a quick escape to the west, no wider than a summer leap for a twelve-year-old, but that spring the rains had thundered down and down like never before. It was Lent and, sealed within the farmhouse, I'd looked out the streaking windows and wondered if God couldn't stop crying for the death of His Son. Maybe He was just pissed off enough to drown us all. The creek caught the downpour and the run-off from forty miles of fields, and on Palm Sunday blew its banks.

Dad's life was quiet and inward: the fieldwork, the Bible and the radio, time spent with my brother and me, all of it fashioned by the clockwork of the growing season. Once or twice a year, though, a need for adventure would put him to something reckless like canoeing a once-harmless creek.

I was in front and we were flying. Newly downed trees slid underneath us. The canoe bucked through troughs of froth, cold foam spilling in. The sun punched through the clouds for the first time in weeks; its brilliance both hurt and felt good. Once, my voice broke as I called out to Dad in the rear, "Big rock on the right!" A few icy drops immediately hit the back of my neck, then I heard his paddle slam against the canoe's left side. The bow jerked hard and safe to port.

We'd just come racing out of a bend and I saw it first: the barbed-wire fence no more than thirty yards away. Its bottom was underwater but it stretched upright probably five feet and spread across the creek like a dam. In front of it lay a strand of electric cattle fence that I knew would kill us where we sat.

I whipped around. When he lifted his head he saw the fence, then me, and froze in mid-stroke. "We gotta go back!" he yelled and began to shovel the water backward. Tendons leaped from the wrinkles of his neck. I tried my best for a few strokes but we might as well have tried to paddle up a waterfall. I yelled back, "It's no good!" I heard him swear for the first time. "Damn!" He stopped and stared ahead, frozen.

I looked at the thin wire ahead, glanced back a last time, then grabbed the gunwale and jumped over.

The water rushed to my shoulders and the freezing cold fastened my hand to the canoe's lip. I didn't take a second to look at him. I could feel his weight, he was still seated. I stumbled toward shore, fingers wrapped hard over the gunwale.

He never even said a simple thank-you, and we spoke of it only once years later. I remember there were friends around the dinner table.

He said, "I honestly don't know what would've happened to us if you hadn't jumped out and pulled us to shore." The pride and appreciation on his face that moment has stayed with me my entire life. I've never seen it on him since.

Duncan and Lars were both eating when I got back. We sat around a campfire and swatted mosquitoes. Duncan is headed southwest out of Canada.

"Started up in Saskwatch, near Regina. Been aiming for Seattle. Girlfriend of mine lives there. I'll hole up for a while then head to Vancouver. Another girlfriend up there."

"Why are you doing this on a bike?" I asked.

"It's all I can do. Couple years ago cops caught me DWI. Took my license. I needed to get to work, so I started riding a bike. Had a good time on that bike going to work, parties, then more parties." He looked at his lap, shook his head and laughed. "Last summer they got me DWI again."

"On a bike?"

"Yeah. Bastards, eh?" He nodded at his mangled Schwinn. "Now I'm ten-speedin' everywhere. Should of thought of it a long time ago, but ten-speeds wasn't cool then."

Why at that moment, I have no idea, but as if by signal Washington's mosquito population swarmed us. Lars dove to his tent. I swatted myself and stamped around the campsite. But Duncan walked placidly into the pines and returned with dried branches and long wet grasses. He laid the boughs on the fire. Sparks geysered into the blue-black sky and the heat pulled the skin tight across my cheekbones. Next came several handfuls of grass. The heavy white smoke smelled like Christmas and summer at the same time.

"There, you bastards" he said, coughing. "That'll keep you down."

I walked into the smoke and watched him layer the fire. His arms looked like cable laid over bone. When we hadn't swatted a mosquito for at least a minute, we both sat back down in the dirt and he knifed open a cantaloupe. "You can come out now," he called to Lars.

Lars appeared wearing this high-tech sombrero that draped a shimmery mosquito mesh the length of his body. He sat away from the fire at first, and the light caught the mesh so that he looked like he was wrapped in aluminum foil. As the fire died back he huddled closer. He nipped blades of grass and dropped them into the smoke. The closer he moved, the less we could see of his face.

"So, how much does your frame weigh on that thing, Duncan," Lars asked.

Duncan looked at his Schwinn. That poor Varsity. Its top tube and chainstays were dented and nicked, its color was indistinguishable. It looked like he'd found it in a Dumpster.

"Hell if I know," he said.

"Brian, you know what yours weighs, don't you?"

"Sorry, I don't. Not exactly. Somewhere around fifteen, sixteen maybe."

"Are you kidding?" he said. "What kind of tube angles you got?"

"Oh, you know, general touring angles. Pretty long. Don't tell me you know your tube angles."

Lars did and was kind enough to fill us in beginning with the seat tube to the down tube. Seventy-three here, seventy-one there. He launched into the components, how much each cost, weighed, blah, blah, woof, woof. I looked at Duncan. He shrugged. This was inevitable. Equipment Wars. My spoke's bigger than your spoke.

The fire was now a bed of coals. Duncan tossed his last two big handfuls of boughs in and they crackled like tiny firecrackers. Lars took off his sombrero. His long blond hair was wet with sweat. "Well, I guess that's about it for me." He walked to his tent and zipped himself in.

Neither of us said anything for several minutes. The silence was pleasant.

"I busted a guy's jaw when I was locked up," Duncan said. "Judge when he let me free said I'd have to go to A.A. every week, and that I get into fights for the same reason I drink. Night I left Saskwatch my stepfather said, 'I hope you find something out there because goddamn you need it.' Suppose they're both right." He leaned back on the heels of his hands and looked up at the stars that were starting to blink on. Then he nodded at Lars's tent. "Wuss over there don't have a clue."

He walked to his bike and rummaged in his bags. He pulled out a small can and a toothbrush. He knelt and I heard a dull crack from the bike as he pulled the chain off the bicycle. He handled it as if it were a snake, swinging it in front of him about waist high.

"Look at that. Stiffer'n a Mountie's dick." I laughed. He unscrewed the can's lid and dribbled liquid onto the chain as if pouring water down the snake's mouth. A sharp gasoline smell wafted to me. "Some of them think they got one this big." Then he coiled the chain on a rock at his feet and dipped a toothbrush into the can.

"You got a dirty chain, you're ridin' uphill all day," he said, and ground the bristles into the links. He then held the chain up to the firelight. The scrubbed links shone.

"You brought a toothbrush?"

"I brought a toothbrush," I said.

"I mean a *chain* toothbrush? You don't have a spare now, do you, handsome?"

I shook my head. I thought I'd made a pretty good checklist. He walked to his bags and tossed an extra at me. It looked as if it'd been chewed by a dog.

"That's my morning one, but I don't seem to use it much out here. On the house. Get yourself a little can of gas and clean your chain every three, four days." He sat down at his rock. "Pretty teeth ain't gonna get you nothin' out here. But a clean chain will."

He gave short, sharp strokes to each side of the chain, then longer strokes for the belly of the links. He held it up from time to time, grunted, then set it back on the rock. The fire shifted, sparked, dimmed down. He laid more boughs and grass on it. The smoke wisped straight up. The Skagit sounded like distant applause. He flipped the chain end over end after he'd gone once down its length. "So, I told you what I'm doing. Washington is a long ways from Minnesota. Pretty boy like you, I bet there's a woman." He looked up with a little smirk. The fire glinted in his eyes.

"Scores of them," I said. He laughed and set the chain down. He layered the last of the pine and grass onto the fire, then resumed cleaning. I watched him for several minutes and almost said, We were together for ten years if you can believe that, but stopped myself and watched him work up the chain's other side. His gas was running low and he tilted the can to reach it. The toothbrush looked worse every minute. From time to time he wiped the chain with a rag. He looked like a bartender drying glasses. I could've tried to tell him at least some of it. It might've even felt good. But how do you start a story that lasts ten years? We held hands in high school and I can still recall the sensation as if I'd stuck my fingers into a light socket. We were engaged twice and stumbled away from those promises each time. Nearly every spring I wrote her a Dear Jane letter, but I always returned. Ten years of ripping apart and coming back built up a kind of scar tissue between us, stronger than if there'd never been a cut. This year, the day before spring, "no more" fell into Dear Jane. I mailed it and drove dazed around the city. Ten fucking years. Late that evening, I bought these panniers and maps. Just a month later I was at Karen's door, flowers in hand.

"Scores of them," I said again to break the silence.

Duncan finished and held it up for a final inspection. "The trick," he said, "is to have lots of girlfriends. You get yourself one in Regina, you get yourself one in Saskwatch." He held the chain up to his crotch and swung it back and forth. It wagged like a puppy's tail. He had that same face-full of smile as this afternoon when we met. "Keep them all happy. My advice."

He dribbled the last drops of gas into the grass at his feet. He lit a pine twig and ignited the gas. It flared into the thin crescent of a new moon. I always feel hopeful at a new moon. He smiled down at it, then crushed it out. He laid the chain on a rock for drying, pulled a sleeping bag from his panniers, and threw it near the campfire.

"No tent?" I asked. "The mosquitoes are going to suck you dry."

"You lay still, they ain't interested. Try it."

I said good night to him and zipped myself into my tent. Quickly, dozens of mosquitoes complained at the screen.

Now I sit cross-legged with this journal and a flashlight between my teeth. I let the first day come back and see shining things: the rim dipped in the Pacific, the silvered Skagit, and Duncan's little moon.

JULY 30

 52 MILES

Marblemount, Washington

When I crawled out of the tent at six, the sun wasn't quite up yet and the camp was covered in white fog. Forty-five degrees on the little jacket pocket thermometer. At the fire ring lay only my bicycle and matted grass where Lars had pitched his shimmery tent and Duncan his mangy sleeping bag. Wheel tracks snaked toward the bridge. Somebody was up there swinging a leg over a seat. Through the fog I watched his first pedal strokes, short strong jabs. It had to be Duncan. I knelt where he'd lain. The grass was still warm.

There was little to see except fog this morning, so what I know of the Skagit River Valley is only how it sounds and smells as it wakes on a summer morning. A heifer bellowing to be milked; her herdmates echoing her as if it were their idea first. The river smelled exotic to me, filled with glacier melt and nothing you'd smell in the brown flat of a Midwestern river. But I get ahead of myself. The first miles I wasn't aware of any of this. The damp put a catch in my right knee at eleven o'clock on each spin, and I worried over that for nearly an hour.

From time to time I thought I saw a biker ahead of me in the fog. I neither called out nor sped up. I'll meet them, they'll go. I'll go. Like life, people just show up unannounced, then leave.

The road lifted suddenly to begin the real climb into the Cascades. A mile up I stopped, panting heavily. The tires had to be low. But the gauge read what it should, ninety-five pounds. I started again and got only a quarter-mile before I had to stop. The bike still dragged as if the tires were half flat. Ninety-five, dead on again. Maybe the wheels were out of true. The front one spun fine and straight. The rear—I could barely lift. Mystery solved. I got on again and discovered I'm loaded so heavy I have to pedal *downhill*. From then on, the morning got cheerier and cheerier. The fog lifted to a concrete overcast. A bee stung my left ear. By noon I was only twenty miles from Sedro Woolley, less than half of where I'd hoped to be. My legs felt like poles.

I filled my bottles and scarfed stale fruit pies at a last-chance convenience store halfway up the Cascades. Junior high boys gathered as I laid the bottles in the pannier. They stood too close and talked too loud, their voices sounding like dentist drills.

"Where you goin'?" a freckled face yelled. He elbowed through them and breathed fresh bubble gum right in my face.

"The Atlantic."

I might as well have told them I'm Jesus. They shut up and parted around me. I zipped the pannier and put a foot in the pedal. All down the driveway, heaving one leaden pedal up after another, I savored the adolescent awe. And that actually helped for a while—yanking myself into the Cascades and knowing that somebody thought this trip remarkable. But soon that evaporated. I pushed up hills into quiet valleys of lush fern and Douglas fir, and hoped for a town so I could ship the extra weight home. But there was nothing. All afternoon, at two and three miles an hour, I climbed into more nothing, only thinning air and pewter walls that leaped higher and more jagged at every hairpin.

I stopped a good thirty miles short of my goal, exhausted and dispirited. It is now 3:18 A.M. I'm too sore to sleep and the place I've pitched this tent feels like it is actually sprouting rocks.

JULY 31

 51 MILES

Rainy Pass, Washington

I've got to get rid of this stuff. I can't pedal one more inch. Today was ten hours for fifty-one miles. Fifty-one straight-up miles. Even I can work the math on that one: a whopping 5 m.p.h. average. I didn't talk to a single person all day, just pulled higher into the Cascades. Head down and in granny gear. Tonight, camp is the men's washroom of a deserted national park. I couldn't even set up the tent, I'm so tired. The sleeping bag is rolled out by the urinal, believe it or not the cleanest spot on the floor. It's drizzling outside, I'm freezing, the bottles are empty, the water here has been shut off, and except for a tablespoon of strawberry jam I'm out of food. I just heard a rustle in the woods outside this john, like a bear shaking a tree or something. I locked the door. It reeks in here.

If it's solitude I came for, I've got it in spades.

Tomorrow, with any luck, I'll be in Mazama. They should have a post office where I can ship stuff back home. Shampoo, contact lens solutions, a washcloth, these maybe add up to a pound. Foam sleeping pad, maybe a half pound. The vise grip, that's over a pound; I better save it, though—I'll need it if I blow a spoke. T-shirts, boxers, socks, spare spokes, I can do without most of this stuff. I might get five or six pounds.

And then there's the book. *Making Peace with God* by Billy Graham. It's got to weigh nearly two pounds. Why on *earth* did I bring it? I guess I thought this trip would be a time to get spiritual or something. I might as well have brought a brick. I remember the morning before I left, getting sucked into the mall's Christian bookstore, like always. I stood in the aisle and looked at the dust jacket. Graham's face feels etched on the back of my eyeballs. Dad wanted the whole family to watch Graham's crusade broadcasts when I was a boy, though it was usually just me stranded in the living room with him. My brother and sisters, even Ma, always found that the best time to start some project outside.

"The righteousness of the lamb, the atonement of our sins . . ."—Words like these made little sense to me but Dad paid Graham rapt attention and sometimes even took notes. At the end of one particular broadcast, as thousands streamed across some cricket pitch toward Billy to get saved, Dad appeared out of the dark and kneeled at my chair. He put a hand on my leg. He quietly asked if I didn't want to get saved too. The choir hummed "Just as I Am, Without One Plea." Nobody I knew was saved except Dad, and some of the kids at school made fun of him for it. I froze. The TV threw an elbowy shadow of him halfway up the wallpaper. I stared at his shadow and shook my head no.

Two or three times before I left the farm for college I shook my head at him, too afraid even to say the word, scared he'd hate me or maybe even hit me for turning him and Jesus and Billy down. Each time he simply stood, turned the lamps on and the TV off. I've always thought that deep down, Billy had the answers; and however uncool it was with the kids at school, that he and my father shared some unseen connection to Jesus. Here in the mall was a book whose title all but said so. *Making Peace with God.* And of all the books in the world, Whitman, Dickens, Hemingway, or even the Bible, I bought Billy Graham. Good grief.

I don't even want to open it. I know what it says anyway: Just bring it to Jesus, or in Billy's Carolina twang, Jus' brang it to Jayzus. I'd actually hear him if I read it right now in this echoing john, probably even hear his wobbly-voiced choir of blue angels hum "Just as I Am."

My God, I've only been alone a few days, but I'm starting to lose it.

AUGUST 1

74 MILES

Okanogan, Washington

I made Washington Pass by mid-morning and, just
before the road took its dive down the Cascade's eastern slope,
had to stop to put more clothes on. Thirty-eight degrees. A
hard northwest wind nudged at the front wheel. I felt as if I
stood in the door of a jump plane, everything all spread below
me like that, the wind, the cold. The mountains looked like
hands, gray gnarled fingers splayed open and pointing to the
sky: jump, jump.

I tipped over the Pass's ledge and the speedometer flashed
nine, then blanked for several seconds as if rummaging around
in its basement for the old double digits it hasn't used for days.
The first numbers it came back with were 37; then, quickly,
40, 45. 50. The bicycle fled the mountain. I let it go down a
long straight and at the first hairpin I grabbed the brakes until
they sang out. Around the turn, I snapped them off and
watched the speedometer zip through all the numbers up to

54. All the mountain crags and fissures I'd gotten such long slow looks at on the way up, now smeared by smooth and gray.

From the cold or the wind, or from the white-knuckled fact that I have never gone anything remotely close to this fast on a bicycle, the handlebars began to shake badly. I caught an image of me smacking into some jutted piece of roadside rock, and immediately snagged the brakes. The bike shuddered to a stop and I put on every last piece of clothing—rain pants, mittens, wool hat, the works.

A long straightaway opened and I leaned forward, back flat, knees tucked into the frame. The bike held steady through the 30s and 40s and after that I didn't look at the speedometer. I only read the yellow dashes on the asphalt. The wind was thunder through the helmet. Near the bottom the dashes smudged to an almost solid line.

Shampoo, contact lenses and the solutions, hairbrush, two shirts, a pair of pants, two pairs of boxers, four socks, the Walkman. I was on a roll, so I even pitched in the floss. Just before taping the box shut, I tossed in the good Reverend Graham. Third-class postage from Mazama, Washington, to Brian Newhouse, St. Paul, Minnesota. Nine pounds. The bike feels fifty lighter.

What was wet and cold and lush with ferns on the eastern side of the Cascades has turned to sand, heat, and scrub pine here on the west. Tonight, I'll sleep in dusty Okanogan. Twenty-three hundred call it home, and there's a bar for almost every one of them. I asked a pair of old thick-browed men outside one where I could camp tonight. They searched the sidewalk for answers, then shuffled away. A third guy directed me to the town park.

I dropped a quarter into the pay phone, and smiled at the sound of my parents' ringing phone. The telecommunications revolution has yet to visit the farm. Their phone rings like a Bronx cheer.

Mother was frantic with worry for the first few minutes. Yes, I'm eating fine, no, no problems with cars, yes, it's fun, no, please don't send me a train ticket.

Dad got on the shop extension. He said almost nothing, as usual, asked no questions about how I am, just chuckled in all the right spots to let us know he was still there. I could see him in his baggy blue overalls, the phone crooked in his shoulder, maybe a piece of gutter in one hand, a tin snip in the other.

The conversation drew on, and I began to wonder about his silence. After fundamental Christianity, his interest lies primarily in his shop—so unlike any other farm shop you've seen. Besides the usual bench full of wrenches and drills, this is where he slaughtered turkeys for thirty years. "Dressed" them is the euphemism of the trade. "He's out dressing turkeys," Ma would say when as a boy I asked of Dad's whereabouts. If he wasn't in the field or garden, he was in the shop, dressing. One of my earliest memories of him is of a fall morning when he picked me up; I was probably three or so, and remember his cheek, bristly with beard and tight-red from the cold—a streak of rust-brown turkey blood drying on his neck.

I was still a boy when Dad retired from turkey slaughter, so memories of the place are made more fantastic by the way death plays on a child's imagination. Five live birds at a time were hung from their feet in a rack that looked like it was straight out of some Vincent Price movie. The little knife he used was no larger than a good-size kitchen paring knife, but it was the Lord's own Sword of Death, the way Dad slid it into the bird's wrinkled orange neck, spewing blood. And all the machinery that goes with butchery, the rack to dunk the dead bird in scalding water, the rotating vat with its black rubber fingers to rub the bird of its feathers, the steel-neck vacuum sealer that sucked the air from the bird's final home, the plastic bag—all perfectly medieval to me then and now.

A large tin trough caught the blood from the turkeys' throats. It had a hole in one end, from which the blood spilled onto the floor. Dad had chiseled a little groove into the concrete, where blood coursed to a hole in the wall, splashing finally into the open pasture. After each day's dressing, he'd throw open the big shop door and hose the whole floor down. I couldn't stand the killing, so this was when I usually showed up. The scent of blood and cold water on concrete is always in the back of my nose, and sometimes just the smell of rain on a sidewalk puts me in his shop again.

But the shop was also his studio for creating. Odd, wondrous machines rolled out its door, including a contraption to detassel corn that looked inspired by Chitty Chitty Bang Bang. It even worked. And a three-wheeled go-cart made for my brother and me out of steel posts, a third-hand lawnmower engine, and a tractor seat. It ran fast as hell until one hot afternoon one of its welds snapped and the left wheel shot clean off, pitching me at 30 m.p.h. into a ditch. My survival made me an instant celebrity to my brother.

Dad worked out his religion in the shop, too. I could walk in there this very afternoon and find, stashed in the tiny wooden drawers of the screws-and-nails cabinet, a half dozen breast-pocket notebooks filled with Scripture passages in his strong, straight hand. The radio was rusted on WMBI-AM, the Moody Bible Institute station out of Chicago. In the rafters rests a life-size cross made of two-by-fours, and around it is wrapped a length of old garden hose, the end of which holds a hand-carved snake's head. I asked him about this once and he quoted a passage from Revelation. That's what life is, he said, the battle between the serpent and the cross. "And we have to choose."

The blood has seeped into the concrete, and even though he hasn't slit a turkey's throat for twenty years, if I step in there on muggy Illinois afternoons when that cold concrete sweats, Dad is once again the man who can make things die, the man who builds you a go-cart, and the man whose religion scares the shit out of you. I turn from the shop, and all these things are mixed up together in my head. His slaughtering and his Christianity. His generosity and his hardness. His whole life and our whole relationship are crystallized there in that shop. It's no wonder my feelings for him are so mixed up. Probably no wonder, too, that he says so little on the phone with me and Ma.

"Bri, hi there! Where are you?" Karen, three time zones away, practically lit the phone booth with the smile I knew spread across her face. She's vacationing in Vermont with her family.

"Hi yourself! Somewhere in Washington. In a desert."

"Washington has a desert?"

"Just east of the Cascades. A real Hoss and Little Joe desert."

"Are you all right, Bri?"

"I'm fine."

"Oh, I'm so glad you called, you sure you're OK? Any scrapes with cars?"

"No, I'm fine, really."

"Are you eating enough?"

"Yeah, a lot of grapes and crackers."

"Bri, you've got to eat better than that."

"No, it tastes good. Besides, it's cheap. It's nice to hear your voice, Karen. Talk to me."

She told me about the card games and boat rides, her dad who this week celebrated ten years of sobriety, her mother who still drinks like a fish. (My observation, not hers; she would never say such a thing.)

After that, silence. I waited for her, I guess, to ask me about something other than food and cars, or tell me something wonderful I could take with me into the desert tomorrow. But the silence drew on and finally I asked her what she'd been doing right before the phone rang.

"I was out on the deck, just sitting there looking at the stars, praying for you."

I dragged my toe across the grit on the phone booth floor and the conversation fell dead. I didn't ask what she's praying for. We'd just get into it again. I squinted at the late sun, thanked her for the thought, and said good-bye.

She has been praying for me, I imagine, since the night we met four months ago. A woman at work first mentioned Karen to me. "She's a sweet Christian woman, and she's been dumped on too many times. She needs to meet good men so she knows they're not all jerks." The next weekend I was invited to a small dinner at Karen's. Lili and I had broken up four weeks earlier, the world looked bent and disheveled still, but I straightened my smile and knocked on Karen's door thinking, sure, I'll go and be nice.

I remember two moments from that night. The first is when

she opened the door. A tall, slender woman with blue-green eyes and dark chestnut hair waving past her shoulders, and regal cheekbones she'd later reveal came from part Cherokee blood. Her smile was broad in the thin streetlight. I stammered over my own name.

The second came halfway through dinner when one of the guests, a dour heavy woman with horrific acne, said, "Let's go around the table and each tell how we came to meet the Lord."

I was pouring milk into my coffee. It boiled into clouds and I wanted to dive in and hide. I felt the exact numbness of fear as when my father asked me years earlier to get saved. From then on I heard only bits. For one guest it had been the crisis of a failed marriage that "led me to Christ." For the dour woman, it'd been more of a rational decision. "You just look at it and it all adds up." Something like that.

Karen had, as her friend said, been dumped on by men, starting with dear old Dad the former drunk. When one day she realized there wasn't a person in this world she could trust, "I turned to Jesus. Since I gave my life to the Lord six years ago I've had such a peace." She must've repeated that phrase ten times. Such a peace. Now she has such a peace.

I stirred the coffee and hoped they'd forget me. God moves in mysterious ways. The phone rang. A minute later another guest arrived and I stood up to give him my place. I made some lame excuse about having to leave.

I went back to her house a week later for a variety of reasons, maybe none of them all that good. She is a strikingly beautiful woman. She seemed kind. She seemed glad to have me at her table. And the slight darkness that came over her when she just sat there, when she wasn't smiling or talking about the peace of the Lord, a darkness that admitted to a hard life—*that* seemed to me to be the real Karen, and even more beautiful than the chipper Christian who professed such a

peace. Like I said, it wasn't the best reason but part of me
wanted to be some kind of an answer for her, to be Good Men.

Our first date three months ago was in her backyard, where
we fired up the barbecue and watched the huge orange neon
Schmidt Brewery letters nearby blink on and off one at a time.
She brought a barbecue sauce from the kitchen, and the smell
of it in the air that night, rising with the crickets' rasp, is still
with me. One of her first stories was of the umpire she used to
date whose idea of a good time was parking her in the stands
while he called a game. She slapped burgers on the grill and
called him a jerk.

Two weeks later she set manicotti before me and the thyme,
rosemary, and basil were nothing short of revelation to my
church potluck mouth. After that, I was at her table most Friday and Saturday nights. Sometimes after supper we'd sit in
her living room filled with antiques and art, and leaf through
the books on the Italian Renaissance masters. She has an MFA
in painting and design, but is now a lawyer. I loved how her
face lit up with stories about this painting or that, why one was
more important than the rest. I looked in her bedroom once
when she was busy in the kitchen. A big black Bible lay on the
nightstand, and the walls held three large Georgia O'Keeffe
tulip prints, the ones that look more like dark and slender bodies than flowers. We'd take long slow walks along the dirty
streets near her house. She has big teeth and when she
laughed they beamed in the street light. One night, kids
jumped from behind a hedge and screamed right in our faces
just to scare the shit out of us. Which worked pretty well. She
locked fiercely onto my arm and held it all the way to her
house. I wished I could thank those kids.

At dawn on a June Saturday, I rode to her door with a quart
of fresh strawberries.

"You called room service, didn't you?" It was a cliché and I hoped she was too sleepy to notice. I held up the berries.

"Bri," she said, and she hugged me, the smell of sleep still warm in her soft tangled hair.

More and more, my training rides came by her house, sometimes even when I knew she wasn't there. I just liked to see it, imagine us in the backyard, then pedal on. My desire to be her savior, to be Good, was still there. But something warmer moved in beside that. Maybe you can call it love, or the beginnings of it.

Early last month I asked her why, with all her art books and her years of study, she had none of her own art on the walls.

"I don't have it anymore. I gave it all away," she said.

"You don't have anything left?"

"I have pictures." She opened an album and pulled out slides. "The work is all gone, but I took these pictures before I got rid of it. They're from art school.

"This is glass I used to blow." There were wonderful bulbs and bottles, abstract little vases, each swirled with colors I couldn't begin to name. "And here are the metal pieces." Whimsical little sculptures, glass prisms set in them.

"These were my best," she said and pulled two slides from the album. "I *worked* on these." A pair of small rectangular women's hair combs, extravagantly detailed.

"You did this?"

"Yeah. Back then."

"Where are they now?"

"Most of the stuff I gave away."

She went to her bedroom and came back with a shoe box. Wrapped in tissue paper lay two combs, cobalt blue and blood-orange glass shards rimmed in mirror-bright silver. They took your breath away.

"Karen, they're stunning."

She scrunched her lips disapprovingly and shook her head. "Here, they're yours," she said, and held out the box. She walked into her kitchen and busied herself at the sink.

"Karen, these are amazing. Why don't you keep it up?"

"That's all behind me now, Brian."

"Why? Why are you even a lawyer? God, you're an artist."

"No I'm not, not now. If I did anything now, it'd look much different."

"How?"

Here she faced me. "I'd want my art now to serve a purpose. See, that stuff was all done before I got saved. That's why I got rid of it. That was the old me. Christ created a new person when I gave my life to Him. If I did anything with art now, it'd be for His glory, to serve Him. He's everything now."

I took the combs home. I love them. Over the next weeks I pulled them from their shoe box and tried to imagine the Karen who used to be. One comb rides in my handlebar bag now.

The following Friday and Saturday nights, I kept hoping the Karen of blues and oranges would crop up. I'd have liked to meet her. But the new, improved Karen was scrubbed white and out of the closet, and more and more she let slip phrases like, "You know, I was telling Jesus this afternoon about my job. . . . I think the Lord is pleased we're friends, Brian. . . . I just felt a closeness of the Holy Spirit all day today. . . ." I'd change the subject. This was the new Karen and she liberally applied the Lord, like salt, to everything. Our suppers were now prefaced with long chummy prayers, as if Jesus were actually perched on the counter licking her incredible tomato sauce from His finger. The week before I left for Seattle, she gave me a picture of her dressed all in white. That, too, rides in my handlebar bag.

One cold, late April evening, on her living room floor with a cup of tea, she popped the big one.

"Are you saved, Brian?"

I let the tea sit on my tongue as long as I could.

"No."

She stared into her cup.

"I thought maybe you were," she said. She blew at hers and steam puffed up.

"There's nothing to be afraid of," she said and sat the cup down. She had her doe eyes on. "God loves you, you know, and wants you to come to him."

"Yeah, I know."

"So, what are you waiting for? He loves you. Brian, we've been getting to know each other these months but before we go any —" She smiled. "Well, I just know that Jesus has his hold on your life in a special way, and he wants into your life. He loves you so much."

The paralysis started in my gut. It always starts there, the same tetanus I felt as a child when Dad knelt beside me during the Billy Graham telecasts. This sensation, though, with Karen, had a different edge, an anger that coursed through the legs and arms. Out the window, the neon Schmidt sign flared phosphorescent orange one letter at a time.

"Can I pray for you, Brian?"

I shrugged.

She knelt beside me, clamped her eyes shut, and frowned.

"Oh Jesus," she started, breathy, "this is your child, Brian, that I know you love so much. So much that you came to die for him, Lord. He comes before you. Lord, I feel he's afraid, Lord. Take that away from him, oh Jesus. Lift it from him, God. I pray you lift it from him. Free him from whatever he carries that keeps him from you, and come into his heart. Yes Lord, tonight. Come into his life, now."

Her grimace loosened but her eyes remained furrowed shut and she looked like she was holding her breath. A minute went by, then two. Then she whispered, "Thank you Jesus, I praise your name tonight, oh Lord, be here, Lord," and waited some more.

Tuck, tucka, tah, tah, tah, tah, tucka, kah, kah . . . Her teeth and tongue clucked in a dry mechanical whisper. She laid her hand on the back of my neck. Immediately, my entire body went cold as if heat fled beneath her hand. I wanted to run, but, as always, the paralysis was total. She took the same authority as my father. They can talk to God. I cannot, and have to wait till they're through.

Tuck, tuck, tah, tah, kuck . . . It sounded like a chain whipping through a rusty derailleur. I began to shiver, and only then did she pull her hand away. I stood and said I had to go. At the door I asked her what those sounds were.

She smiled tensely. "That's my own prayer language. God gave it to me to talk to Him. It's prayer too deep for words. Pray to Jesus tonight, Brian. I'll pray too."

We didn't talk that week until she came to my house, sat on the couch and put her face in her hands, and started to cry.

"You aren't saved, Brian. God won't allow me to go on getting closer to you if you're not saved. I just can't do this. I've been praying for you, but you've got to make that choice for Him yourself."

This is my story, I'm afraid—this is the minute my duplicity really began. I touched her shoulder, helped her get up, and we quietly hugged at the door, while inside I was screaming, "Who the hell are you to judge me, to do this to me? GET OUT OF MY HOUSE AND STAY OUT!" A minute after the door closed she came back, still crying.

"Brian, I'm not going to abandon you. I know God wouldn't want me to do that. He probably wants me to stick by you more than ever. I'm gonna be here for you, Brian." I nodded. She hugged me and left. I shut the door and wanted even then, in the silence of my own place, to let that scream go, but couldn't.

Tonight, I sleep with a drunk.

He slurred "whathell time zit?" when I asked if I could join him in this gazebo. Two picnic tables stand between us, and all I can make out in the street light is a huge humped darkness against the wall. He just turned and I heard glass against wood, saw the bottle roll into the shadows. Whether he's passed out or asleep, I just hope he's deep enough gone to stay on his side of the tables. Good night to him.

AUGUST 2

74 MILES

Republic, Washington

I felt a jolt in my back and jerked awake.

"Whatime zit."

Another jolt. Bearings coming slowly through the fog. Bicycle trip. Washington state. Gazebo. Large drunk a couple yards away.

"I said, whatime zit."

I squinted at my watch. "Four-thirty."

Gradually he came into focus, such as it was. A hump on a bench. The jolts had been his feet striking the gazebo's wooden floor. He stood and stumbled my way. The boards groaned. He must've been six and a half feet tall. He stopped and leaned onto the nearer picnic table. The bag was zipped to my neck but I got an arm out and patted the boards until I found the tire pump. He turned backward a bit, then fell to the bench. The whole gazebo shuddered. He tilted a bottle to his mouth and I heard teeth against glass, then the bottle shattering as he threw it where he'd slept.

35

He pivoted and faced me. I grabbed the pump. He leaned forward. I tensed and could only think of, Go for the eyes.

He stood and shuffled till he was right over me. I put my left hand on the floor for leverage. He wove above me in the dark. Then he turned and his foot grazed my sleeping bag. He lurched down the steps. By the time I sat up and got my glasses on he was on the sidewalk toward downtown. He walked as if it were a ship's deck in high seas.

I wanted to get out of Okanogan, so I was the first customer at the diner downtown. Six o'clock sharp. The kitchen was partially hidden by a long, yellowed mirror. An old Native American woman stepped from behind the mirror, looked at me, and stepped back. Coffee smells and muffled voices floated around the mirror.

I waited ten minutes, the place filling with the odor of fried onions and potatoes, the day's fresh-baked rolls. Another ten minutes passed as I reread the menu and my maps, then cleaned gunk off the helmet strap. A brickish woman with gray hair stacked high above her slid from behind the mirror and one-eyed me. As soon as our eyes met, she leaned back. Finally, a young Native woman with long black braids came to take my order.

Locals entered around seven. Each time, I heard their conversation from the entryway, then, as they caught sight of me, it shifted abruptly to whispers. I'd look up and they'd jerk their eyes away. It was my riding clothes, I know, that and the fact I was a stranger: when in doubt, stare at it, it might go away.

It says somewhere in one of the Gospels, doesn't it: "When you leave that town that has not welcomed you, shake the dust from your sandals. . . . Sodom and Gomorah will fare better on Judgment Day than that place." Something like that. I banged my cleats against the bike frame at the city limits of Okanogan, pop. 2,307.

An hour outside Okanogan and the desert sun was warm on the shoulder. The Cascades' damp cold blew away. Around me spread an honest-to-God desert. I've only seen them in picture books before and didn't know they could be so beautiful. Peach-colored earth, dry gulches a shade deeper. A fierce little red bush clinging to the creekbeds. Ashen cow bones. And lush apple orchards tucked next to the Okanogan River, their deep green speckled with early fruit.

In the late morning a figure appeared in the handlebar mirror. Another rider, a half mile or so behind. Instinctively, I picked up a gear and pedaled harder. I didn't want him. Maybe like Okanogan didn't want me. No. It was everything, the desert, the way the tires hummed, the way they giggled when they hit a soft stretch of road fill. These were all I wanted.

I picked up another gear and quickened the pace. That's what it's all about, pace. Strangers meet, ride together as little as a mile, and sure as the sun rises they'll start to sprint around each other to see who's bigger and stronger. Most times they won't even introduce themselves—just make absolutely sure they don't look like they're breathing too fast as they try to pound each other. (Another tip: flex the biceps almost imperceptibly when you pass; you'll feel like a schmuck at first, but that lasts no longer than when he blasts by you.) Eventually, a winner is declared and the wimp hangs on, if he can. I usually can't. Pace is everything. Pace is ownership.

He was still there and no further back, so I shifted again and checked the map. No towns for miles, and only a few gravel roads off the highway. If he caught me I'd be stuck. I grabbed my biggest gear and nearly killed myself for an hour. He started to gain on me.

"Where you going so fast?" he eventually called, just within earshot. I faked surprise.

"Huh? Oh! East." Touch the brakes, check my own breathing. He glided up.

"You haul, guy," he said. He smiled and was panting hard. My first impression was that he looked like the guy in the Marlboro ads—square jaw and everything. His bike wasn't quite Marlboro, though, a dirty violet color, all beat up. He had panniers the same make as mine.

"East? Where east, Spokane?"

"No. East Coast."

"Whoa. One of *them*. Hats off to you." He pulled his water bottle from its rack. He had to wait for his breath, then he raised the bottle to toast me.

"How about you, where you heading?" Please oh please not east.

"I just started this morning from my grandma's in Okanogan. Not really sure. Somewhere in the Canadian Rockies, maybe Banff. I'm due back in school the twenty-fifth. A loop in the Rockies probably." He squinted at me in the bright sun. "So, you really going all the way across, huh?"

I didn't want to give him more than that. The pleasantries were out of the way, he'd had a drink to catch his breath—any second we'd start the ritual.

"My name's John Runmann. I'm from Portland. Mind if I ride with you a bit?"

He held his gloved right out. I gave him mine and we coasted a few sweaty-handed seconds down the highway together.

During the next few hours, I heard about his anthropology Masters program at "U-Dub" (University of Washington), the girlfriend that waits but doubts his return to her, and how, at twenty-five, he doesn't have the slightest idea of what he wants to be when he grows up. He rode the gentleman's spot—out left, a half wheel behind—the whole time.

Suddenly, though, in the wooded hills east of Tonasket, he jumped ahead. "Loggers," he said, sprinting. He looked frightened. Seconds later, a semi loaded with Douglas fir flew by our left elbows.

"Watch those bastards," he yelled through the billowing dust. "Loggers don't budge an inch and nobody drives faster. You're just another speck . . ."

His last words were lost. Another log truck blasted by. John waved me off the road. We got onto the gravel shoulder fast, and then—it must've been quitting time—a wave of trucks descended and the air hurt with pulverizing noise. This was the first moment in hours without his voice or my own in it. In the teeth-rattling gravel, he pedaled easy.

When the trucks had gone, he fell back and spit. "Just another speck on their radiator."

Midafternoon and the village thermometers rose into the mid-nineties. As we climbed the low mountains near Republic, the sun nodded down to meet us. John's face took on a redness as if he'd been slapped. We came along a fast clear creek and he asked if we could stop.

"Try this," he said. "Shock the shit out of you for a second, then it feels good. Save you from frying out here."

He peeled his T-shirt off and dunked it in the creek. His torso was that of a gymnast or a swimmer. You could count the ribs and those tiny muscles between them. He didn't wring the shirt out, but wriggled back into it gasping and blinking.

"Try it, it'll change your life." He grinned, hair dripping.

I did, and it did. Like a roll in the snow right out of the sauna door. My yell shot up to soprano and echoed around the valley beneath us. He laughed.

He pulled three bandannas from his panniers and dunked them in the creek. Winding them into little ropes, he tied one around his forehead, the other around his neck.

"Here. This is the best feeling of all." He came behind and tied his third bandanna loosely around my neck.

As we climbed, still closer to the sun, the T-shirt started to dry and lift off my back. It turned the mountain's oven air into an April breeze. Best of all, though, just like he'd claimed, was the bandanna. The T-shirt dried too soon but the knotted wet cloth at the neck dripped slowly for nearly an hour. A single drop of that freezing creek sliding down the back or chest was heavenly.

Time to start thinking about camping for the night. That made me itch. OK, maybe he'd saved me from a logging truck, and maybe he was an interesting ride, but if we camped together there'd be *no* owning this thing. I looked for a graceful way to leave. There were still no other roads, though, only graveled paths into the woods.

Surprise number one: a roadside café, literally in the middle of nowhere.

Number two: the daily special, blueberry cheesecake shakes.

Three: he offered to buy and I didn't take the opportunity right then to leave.

Numb from the heat and an ice cream headache, I watched him read the local paper. With the right mustache and hat, he *could* be Marlboro Man, or maybe Son of Marlboro Man because his nose is kind of pug and too cute. Those eyes, though, they're almost jade. They moved quickly across the paper, even faster when he came to the editorials, muttering, "Damn Republicans, can you believe them?

"And the damn Twins, too," he quickly added.

"What," I asked, "they beat your Mariners?"

"My Mariners! Piss. They lost to the Mariners," he pointed to the article. "Seven-four, for crying out loud. To the Mariners! The first game I ever went to was at Met Stadium in Minnesota. My grandpa took me. Double-header, Twins, Yankees. I was a kid. I've been a Twins fan ever since." He looked at the stats.

"No kidding. The first game I ever went to was the Twins, too. They played the Royals at the Met, even though we lived closer to Chicago and the Cubs."

"What was the score?"

"The only thing I can remember is somebody hit a high foul pop—up to the second tier. There was nobody up there, but this little kid ran over to the ball and drilled it right back to the pitcher. The pitcher didn't have to move an inch. He took his cap off to the kid and the crowd went nuts. Don't tell me *you* remember the score?"

"First game four to five, Twins. Second game was eleven innings and Killebrew broke it open with a two-run shot with two outs. By that time I'd had three hot dogs and I threw them all up on my grandpa's knee. Helluva game. Seven-five, Twins."

The waitress came, smiled at John, and tugged smooth her blouse. She laid the check facedown in a little puddle of condensation.

"You want to find a place to pitch our tents tonight?" I asked him. Surprise number four. He looked kind of shocked himself.

"We can pitch our tents in back of the johns," he said. "The cops'll cruise this place but they won't see us." He stopped at a picnic table behind a brick outhouse.

The Republic Fairgrounds used to be a logging camp, he said. One hundred years ago the town of Republic boomed with gold, lumber, and dozens of saloons and dance halls. Now, Republic was paved streets and the peace of suburbia. Posters told us the county fair would start in ten days: See the Shetlands, ride the rides, judge heifer of the year.

"How do you know so much about this place?"

"My grandma had some land not far from here. First night for a lot of bike trips. Every year before the fair starts they water the hell out of the grass, that's why it's so plushy. Sleep great here this time of year. This is my picnic table, best one on the grounds."

We set the tents up. His is a tall yellow two-man, and he laced one of its ropes through his bike frame, then staked it. "Kids like to come through here, too," he said. He set the whole thing up in two minutes, his movements as easy as if he were tying his shoes.

He made supper on his gas stove—mac and cheese with peas, *lots* of peas, and a can of tuna. We ate like kings, or hogs. I washed dishes.

"How do you *do* that," he said as I spat a watermelon seed ten feet to the outhouse wall. We sat on top of the picnic table. The sun was low.

"All in the teeth."

He slurped the melon and stored the seeds in chipmunk pouches on either side of his face. With a great sucking of air and straightening of back, he let one fly—PEWFFF! A couple hit his feet, one dribbled down his chin.

"One at a time, John." I banked another off the wall.

"How?!" He slurped up more seeds.

"Try more air, less spit."

It was a small victory. Not that I was looking for one—but John seems to do everything so well, so easily. There is a grace to him I have rarely seen in a man. I wouldn't mind if a waitress smiled at me like that either. Until he gets the hang of it, which probably won't be long, I am the champion seed spitter.

"Lift your chin a bit."

At least that one cleared his feet.

"Now aim. Visualize the wall, John. The wall is yours."

We belched and worked on it through one whole watermelon. His best was halfway to the outhouse.

AUGUST 3

 51 MILES

Colville, Washington

The Kettle River range met us outside the fairground gates and had us each in granny gear all morning. The air was cool, and ragged balls of fog rolled down the wooded hills. At the steepest parts, John would check for traffic, then turn out into the other lane and weave back. Again, out and back. Cut the hill, he said, cheat it. It worked like a charm.

For the most part we said little. The climb was work, and talk was simply more work. At a little flat spot, though, I asked John who taught him that trick.

"My dad. We used to ride here all the time."

"Used to?"

"Yeah, used to. He died when I was eighteen."

Sweat dripped into my eyes and I rubbed my T-shirt tail into them.

"What did he die of?"

"Heart attack. Mom called us to supper one night and he stood up from the La-Z-Boy and that was it. He didn't even

44

put his arms out. The doctor said he was gone before he hit the carpet."

John's face registered nothing. I said I'm sorry, but I don't think he heard me, because he passed and climbed ahead without a word. He stayed ahead to Sherman Pass and down the twenty miles of swooping curves to the Columbia River. The river was as wide as the Mississippi there, the sky a harsh blue. On the bridge, John turned his face to the bright water. That image of him, blanched white by the sun, then darkened with the flitting shadows of the steel girders—he suddenly looked so hard. Marlboro Man for real.

East of the bridge we climbed a smaller range. The air was hot and dry, the pines browned. A faint crackling sound rode on the wind, the sound bread makes in the toaster.

"My Dad had a heart attack, too, last year," I said.

John stared straight ahead. The sweat collected on his forehead. The road bent stiffly upward and we climbed side by side without a word. The bikes rocked, the frames creaked, and I saw in my mind's eye the day before Easter, warm and overcast. Saggy gray piles of snow. I was at my brother's farm for lunch, watching in amazement as Marshall opened the mail. Seed, the new tractor, fertilizer—by the time soup and sandwiches were passed the bills totaled nearly $100,000. In a rare fit of goofiness he opened each envelope, yelled "Yippee!" and threw it over his shoulder. His two kids thought this great fun.

But the phone rang and when his wife answered it and said, "Is it bad?" we all turned to her.

Dad had been getting everything ready on the farm, lifting, greasing. The pain had started in his left arm, moved to the stomach, then landed on his chest. He'd walked gingerly from the shed to the house and leaned on the kitchen counter and told my mother he thought it might be a good idea if maybe they went to the doctor's.

They went straight to the emergency room. By the time we got there he was hooked to the monitors, surrounded by white coats.

"Hey, come on in," he greeted us. He was a little gray under the eyes, but other than that appeared normal. Friends had always remarked how he looked twenty years younger than his age. Even in that gown, at seventy, he still did. Ma looked a lot worse than he did. Her eyes were bleary and she clutched her purse as if it were a life raft.

"It was fairly slight, we think," said one of the doctors. "We're running some blood tests right now to determine if it was an actual M.I. or angina."

"I tell you it was just a little tight in my chest," Dad said for, I imagine, the thirtieth time that day. His pain threshold is remarkable. When I was sixteen he'd gotten into a motorcycle accident and fallen on his hands into gravel. I remember walking into our bathroom and he held up what looked like a handful of uncooked sausages over the sink. "Look what I did." He grinned. I shut the door and grabbed my stomach.

So here he was again, just a little tightness, nothing to worry about. As always.

We hovered around his bed until evening. The attention made him squirm. "Go on now, you've got to get that John Deere ready," he told my brother. To my mother, "There's Easter service tomorrow and they probably need you at the church, so you go on. I'm fine." He waved us out the door with a smile.

By 5:30 next morning the whole little Lutheran congregation knew. Before and after the sunrise service many squeezed my elbow with barn-strong hands and told me they were praying for him. When we returned to the hospital that afternoon Dad was only cheerier.

"I'm out of the woods. They're going to let me go tomorrow or Tuesday the latest."

The grandchildren gathered around the bed and peeked up at Grandpa, dazzled by the lights he made in the machines behind him. Their parents, my brother and sister, answered their questions, the best of which was, "Where do we put the quarter in to make the lights go faster?" He had us all fooled.

"OK, Dad, you promise me you're out of here by Tuesday," I asked him.

"Oh, of course."

I draped his wires back and he moved his IV and we hugged good-bye. The Newhouse hug lasts anywhere from a half second to a second, its end telegraphed with a flutter of back pats. Arms are never wrapped all the way around. But this time he didn't let go.

Ma drove me to the Greyhound station the next morning to go back to St. Paul. At the counter the clerk wide-eyed me, turned to Ma, then pulled a paper from his pocket.

"Are you Mrs. Newhouse?"

"Yes," she answered, her voice already shaking.

"You're to call this number immediately. There's been a problem. You can use this phone right here."

A driver stepped in. "Seven-fifty for St. Paul and Minneapolis! 'Board!"

Ma dialed fast. "Yes, hello. I'm calling about my husband in the cardia—yes. Yes? I'll wait." My mother, always so proper and polite. The rims under her eyes suddenly looked raw. "They moved him. To intensive care," she whispered.

"Last call! Minneapolis and St. Paul!"

I didn't know what to do. Any good son would've ripped up the ticket and raced his mother to the hospital. I froze and watched the driver leave and the station door swing shut. Mother stared at the wall in front of us.

"What's happening, Ma?"

She seemed to snap back from a faraway place. "What? Oh. Nothing yet. They're trying . . . they're trying to get Dad's nurse on the line. I think it'll be OK. You should . . . I think you should get on the bus. We'll call if there's anything serious."

I didn't really believe her. She didn't even believe herself. But at such a time you simply do what she says. You're kind of a kid again. Ma is Ma and Dad is Dad and if she says get on the bus—I found myself halfway to Madison before I knew it. I'm ashamed of this.

Dad'll tough it out, he always has, I thought. *I'll just go back to my city and everything'll be fine, it always is.*

The bus stopped in Madison, and as soon as the door opened a man trotted up the steps.

"Is there a Mr. Brian Newhouse on this bus?"

He handed me a piece of paper outside. "Your sister called," he said. "You're supposed to take the next bus back." A cold mist fell and smeared the ink. "That's a phone number where you can reach her. She wants you to call as soon as you can."

Ginny answered on the first ring. "Damn him," she said. "You know how he takes pain and doesn't want to bother anybody. He had a real heart attack overnight. He thought it was just a little stomach problem so he didn't even call the nurse. Can you believe it? A heart attack, and he didn't want to bother the nurse." She started to cry, the hospital P.A. system squawking behind her.

"How's he now?"

"He's in ICU and I think they've got him stabilized. I think. Maybe you should come back." Then her voice wobbled away.

During the ride home I didn't cry or beat on the driver's shoulders to go faster, faster. I sat halfway back and simply stared out the window, watching the rows of tan corn stubble, and the mist as it formed tears on the glass. The telephone poles and their swooping wires ticked like Dad's heart monitor, only a little too fast. I felt only the pressing of what I didn't feel.

If his number's up, his number's up. There's not a thing I or anybody else can do about it.

I felt rotten thinking these words, but they were all that came to me. Over and over, they were all that came.

He was flat on his back when I walked in. My family stood behind the doctors, whispering nervously. The web of tubes and wires above him scared me. Marshall motioned me out of the room.

"It was a heart attack all right this time. They think he's gonna pull through, but I guess it was close. All that ice cream finally caught up with him."

He smiled a little. Like the old man, Marshall is an amazing stoic. He stood solid and straight as a fence post. But he gave himself away, too, as Dad does: his eyes said he hadn't slept since yesterday.

I walked in and leaned over so Dad could see me.

"Brian!" His eyes lit again with tears. "What are you doing here? I thought you took off."

"I did, but I heard there was more excitement back here, so I thought I'd check it out."

"Oh, you didn't have to come back for—this is silly!" His voice was raspy, and I could tell the tube that ran into his nose made swallowing difficult. He tried to sit up and, with a look, place a little blame on Ma for my return. The doctor's hand pressed his shoulder to the mattress.

"Oh for cryin' out loud . . ." he whispered, then laid his head back. He smiled, pleased to have us all around him. He looked old and fragile for the first time, ever. The doctor nodded us all out of the room.

By summer he was taking nice slow walks to the bean field; he'd stand there a minute, surveying, then wade into the waist-deep green until he found a stalk of volunteer corn, which he'd gently pull and heave over a couple rows. By fall, he was chopping wood for the stove. Winter found him on the exercise bike with a mason's brick in each hand; he pedaled them in the air in time with his feet. "He is one tough Norwegian," the neighbors said, to which my siblings and I could only add the cliché, "He'll outlive us all." The thing is, we are reasonably sure he will.

But, over the course of this year, that bus ride home has haunted me: this was my father—how could I be so ready for him to be taken from us, from me, just like that?

"I really felt nothing," I muttered out loud, as if John also had been watching the scenes unfold in my head. "You know, if his number's up, his number's up."

John's face was flushed and dripped sweat. He didn't say a word, didn't look up, right, or left, just stared at the gray-black asphalt sliding steadily underneath us.

We topped the long rise in early afternoon, and the land opened to wheat fields edged in pine. After the dark and dank forests and the harsh deserts, the fields were a reassurance, and I felt the muscle along the top of my shoulder blades loosen for the first time in days. The wheat waved gold and lemon.

Ahead stood another range. I checked the map. One of the smaller ranges that lead to the Rockies. The thought that I am going to cross the Rockies on a bicycle is as absurd as it is exhilarating.

"Colville's just ahead," John said, with one finger on the map in his handlebar bag. "I know the city park there. There's a decent spot to camp in some trees." Here, his face looked softer, as if he were the one asking me to camp with him this time. "It'd be free too."

AUGUST 4

29 MILES

Kettle Mountains, Washington

Two weeks ago forest fires flared up east of Colville and charred eight hundred acres, John said. At first, the Forest Service thought they could handle it with the usual crew, but last week when it got away from them "they had to call convicts, wetbacks, some students." Now, with the fire out, these fine boys were going to hit Colville and see what she had to offer.

From the sound of it, they'd each gotten their checks, closed the bars, and come to the park blazing drunk. Bottles smashed. Voices wallered. Like John, I'd staked a tent rope through the bike frame, which someone tripped over around 1 A.M. Around two, I peered through the net at a man kneeling beside my bike. The man turned to me and showed me brown stump teeth. Slowly, I laid my hand on the tire pump. He swayed to his feet and staggered away. Around four, police lights flashed red and blue across the tent wall. Some garbled

bullhorn threat must've done the trick, because it was quiet
then until dawn.

Nine o'clock came and I folded stiff legs out of the
tent and put on my blue button-down shirt. At a phone booth,
the yellow pages listed the local church options: two different
synods of Lutheran, a couple parishes of Catholic, two Methodists, one Presbyterian, and several Assemblies of God. A map
in the back of the phone book showed one of the Lutherans
and an Assembly of God equidistant from the park, and each
of their services started at ten. How perfect.

Most of my life I've seesawed out of Lutheran churches,
over to Holy Rollers like Assembly of God, and back again, trying to find a home. As has my father. I know this morning
exactly where he sits in his little white country Lutheran
church, how he holds his choir folder, that his blue robe is
skewed slightly off his left shoulder. And that he's bored out of
his skull.

He's never missed a Sunday at his little church, except
Easter a year ago. It's odd, because he's been so unhappy
there. Even though he is a born-again Christian, he still at-
tends the quiet Lutheran church of his long-dead parents. My
uncle told me once that, years ago, after Dad had gone through
a wild stage, Dad repented and got saved. He'd always gone
to that little church, and after his conversion, to everyone's
surprise, he stayed and didn't forsake her for one that better
fit his new faith. As I grew up, he taught Sunday school there,
chaired the council, and brought us weekly without fail.

But he should've gone over to the Holy Rollers, because
there at the Lutheran church he's been a pain in the neck for

each pastor. He rails against infant baptism ("It's not in the Bible!"), sloppy Sunday school lessons ("They'll let anybody teach!"), the bumper pool table in the church basement, the stilted liturgy, and in general the whole errancy of Martin Luther. Forty-some years and hardly a moment's peace for him there, but he's never left.

My uncle, my mother, and some of my siblings remain as unsaved as me, a fact that causes him continual silent heartache. We all know this and never speak of it. As I was growing up, you could see his deepest wish was for us to know God as he knows God. Which meant us making a Decision for Christ. Given that I'd turned Dad down after the Billy Graham TV crusades, coupled with our Lutheran church's doctrinal flabbiness, three or four times a year he'd drive us all to the nearest Assembly of God church where they had a proper altar call. There, it was up to us to make that decision.

Those trips are scratched into my memory. My brother and I would ride in the back of the old black VW, on vinyl seats that in winter felt like wood. Once at the church, the memory gives way to blinding lights, the heat of hundreds of bodies, and crying. Adults, so high above me, would raise their hands toward the ceiling and wave ecstatically to someone I could never see. Once, a tall man next to me jerked stiff, his eyes rolled all white, and he fell to the carpet.

Often, a woman's voice would start to climb above the babble. She'd be down front and though I wasn't able to see her, I could hear her weird, water-language cries of "Ahmbalasulalbala, shimwolsounfo—hai, ahai, hahihahi!!" Suddenly she'd stop and the place would fall absolutely still until a male voice boomed, "I am the Lord your God, and I am come tonight to say . . ."

The words were always fierce, grisly. "The lamb slain for you . . . a righteous sacrifice . . . my Son's precious blood."

The choir swayed in shimmering blue. A man behind me yelped as if knifed. Men wept freely. Salvos of "Hallelu" and "Thank you Jesus" wailed overhead. I scrunched down in the pew, afraid I'd be hit by some stray Holy Spirit torpedo and made to stand, scream, then fall paralyzed to the ground and later wake up some sort of zombie and all the kids in school would laugh at me forever.

I wanted Dad to drive me back to our farm, back to the trees and the corn, but he just stood there and whispered quietly in the righteous storm around him. One of his tanned strong hands was usually upturned, slightly raised. I could never hear his words, but he pleaded for something with such an anxiousness, such a desire in the lines of his face. He never got what he asked for, though, and a sadness always came over him. He'd put his hand down, and his face would become hard set like the skin of the maple in our front yard. We'd drive without a word back home.

Church. I've got church in every bone.

John gave me a look this morning when I told him I wanted to attend a Colville church. We agreed to meet a few hours east of Colville.

Why another Sunday in another church? Maybe here, after I've sent Billy Graham packing for St. Paul, after leaving Karen and Dad and everything that has pushed me toward Jesus all my life, maybe here on my own I can figure out this God whom I've hated for being so damn *necessary*. Maybe I'll finally get in Karen and Dad's boat.

Or jump ship altogether.

Lutheran or Assembly of God? I tossed a quarter and watched it spin into the pines and felt the tug of each—one offered tradition, the other, rapture. Heads. Holy Rollers.

Pew eight. An immense white cross at the front. Hollers. The same fear I felt as a child. The same vast emptiness in my chest that I've felt my whole adult life when the pastor reads the words: "He came so that *you* may have abundant life."

The preacher went on, "Remember. He told the thief on the cross, 'I tell you this day you shall be with me in Paradise.' Paradise! Do you hear that? Paradise!"

Oh, God, my life seems so unabundant! *So* bound! I want to be alive with spirit, *your* spirit, really free, where are you?

"Who wishes to give his life to Jesus today?" the pastor called over the congregation. "Who wishes to know all the everlastin' joy and peace that comes from him? Just come forward and kneel at the rail."

The people of Colville walked to the rail, tears in their eyes. A voice said stand and walk, and my father's hand on my back urged me forward with the others to Eternity. The voice started to get pissed off. It demanded I go. But all I could do was sweat-grip the pew and wish to God I'd never come.

I forced a smile and a manly handshake at the door, then ran to my bike and flew into the charred forests east of Colville.

AUGUST 6

156 MILES

Bull River, Montana

Two notches on the stick: a big one, Washington, and a smaller one, only a nick—Idaho.

The first took 430 miles and eight days; the second, fifty and an afternoon. Far north where we crossed, Idaho is like a chimney of low mountains. Local myth says the original surveyors were drunk and made the Bitterroot Range instead of the Continental Divide the state border—the difference being 120 miles. Had they been sober that extra real estate would've squared out Idaho, maybe done something for its lard-butt shape. As it is, we crossed it so quickly that my memories of Famous Potatoes are only of its sky, blue as the bitterest Minnesota winter afternoons; of the honey-tanned women who shopped Sandpoint in tight pastel T-shirts; and of the occasional cardboard sign that swung from mountain café doors: Closed. No Water. Giardia.

In and out of the smaller ranges that point to the Rockies, John and I have stayed no further than a foot apart. We watch our mirrors for the looming log trucks and talk of everything except fathers.

We've developed a rating system for the cars as they approach: a "grandma" gives a whole lane; a "salesman," half; a "dink" aims for your elbow.

"We got a dink closing fast," one of us announces and slides in behind the other. The driver invariably death-grips the wheel as he blasts by.

"You have to watch their passengers too," John said, and bandanna-wiped the grit from his mirror after a particularly close dink pass. "If they're going to heave something, the passenger is cranking like hell to get his window down. Get in the ditch and duck. I was in Nevada last year and these guys lobbed a full bottle of beer out the window at me. The bottle wasn't even opened. They must've been doing eighty and it exploded all over the road."

We wave at the grandmas, nod at the salesmen. Sometimes they wave back and smile with a look that's part sweet, part sad.

All these miles across two states and you'd think I'd have more to write about. But what looms largest in my mind these days is John. We have struck a rhythm. In camp, he drops and rolls my tent while I pump his tires; I stir the mac and cheese while he tries to relight the stove in the rain. The rhythm is there on the road, too. We take half-mile turns pushing the air aside for each other—one rider's front wheel inches off the other's ankle.

There's rhythm in the talk, too.

"She loves it when I come home. She's usually at the door. I come in, drop my stuff, and roar. It's crazy, I mean it's like right out of the movies, but she loves it when I roar. I carry her into the bedroom. Then we play Tarzan and Jane. She loves when we play like that."

The sun has picked us out. We're drenched in sweat. John sits up as we near the Montana state line and lets a Tarzan yodel fly.

"I admit there's a pathology to it," he goes on. "I mean, like, I'm drawn to women who'll worry about me. I want them because they're nice and stable and can give me something—I don't know, something like a sense of home or something. And they, at least in their heads, want someone who's adventuresome and who'll go off for three weeks at a time, but when it comes to the actual leaving, that's different. This girlfriend, though, she is *thrilled* when I come home. I've had some great homecomings. You know what I mean?"

Sun and sweat make me horny. And this gorgeous mountain air and our talk, which has led more and more from the head to the crotch—all this is starting to make me itch.

"Yeah. Well, not really. My girlfriend and I are, well—how do I say this? She's born again. And, you know."

"You mean, you don't?"

"No, I'm sorry to say, we don't. God's plan."

"Some plan."

"Well, she seems to want it that way, and what am I going to do? We're not going to break up just because of that. That'd be pretty crass."

"Crass or no crass, look at you. Twenty-eight, twenty-nine, you ride a hundred miles a day, you eat like a camel. You've got appetites God himself gave you. Are you supposed to pray all that away?"

I caught myself in the handlebar mirror, my face red from sun and embarrassment.

"Does she swear?"

"Not that I've ever heard."

"Man. She must be something. Ah, don't listen to me. You

do what you have to. But she doesn't swear? I don't think I could date a woman who doesn't swear."

Actually, swearing is one of our most frequently ridden merry-go-rounds. She says the Lord wants her holy. I say that I'm not so sure swearing makes us *unholy*. "Let no evil word cross your tongue," she says, or something like that, then gives me the chapter and verse.

But Karen, when you drop a casserole or bloody your thumb with a hammer, what are you supposed to say?

I know it's hard, but as soon as something like that happens, I just try to give it to the Lord, she would say.

You're kidding.

No, really, I just give it to Him.

"Speaking of God, how was that church in Colville Sunday?"

"About what I expected, I'm sorry to say."

"Is that what you were raised, Assembly of something?"

"God. No, I'm Lutheran, but every once in a while I try to branch out a bit." I didn't want to start the whole messy history.

"I like branching out, too. I was raised Presbyterian, but my parents just kind of lost the oomph for it."

"I can't imagine Tarzan in a Presbyterian church."

"Ah, it was OK, growing up, kind of a pleasant country club church. Man, during coffee hour? More business deals got cut there than downtown. Actually, I'm kind of proud that my parents drifted away."

"And now?"

"Right out here. This is where I worship."

John opened up his arms and Montana, just ahead, seemed to issue forth from them, everything, the craggy white helmets of the Cabinet Mountains, the Kootenai River glistening in the sun, like he'd created them that instant.

"That's why I come out here, Brian. It's worship. Nobody'll call it that, but that's what it is."

How preposterously simple.

"Here," John said, and reached behind and pulled a water bottle from his panniers. He held it out to me. "Communion." Buried deep in his smelly T-shirts, the bottle had kept its cold all morning since he dunked it into a stream. The cold made my teeth ache.

"I like fringes, Brian, the edges of things. You don't get that in *any* mainstream church I've ever been to. One day I'm going to make up a religious business card for myself." He rode no hands and held the invisible card over his handlebars.

"John Runmann, First Church of the Absurd. Wherever there's a rip in the cosmic fabric, I'll be there."

He lifted his face to the sun. I laughed for a mile and finally passed the bottle back to him. He sprayed his head and shook the water from it like a dog.

And thus it was that they passed into the promised land of Montana—a halo of sun around the Right Reverend Runmann, First Church of the Absurd.

I didn't think that Karen had gotten so deep under my skin already, but last night's dream tells me otherwise.

She and I are driving down a rainy street late at night. She is crying. She wipes her tears away and each time steers right a little too far. We're coming on a row of parked cars up ahead. I've asked her three times what is wrong, but she can't answer, just shakes her head and keeps driving. The cars are getting closer.

"Karen, how about here, in the White Castle lot. Just pull in."

Without signaling she veers in. She turns the wipers off but leaves the motor on.

I hear "Oh Jesus" whispered a couple times, then that's it. She rocks in her seat for a second, then her whole face furrows into itself and she suddenly bends forward as if she's been punched.

"Karen, tell me what's wrong."

She says into the wheel, "I don't know. Just something bad is all."

"What do you mean, to your body? Are you sick?"

"No. I mean, I don't know. All I know is something is happening *to me*."

I still have no clue what this means, but I imagine she's talking spiritually here. I resist the temptation to roll my eyes and instead watch the rain through the window. I look back at her. I put my arm around her. She shakes it off. I try to put my windbreaker around her and she shirks it away. I have no clue what to do.

"You want me to drive to the hospital? Is it your stomach?"

The rain drums her car roof. The motor throbs quietly. She shakes her head. Raindrops wobble like broken marbles down her windshield, blue and green cat eyes under the parking lot fluorescents, and I wonder if she's going to break up with me. Is it appendicitis? I *really* have no clue what to do. I rest my hand over hers on the parking brake but she takes no notice of it. And in the next few minutes, for once, I try not to think about her tanned body or her wacked-out religion. I don't really think any *thing* about her. I just sit there with her. I close my eyes and listen to the rain drum the roof.

Then I feel air moving on my chest. I check the window but it's rolled up. Now it feels like air is moving *through* my chest; not down my throat but passing directly into my lungs, as if the skin and sternum and ribs had all turned to gauze—now as if even my lungs themselves are gone. My chest feels—man, this is weird—but it feels like a window left open the first warm spring day the snow melts. I feel no panic about any of this.

"Karen, look at me." Her head is now against the steering wheel. She doesn't move.

"Karen, please."

She does and I see tearshine in the dash lights.

"Karen, you're going to lose your job. You are going to lose your job. I don't know how I know this, but I know it. You are going to lose your house. You'll have to ask family and friends for money to live. You will survive. But this *is* going to happen to you."

Now she is sobbing. The car jiggles slightly with her cries and the storm. When she comes out of it, she turns to me and all her Pollyanna is scrubbed away. Her past and darkness and fear, all the reasons she runs to Jesus, her whole messy life— it's all laid out right there. We hold hands for a few precious minutes and I feel like maybe she *is* the one. We listen to the rain slacken. I so want to hold on to the closeness that wraps itself around us.

I woke and had to talk out loud just to make sure it was a dream. They come like this once in a great while. I don't even want them, but they come. I wake with the feeling that I heard, not dreamed, but actually heard the rain on her roof, and felt her long, cool fingers. More real, though, is the certainty that all of what I said about her job and house will happen.

AUGUST 7

75 MILES

Lake Koocanusa, Montana

It happened at the Libby Dam. The Libby is a concrete straight-edge rammed between two walls of the Purcell Mountains. The canyon narrows to the dam, strengthening the wind as you approach. Pushed by a warm southwest wind, we pedaled easily toward the Libby. The closer we got to it, the easier. By the time we reached the dam, we were barely pedaling. When the wind hit the dam it had nowhere to go but up and over, which it did, howling at probably seventy miles per hour. We wheeled the bikes onto the dam's top. The noise was like a runaway train.

"When was this built?" I yelled, inches from John's ear.

"What?"

"Built. THE DATE!"

"Why, thank you!" He bellered into my ear. "I've been waiting for you to ask me out!"

I grabbed his throat and bent him over the Libby's front edge. There must've been a quarter mile of concrete below us.

The wind rippled his cheeks and made his hair stand at a straight angle. His lips moved and I let him back up.

"Nineteen forty-eight!"

I looked down the Libby's long beige wind-scoured face and marveled at its sheer straightness. John's mouth said what looked like, "Watch this!"

He jumped on his bike and aimed it north onto Highway 37. The wind flung him from the dam. His feet were not in the pedals; he held them wide open by the front wheel. The road bent uphill and *still* he had his feet out of the pedals. He was even gaining speed.

Wind strong enough to push a fully grown man on a fully packed bicycle *uphill*. I now know why I have come on this trip: to see this.

I jumped on mine and kept my feet out. It was like riding a broomstick horse, a *flying* broomstick horse! Blasting up 37, John slapped his bike's fanny while I kicked the flanks of mine and yelled "Giddap!" We lifted off. We were outlaws. No, he was the outlaw, I was the sheriff! Over his shoulder, he fired off a half dozen thumb-and-forefinger bullets. Piss-poor shot. Missed me by a mile.

High above the Kootenai, we leaned the bikes against a guard rail for lunch. Our first three or four days together, it's been peanut butter and jam on wheat, with bananas and granola bars. Fairly straightforward. No grace. The longer we ride, though, the more our appetites increase. Here at the guardrail we set it all out like a poker game. I pulled a pound of green grapes from my panniers, he produced a stick of salami. I countered with three big apples, he with two Hershey bars.

"I'll see your cheddar with these crackers, the peanut butter, and jam."

"I'll call your jam with this bread and the water bottles."

We sat cross-legged, laid the sandwiches right on the asphalt, and dove in. A half hour later it was all gone. John declared himself winner as we belched like hippos amid the wrappers and empty jars.

I closed my eyes and stretched out on the pavement. The road was warm and its heat rising into my body made me feel like candle wax just beginning to melt. John walked a gentlemanly distance downwind, humming, and unleashed a fart of four or five seconds' duration.

"I want to teach you something," he said.

I was almost asleep. "Can't wait."

"A couple years ago I was up in this dinky town in the mountains near Vancouver. I'd banged up my derailleur and thought I was dead, being so far from a shop. But I found this place. It was like a library and a Chinese kitchen and a bike shop all in one. Books on every wall, woks and spoons hanging from the rafters. The owner had never had a family. He toured all his life. We started talking about how great it is to live on the road, about how you hardly need anything out here—food, water, a place to sleep, that's about it.

"I told him I believe man is basically a hunter-gatherer and whenever we can get back to that, doing those basic tasks, we're most at peace. He liked it, then he waved his shop rag for me to follow him.

"Above the work bench he had this plaque. The bench was a mess. Spare parts and travel books and oil cans. But this plaque was absolutely clean, all scratched up, but clean, polished."

I sat up and watched John's hands describe the thing.

"Four sentences carved into this beautiful script forest

scene. Vines and trees and everything. It said: 'I gather wood. I build fires. Oh what happiness. Oh what joy.' "

John emptied the last swig from his water bottle. "He said when he was a boy his father, who studied Zen, made it and gave it to him, and that he'd had it all his life. Took it with him wherever he'd moved. Said if the place was ever on fire he'd let the whole goddamn mess go up, but he'd grab that plaque and run."

I lay back down and closed my eyes.

"That's all we're doing out here, Brian. Motion and food, motion and food. Everything else is gone."

The wind blew in the pines. I felt the food in my stomach, the warmth of the asphalt rise into my thighs. I sat up into a Buddha position and said, "I gather wood. I build fires. I fart like hippo. I am at one."

John emptied his water bottle on my head.

AUGUST 8

61 MILES

Dickey Lake Camp, Montana

In the northwestern corner of Montana. Days of white crosses and gray circles.

On the right, a perfect mountain stream tripped over brown round rocks. On the left, a curtain of ferns and fir trees. A dirty white cross jutted from the curtain, about eight inches tall and a half foot wide.

"Funny place for a grave," I said.

"It's not a grave," John answered. "It might as well be, though. It's where a traffic accident happened. One cross equals one dead body. The state puts these up to mark the exact spot. Folks out here drive like hell and it's supposed to slow them down when they see a cross." His voice got louder and he glared at the cross, almost scolding it as we approached. "Doesn't work for crap, though, drivers don't see them after a while. Bikers are always getting picked off in Montana." He craned his head around and stared at it even after we went by.

This was the first one, but he was right; after a while you started to not notice them, just another kind of fern. Until east of Libby, where 37 hugs the Kootenai. The road is a good twenty feet above the river there and, incredibly, there are no guardrails, just a straight shot out into the water. There, we came upon not one but four crosses welded together on a steel rod. The rod was jammed into the cliff over the river. No names or dates, just crosses over the sparkling water. You could practically hear the car go over.

And the gray circles: After John and I settled in this campground I went looking for a phone. The maintenance guy picked at the paint on the camp well and nodded me south.

"Just turn left at the end of the drive and go a couple miles. S'called Trego. The mercantile is just beyond it. Pay phone out back. Can't miss it."

I checked my map. "There's nothing on my map here that shows Trego. How far again?"

"Two miles, maybe three. There ain't nothin' there 'cept Trego. You'll find it."

He had his distance right: 2.45 miles south, a rusty yellow sign announced "Trego, MT." Behind the sign there wasn't much—he got that right too—just a clutter of pumpkin-shaped trailers strewn like marbles in a large curve in the road. They were decrepit and I wondered if Trego was abandoned. A Jeep rusted in shin-high grass and an emaciated Malamute tethered to it, lifting its head, seemed to be Trego's only sign of life.

At the end of Trego's grassy main street lay an old Chevy wagon. A flickering movement inside stopped me. I got off the bike. The windows were all up and lightly fogged. Tin cans lay outside the driver's door. I peered in the back. Candy wrappers, blankets, an orange Nerf football ripped in half. I walked to the driver's side, rubbed the glass with my sleeve, and peered in.

Muddy clouds blocked the sun, so it took a second to realize that two tiny eyes peered out at me. They may have been green or blue or brown but I remember only the gray circles under them, and then the skin, pale as a fish belly. Was it a boy, a girl? I could make no guess at this person's age.

"Can you tell me where the mercantile is? I need to make a phone call. I won't hurt you."

He or she slid quickly down the seat, panicked eyes fixed on me.

I took a step back. "It's OK, really, I'll leave in a sec."

The child clutched a tattered blanket and hid its face. A half minute may have passed before the blanket slid back down, and when it did the eyes were softer and less afraid as they glanced through the windshield.

"OK, I'll leave if you'll just point me the way toward the mercantile."

The child coughed twice, a pathetic wheeze.

A Doberman exploded from the rear seat and threw itself against the window. I jumped on the bike.

"The store!"

The Doberman clawed at the glass, howling, and the child slid even lower in the seat, eyes scrunched almost shut but still locked on me. A tiny dirty finger pointed the way. I didn't let up until I closed the phone booth door.

"Bri, hi! Where are you?"

"Friendly Trego, Montana."

"You sound like you're next door. Are you all right? You sound a little, I don't know, something, out of breath."

"Yeah, I'm OK, I just wanted to hear your voice again."

"That's nice. It's good to hear yours."

"Talk to me, tell me anything. What's the weather there, it's cold here. I took a sponge bath at a campground pump tonight. Was that cold."

"It's kind of a sweaty summer night here. It's about to rain, I think, I can see some lightning in the west. My Bible study group just left, and I'm sitting here."

"What are you wearing?"

"Wearing? Why?" I could hear her smile.

"I don't know, I just want to see you. Tell me."

"Well, pretty much the usual. My blue top and white shorts. Nothing too special."

Sleeveless. Top button open. Her arms dark brown against the faded robin's egg blue. Her legs even darker against the white. They'd be curled under her, one hand resting on an ankle.

"What are you doing right now?"

"Aren't you the curious one. Well, do you really want to know?"

"I'm asking, aren't I?"

"Well, to tell you the truth, I was just having some pretty nice fantasies about you and me."

"Karen," I said, scolding. "Your Bible group just left. I'll pray for your soul. Tell me."

"Are you sure?"

"Oh man am I sure." I could see my breath in the phone booth.

Her voice didn't so much come through the phone—it seemed more to enter my stomach, and the warmth spread in every direction. We lay in a cave behind a waterfall, moonlight shifted through the water, a small campfire burned, and we were surrounded by fresh flowers.

Riding back to camp, I pulled her comb from my handlebar bag. I turned its blues, oranges, and silvers over and over in the sunset. The Karen inside the blanched Christian shell, the artist, the dark Karen who has fantasies she can't tell her friends—she's the one I want.

John was frying brats and sucking down a can of Coors. Neither of us has touched meat or alcohol since we started.

"Courtesy of our neighbors," he said and waved the can at the next campsite. A heavy gray-haired couple smiled and waved back. Beside them stood a silver and black Harley with a matching trailer. Four cans of Coors sat on our table. The brats were monsters, nearly eight inches long. They smelled delicious. "You should see it," John whispered. "That trailer is stashed with beer and brats. They said a person can't camp without beer and brats, and then unloaded all this stuff on me. She said I'm too skinny, wait till she sees you. She's gonna *love* you." The couple raised two Coors at us. John flipped the brats.

"Yoo-hoo," the woman called. "Potato salad? We've got plenty!" She trundled into our camp with an ice cream bucket. She wore a black leather jacket with red fringe shimmying wildly across her chest. "You didn't tell me you had another guy with you," she said, laughing and scolding John. "And look how skinny *you* are. You must be *starved*." She mounded salad from the bucket onto a paper plate. Her chins flapped like fish gills. "And here's a couple more brats. These big ones we get made special in Milwaukee. You're probably thirsty, too." She pulled four more Coors from her pockets and set them next to the salad. We thanked her and she went back to her husband.

I am no great beer fan but the first can went down surprisingly easy. Halfway through number two I began to feel burpy and expansive. I watched John turning the brats, and decided he could benefit from a few of my larger life experiences.

"Have you ever done it in a sauna?"

He was in mid-swig and sprayed it into the weeds. He wiped his mouth with a forearm, laughing. He swallowed and drank again and looked into the pines. "A pool, but not a sauna. It'd be kind of hot."

I finished the can. "All that steam. It's great. How about in your front yard?"

"No. God, a fellow has some decency."

"Oh, come on, Tarzan. How about behind a waterfall in a cave?"

John sat down on the bench and finished the can. "In a cave behind a waterfall." He looked at the lake near our campsite, then studied me for a second. I just smiled. "You are so full of shit," he said. He laughed. "Two beers, two lousy beers and you're shit-faced." He cracked his third open. "You and that little dangly thing you got between your legs." He forked a sizzling brat and held it up to his nose.

"Last summer I worked with a Japanese fishing crew off Puget Sound. The government paid me to make sure they caught only what they said they caught. When they weren't fishing, the crew watched American triple X movies on the VCR. You come in the galley at six in the morning and they're eating their eggs watching *Debby Does Dallas*. And I shit you not, they were convinced that the American male is hung big as this brat."

"Well, John, just because *you're* not . . ." I left the rest of that trail off and cracked open another can.

We plowed through the brats and the rest of the Coors and told great and awful jokes. After four beers, the wind kicked up and the trees started to swirl around the table and slap their tree knees. The Harley neighbors swirled with them, and grinned at us, raising their Coors.

"OK, OK," John said. His hair stuck up funny. He said, "Bikes and sex aside. Look at me. I'm trying to be serious here for a second. Bikes and sex aside. Come on, focus. Bikes and sex aside, what do you love to do most in your life?"

"Oh, John. How should I know. Breathe? I really like to breathe." I lay down on the table and watched the pines swing. Their boughs looked like conductor's arms leading a big noisy symphony. "You go first."

He blew a massive belch out of the campsite and down to the lake. It struck the pines on the other side and echoed back to us. He said, "Let me think." A couple of smaller after-belches.

"That summer with those little Japanese guys. That was great. All that water, that space. Those guys were rednecks. I mean they were real Japanese rednecks, eighth grade education and didn't give a damn about much of anything. But they were sweet, too. They called me John-san, which means something like sir John, and they'd always stand up whenever I came in the galley. Sweet damn little rednecks. I loved that."

The trees swayed wildly now, as the wind came to play the big stormy part of its symphony.

"Your turn."

I watched the boughs and hummed along.

"I love to sing," I said.

"Sing?"

"Yeah, sing."

"What do you mean, sing?"

"You know, Bach, Mozart? You are in the presence of a trained classical singer, my good man."

"You. Are. So. Totally. Shit-faced."

"Nope. I sing."

"OK. Sing me something."

"I'm rusty. I haven't practiced. But Scout's honor. Sometime I'll sing for you."

"Ain't gonna believe it till I hear it."

I tried to think of a song. I couldn't think. I cleared my throat. I could give him "Ninety-nine Bottles of Beer." No. If I was going to do it, I wanted to wow him. But the piano bench was empty. I thought of the college recitals. I could see myself standing in the crook of a Steinway, and the crowd out there, and my mouth moving, but I couldn't hear a damn thing. Not the German songs, *definitely* not the French ones. I could recall only a few notes and a couple words of the English songs. Finally, I remembered my encore. That one I could hear. Oh, it's a great song.

"OK. Here's one. Stand back. This is my favorite."

I stood and placed a hand on the nose of John's bike seat as if it were the Steinway.

> *Sweet chance, that led my steps abroad,*
> *Beyond the town, where wildflowers grow.*
> *A rainbow and a cuckoo,*
> *Lord, how rich and great the times are now!*
> *Know, all ye sheep and cows, that keep*
> *On staring that I stand so long*
> *In grass that's wet from heavy rain,*
> *A rainbow, and a cuckoo's song*
> *May never come together again,*
> *May never come this side the tomb.*

I, or the beer, was on a roll and I stumbled down to the lake's edge to belt my favorite lines across the water.

> *A rainbow, and a cuckoo's song*
> *May never come together again,*

May never come this side the tomb.
Lord, how rich and great these times are now!

"Now" echoed back across the lake and John pounded an empty Coors on the table and the Harley couple clapped and I took a deep bow and that was that.

AUGUST 9

62 MILES

Lake 5 Camp, Montana

Last night before we hung up, Karen invited me
to her best friend's wedding. It's in St. Paul on the twenty-
fourth. Quick math: Washington's 430 miles took seven days.
Montana, though, Lord, it stretches for almost 800 miles.
North Dakota, another 400, then western Minnesota—maybe
if I pull a hundred miles a day, every day, I'll get close. I told
her I'd try.

This morning in the tent, I flattened the Montana map on
my sleeping bag. Hail poked long, thin fingers at the tent wall.
Then came the hard rain. On a good day across Washington
I'd been able to mark my progress with two folds of the map.
Seven days, fifteen folds. Montana would take thirty folds or
more.

She'd said, "I'd love it if you can be there, Bri." I don't let
anyone shorten my name, and she only does it when she's
feeling funky. But last night I actually liked it. "I want to stand
there and brag about you to all my friends."

Damn. She says that kind of stuff from time to time and I think, again, that maybe there's hope for us. On the tent wall I can see her sunlit in a gorgeous blue dress. I want to be happy with her. I want to impress the hell out of her. I want her to know I'm decent. That I may not be saved, but I'm not a bad person. I'll be at that wedding.

Outside, John shivered silently over the stove trying to light it. It was forty-eight degrees. He got it hissing and made oatmeal and hot chocolate. When the cups clinked empty, his cheeks were beet red. Rain dripped off his nose.

"So"—he leaned on the table—"too cold to ride today? You want to maybe find a nice warm lodge?"

"I'm from Minnesota, remember? God made cold there."

"Just checking," John said. He looked furtively around the camp and zipped the collar of his jacket tighter.

" 'Course, if you did want to stay," he said, avoiding my eyes, looking down into his cup.

"No, John. I've got a date in St. Paul."

Highway 93 hugged the Stillwater River forty miles southeast into Whitefish. We always aim for these river roads because they roll gently, unlike the steeper mountain roads. But this was hands down the worst forty miles of my life. I wore top and bottom thermals, the rain suit, the mittens, but I might as well have been buck naked. Soaked in minutes. The rear wheel flipped ice water up the length of my spine. The wet pavement felt like flypaper, and we drifted apart constantly. The clouds were so thick that the mountains, when we could see them, looked charred.

After ten miles, John's thermometer read an even forty degrees. Shivering, we took a short break on a logging road. He handed me a small box of raisins from his handlebar bag. The gesture was touching—you keep only the most important items in the handlebar bag. I peeled off my mittens, the fingers were wrinkled and faintly blue. The little scar in the palm of my left hand, the one I got in a farm accident years ago, stuck out bone white from the rest of the hand as it does when really cold. I couldn't dig the flap up on the raisin box. John tried, failed, and handed it back. I bit through the cardboard and showered half the raisins into the muck. The rest we split.

Another five miles and my right knee started to stiffen, and the ball of it kept catching the kneecap at its favorite spot, eleven o'clock. The temperature dropped another two degrees. Approaching cars sounded like bed sheets ripping and they threw water on us by the bucketful. In the mirror, John's head was cocked slightly to the right, shielding his eyes from car splash. He looked pitiful, absolutely pitiful.

Now this seems practically inexcusable, but I dropped my head and pounded the pedals in rage—to get away from John, get away from this cold, get away from freezing to death in these mountains! The speedometer climbed through the teens and John shrank in the mirror.

I was screaming, "I hate this! I hate this!" when a tidal splash from a log truck nearly knocked me into the ditch. I got off, dripping silt and rain from every body part, and waited for John. He came a few minutes later, riding no hands. He ped-aled that Sunday morning cadence of his and gestured to the pines on either side of the road. He was singing.

"I'm sorry for taking off like that," I said. "It's just this damn rain—"

He rode right by. He didn't even look at me. I got back on.

"I will sing a tale of two mud-spattered men," he cried, "and their danger-filled ride to Tibet."

"John, I'm sorry," I called up.

"There is danger, forsooth danger"—he held a palm up to me—"but rewards for sure, yeah, you bet."

I stayed behind. This is roughly what he sang, though to call it singing is a bit of a stretch:

> They crossed Tibet on their ten-speeds
> in search of passage to the east.
> But the season was rainy, the temperatures frigid,
> and of their fate they knew not the least.
>
> The rains came down and the mud flew free,
> and they swore they'd see America again.
> But was it to be?
> Oh listen to me,
> and I'll tell you the history,
> of the mud-spattered men,
> who were manly.
>
> Mud flew to their manly legs and proud pectorals,
> the jungle rose high over them,
> and invisible eyes watched their every move,
> until one night their masculine mettle they were forced
>   to prove.
> Oh, woe to the mud-spattered men,
> who were manly.

He lifted his tire pump from the frame and held it aloft as if he were a medieval knight brandishing a lance.

> There swarmed through the pines thousands of Mongols,
> to capture the mud-spattered men.
> The battle was fierce, damn, it was fierce, yes it was
>   altogether fierce.
> And they used their tire pumps.
>
> As dawn's rosy fingers opened the day our heroes were
>   bound, blindfolded, and led to the Mongol's den.
> There stripped to the waist, their captors made haste

to quickly paste, uh, paste their behinds to a pole.
And then, oh then, what unspeakable acts were done to
*   our mud-spattered men. Oh, these men of the proud*
*   pectorals!*

"Here, you take it for a while," he said and tossed a hand
at me.

"Well. These two guys, these, um, mud-spattered men
were in a terrible situation. They were in a far-off nation. It
was Asian. Um. The Mongols—I can't do this!"

He hollered,

Excrement! Excrement and filth of every sort
clung to their proud pectorals and chest hair.
And as the temperatures fell, it got cold as hell,
and this poop froze there.
Oh the mud-spattered men who were manly.

Like I said, this is roughly what he sang. Thunder, ripping
sheets, and car-splash in my left ear obliterated the rest. I do
know this: at the climax of the story our heroes were doused
in a very precise combination of cat urine and mud, and left
to freeze to death. I was shivering from the inside out. I was
also laughing so hard I couldn't keep a straight line. John sang
it out for nearly twenty miles, all the way into Whitefish, and
paused only to wipe the mud from his face.

At last, when all hope was gone,
when their courage was none,
there appeared through the pine a vision divine.

What? What was this? Two gentle and bare-breasted
*   women drew nigh. They advanced and with smolder-*
*   ing passion and wanton fashion laid their ample,*
*   olive-skinned bosoms upon the mud-spattered men*
*   who were manly.*

Free! Oh yes, free again! The cords that bound them fell
  'way,
and the happy four flew far and free on, on, uh, fierce
  fillies!
And then were our mud-spattered men content,
and they knew not the spatter of mud ever again.

They wintered most sensually with these bare-breasted
  saviors anon.

He turned and looked at me for a second, rain pouring off his
nose. "I've always wanted to use the word *anon.*" He pointed
his tire pump through the driving rain.

But when westerly breezes rose from the dawn,
they mounted their bikes and rode, yes, rode again, on
  and on and on . . .

AUGUST 10

 3 MILES

West Glacier, Montana

Thirty-nine degrees at 7 A.M. I didn't think rain could fall any harder than it did yesterday, but this morning the water arrives in near solid waves. We crawl toward Going-to-the-Sun Highway and Logan Pass, the best road nearby to get over this stretch of the Rockies. The rain is a gray door slammed shut in front of us. Car lights appear from nowhere, horns blast at my hip. The drivers pass slowly—even they can't see a thing. John's up there somewhere, I guess, on the other side of the door.

I have no idea why I am doing this.

Three miles and an hour later, we're at the village of West Glacier. A motel-café in the center of town.

Over steaming cups I tell John about the wedding, and how, if I pull a hundred miles each day between now and the twenty-fourth, I might make it. He thinks this is crazy. We're in the middle of the Rocky Mountains, he says, though we can't see them for all this muck. He wants us to stay here at

the motel, wait the storm out, and says the wait will be worth
the scenery. Maybe tomorrow it'll clear. I want to go to Logan.
To the Midwest and Karen.

"Brian. Look at it. For Christ's sake, just look. You can't
even see across the street. If we don't freeze on the way to
Logan, somebody's sure as hell going to hit us. What are you
trying to prove?"

"Are those your bikes?" A park ranger in a poncho nodded
out the window.

John answers. "Yes, sir."

"Are you going to Logan?"

"We're thinking about it," John says and looks at me.

The ranger checks his watch. "Sorry, but I can't let you
go," he says.

"Why not?" I ask.

"You've got about twelve miles ahead of straight climbing.
It takes about four hours in good weather. But it's nine-thirty
now, and we have to have all the bicycles off Going-to-the-Sun
Highway by eleven-thirty. You wouldn't make it, especially in
this. There's even some snow falling up there now."

"What happens at eleven-thirty?" asks John.

"That's when the R.V.s start coming through. You know,
the Winnebagos? Texas mirrors stick way out and knock you
guys over the edge and that's the worst part of this job, scrap-
ing bikers off the rocks down below." He looked at his boots.
"So, I'll give you a ride to Logan in my pickup, or you'll stay
here and start early tomorrow. Your choice. I'm gonna pay my
bill. Be right back."

Neither of us had to say it. No rides.

John and I spent the rest of the morning in a moldy
hotel room doing maintenance on the bikes, and watching

sheets of rain batter the window. He has this high-tech plastic thing that clamps over the chain. Rube Goldberg would've loved it: you crank the handle that turns the gear that pushes the brush that pulls the links through solvent. The chain comes out gleaming. The real beauty of the thing is that you don't have to crack the chain off the bike as Duncan had done. Good old Duncan, what was his phrase, "Stiffer than a Mountie's dick"? He had it about right. I could barely crank my chain through the solvent. With daily touring you can't feel it stiffening up. The rigidity comes slow and quiet like arthritis.

Next, the wheels. Mountain work is fierce on wheels; the constant yank back and forth; the million little divets you whack into at fifty miles an hour. If the wheels are out of true, a spoke or tube will blow in a second. We need arrow-straight wheels if Logan Pass is as steep as John says it is. His bike wobbled this morning, so he spent an hour meticulously tweaking spokes until both wheels spun straight.

He offered to do mine but they were both still true. He knelt at my rims.

"This is freaky, they shouldn't be this true," he whispered at the front. He spun it.

"Custom," I said.

"You ain't got that kind of money."

"I sold my high school trumpet for those hubs."

He fingered a patch of grit off the hub. "These are Campagnolo!"

"Everybody said if I'm going to do this I've got to get the best wheels I can. A friend of mine offered to build them if I gave him the parts. I saved a lot of money that way."

John wiped more dirt from the rims. "These rims are weird. They got this little dip in them."

"Those are concave rims. Weinmann, handmade in Germany. That little dip in the metal makes it stronger than if it was just flat across. The same reason bridges are built in an arch."

He straddled the front wheel and spun it again.

"I've never seen wheels like this. Boy, nice friend to have who can build you this kind of wheel. Is he a pro?"

"Believe it or not, he's a Lutheran preacher."

"A Lutheran preacher." John spun the wheel again. "Right."

"I'm not kidding. Wheels are like therapy for him. He's got this long workbench in his basement and he heads down there usually after a funeral. You sit there and pretty soon he starts telling you about the drunks and crazies he used to work with in the state hospital. How all of them and everybody in his church, and himself most of all, need God's grace. Once he starts talking like that, he's pretty deep into the wheel. You know it's going to be a good one."

"The sermon on the workbench?"

"Either that or a dirty joke. He likes to tell this one about two guys at a urinal. I can never remember it, but the punch line is something about, 'I wasn't going to touch it until you did.' "

John spun the wheel hard a last time and set the bike down. It hissed into the ancient, burnt-orange shag. "Anybody builds wheels like that, *I'd* go to his church."

John left for the hotel sauna. I rubbed paper towels against the rims to shine them. I've taken them for granted out here. They were so *perfect* when I pulled them from the box. Andrew, my preacher friend, had shipped them to me a couple weeks ago from his Illinois parsonage and I remember marveling at the shine on the metal, their spiderweb lightness and strength. It must've been a bad month at church: a note taped to the wheels asked if he could ride with me across Wisconsin.

I left our Illinois family farm at eighteen for college in Iowa and got my first job after college back in Illinois, in his town. One rainy night during Lent after Lili and I had called off engagement number one, I stumbled dripping into his church and found a religion that finally made sense to me. Here was a preacher who built bicycle wheels.

He also raced, and twice a week he tried to teach me everything he knew by badgering me around a seventeen-mile training loop south of town. He is fifty-three, the father of six, and could kick it out in just under an hour. My best was sixty-four minutes. The smallest hills always seemed too steep and at their bottom he'd call out to me *"Sisu!"* and be way out front by the top. *Sisu* is Finnish for "guts." Andrew is Finnish like the Pope is Catholic.

"Ride *through* the hill, Brian, as if it weren't there. When you're at the top, when you want to coast down, grab a bigger gear and pedal hard." That is *sisu*. And whether I lacked legs, lungs, or *sisu*, it was all I could ever do just to hang on to him.

His other word is *tervetuloa*. Winter nights when Lili and I had problems, he would often call for me to come take a sauna. He always seemed to know when. In his basement strewn with bike rims, he'd hang his blue-checked boxers on a peg and I'd lay my glasses on the washing machine. I have the sharpest memory of the first time, just standing there reading the big letters he'd carved in his sauna door. TERVETULOA. WELCOME. The memory isn't so much of the words as it is of the feeling, how it *feels* to be welcome.

"This'll bake the sin out of you, Norwegian," he said.

A painting hangs inside of two old Finns, a man and a woman, buck naked and grinning beside their forest sauna. The caption reads, *"Muuista, oi syntinnen, muuista . . . ,"* then more Finnish. I tried to pronounce the words, but in the simmering airlessness only croaked. I rapped it with a knuckle. Andrew was just laying himself out on the top bench and, with one finger raised, sat up and proclaimed in his best fake stentorian preacher voice, "Remember, oh sinner, remember the fires of hell when you climb to the sauna's top bench!" He sighed and lay down.

This, then, is the extent of my Finnish: remember, sinner, guts, welcome.

He still preaches a monthly service in Finnish to the old ones, and when I lived there I'd sit in the narthex and listen. Finnish is almost music, and his voice, gnarled by thirty years of two packs a day, became almost that of a singer's when he reached the heart of his sermon. I'd heard it an hour earlier in English, and knew that here, at his most passionate, he was preaching grace, God's unmerited and unstoppable favor to us, how we can't do a thing to earn it, it just is. Afterward in the church door he'd bend to the oldest and the deafest and holler till his face reddened. Then in the little room where the communion cups are stored, he'd change into his orange jersey and kick my ass through seventeen miles of cornfields.

I directed his men's choir, taught Sunday school, led youth canoe trips—and if I didn't exactly find myself there, at least I had a place to be and be happy. He even gave me a church key. When I moved to Minnesota two years ago he said it was like he had lost an assistant pastor. The day I moved, I taped the key to a piece of paper and wrote him that his church was where religion had come alive for me. I didn't say that it was all pretty much because of him. I still miss that place and the way I felt then.

We'll ride Wisconsin, the only exception in my No Hangers On rule. Besides John.

Dear Andrew:

Stalled in Montana. Picture on the other side of this card is bullshit. Sun doesn't shine here. In the middle of August it is thirty-six degrees. In West Glacier we've got everything but snow and they say that's just up the road some. I can barely get my brain wrapped around that one, August snow. I have just taken the longest, hottest shower of my life. All I want right now is to ride through some hot humid cornfield. See you, if the snow holds off, in Wisconsin.

John was gone for hours. I finished some more postcards, then sat in front of the picture window waiting for a break in the rain. The scene remained unchanged all afternoon. The rain never let up for a minute. I thought of Karen, of wanting to impress her by standing next to her at her friend's wedding, and of the huge miles I'll have to pull each day to make it.

About 4:30 I couldn't stand the smell of my own frustration or of the soggy room anymore, so I wandered into the local gift shop. Big shellacked Douglas fir slices, $25; with Elvis, $50; Elvis and a clock, $75. I bought a magazine. Crack wars, famine, and budget hopelessness. Back in the room and I took one last look out the rain-streaked window. I snapped the curtains closed and flopped on the bed.

But even in my dream it rained. I was alone in the ditch of a gravel road. Both my tires were flat and I had no tools. Through the storm, a pair of headlights approached. I dragged my bike out of the ditch to the road. It was a black VW, the car my dad taught me to drive in. A door opened. I couldn't see his face through the rain, but I knew the voice. He said, "You need to learn what the word *finish* means." He drove away. I tried to wipe the rain from my face but it came down too fast, and the ditch water was rising. I woke with a start.

John snapped back the curtains. Over his shoulder, a stamp-sized break in the clouds blossomed. It quickly closed. A wink of blue.

AUGUST 11

110 MILES

Cut Bank, Montana

John's alarm clock struck at 3:45 A.M. A hand
bounced the foot of my bed. "C'mon, Brian. Minnesota's calling." A half hour later we stepped into the pedals.

"I've been thinking," John said. "It's time I head back.
School starts in a couple weeks, and my mother probably
thinks I'm dead out here. I'd like to spend time with her before
then. There's a little town the other side of the Rockies called
St. Mary. We should be there by early afternoon. I'll stop there
for the night, then go north into Canada before I swing west
for home."

We started from the motel. Wet gravel snapped under our
tires and I wanted to say something about how he could stay
on all the way to Maine if he wanted, just blow off school. We
drew along Lake McDonald, a skinny eleven-mile finger
draped in weepy fog. One look at it and you could tell there'd
be another downpour any second. Great. We pedaled past
pumpkin campers. Fluorescent zappers smoked horseflies.

Our derailleurs ticked off the seconds until sunrise or another deluge.

The road suddenly pulled off the valley floor. We climbed quickly out of the fog into heavier clouds and John evaporated into the gray. After a mile, a dome of pale cream light faded in overhead, hung there for a moment, intensified, then spilled down coils of cloud. Higher, the light brightened, the air thinned. And suddenly the cloud yawned and at once I was through it.

Good God. Mountains. Mountains everywhere. A crowd of mountains, dressed in wildflowers and jack pine, and—

And light, honest to God real light. It has been days! The sun was still below the peaks, but you could see the sky filling fast with actual light!

I stood in the middle of the road, my mouth open. John came out of the mist and stopped next to me.

"John."

For a minute he said nothing, but looked down the valley of scattered ponds at skinny Lake McDonald, then up to the gray peaks. "Yeah, I know." We stood there and gawked for several minutes, then got on again and pulled ourselves side by side up the steep slope, matching each other deep breath for deep breath, stroke for stroke.

We took a water break and dangled our feet over a retaining wall. Miles of air swung beneath us.

"Up there? That's Logan Pass." I followed his finger up the zigzag of Going-to-the-Sun. It couldn't have been named more perfectly: at Logan the road sliced between two peaks; behind it, brightening sky.

"I think we can make it by eleven-thirty before they sweep us or those Winnebagos shoot us over the edge."

I started to get up but John laid his hand on my arm and pulled me back down. "Watch this." In another minute, the sun broke through Logan. It teetered up there like a precariously balanced bowl of milk, then spilled white down the valley.

Now was as good a time as any. "So, you really have to get back to school?"

He waved his hand dismissively, said thanks, and looked down kind of embarrassed at his lap. There wasn't much to say after that, so the rest of the way we climbed silently.

At the sign "Logan Pass—1 mile" the road bent up stiffly, aimed directly at the sun. The strangest sensation shot into my legs—a sweep of adrenaline that yanked me out of the saddle to spin faster and faster. I shifted to a bigger gear, spun again, shifted again, and spun harder still. It felt as if this was not my choice, as if this was all happening *to* me. I sprinted, bellowing I don't know what words all the way to the top, going toward the sun.

I've always heard that water poured one way from the Continental Divide will wind up in the Gulf; pour the other way and it'll flow to the Pacific. Lord knows when I'll get another chance, so John and I tested the theory behind a shrub. Steam rose from our necks as we stood panting. Back to back, we dropped our shorts and let fly—I to the east, he to the west. It seemed to work.

We leaned the bikes over the eastern edge of the Divide. The speedometer ripped through the digits. All the little idiosyncrasies—how he swerves for the potholes, shifts and pushes ahead at the steep parts, how his index finger shoots out at the last second to brake for a hairpin—returned in a

flash after our grindingly slow rain days. I tucked behind him.
53. We flew like planes in formation, locked together down the
switchbacks, passing cars in our own lane. Barreling down. 58.
Hooking back and forth against the gray walls. 60. Like ice
dancers, swinging and diving.

Tools. They've mingled together over the days, his
tools in my bag, mine in his, so this was time to sort them and
say good-bye. We had two piles on the campground table: my
vice grips, screwdrivers, and tire irons, his needlenose pliers
and spoke keys. They were greasy with our fingerprints. We
were in St. Mary, a brown and dusty oven fifty degrees hotter
than Logan. John's campsite was intentionally chosen for a
single tent. He'd save a couple bucks that way. I'd get a good
fifty, maybe sixty miles if I kept on.

I rummaged through my bags for strays. We spoke nervously of easy stupid things, the heat, the closest laundry, like
two old mechanics who compare gas mileage at a funeral.

"Is this your water bottle, John?" We'd passed it back and
forth so many times I had no idea.

He gave it only the quickest glance. "Guess so."

I turned back to the bags and reached inside for more tools
and a few perfect words. I put my hand on a couple spokes and
a spare map, all his.

"Here, these are yours," I said and clattered them onto the
table.

"Oh. Thanks. Forgot I had those." He unfolded the map
and studied it for several minutes. "I'm beginning to feel the
loneliness of the solo expedition biker," he said, more to the
map than me.

"Me too," I said, still looking into my bags.

A feeling as sudden and surprising as the adrenaline at Logan washed over me then. I wanted to hug him. But I cinched my bags, thumbed the tires to check for pressure, and swung a leg over the seat. He scribbled his name and address on a scrap of paper.

"You don't write me, you're roadkill, Brian."

I laughed. "Check." He thrust it at me. John R. Runmann. His hand stuck out with the same sweaty friendliness as it did back in Okanogan, what seems like months ago.

"Here, what's yours," he asked and looked up at me, his pen poised above a scrap of paper. I think I'll always be able to see that face. The green eyes. The foolish pug nose. Strands of fine red and brown hair.

I gave him my address and he stuck the paper in his handlebar bag. All I could do was nod to him and head the bike into the brown and beige eternity of Montana.

AUGUST 12

105 MILES

Gildford, Montana

What little the grasshoppers have left in these fields the combines are now trying to scrape up. Huge powerful machines scratch for almost no crop—they look pathetic. All day they marched up and down the fields. The wind brought the chaff and silt to the bicycle, and if I opened my mouth I got the taste of sadness in a second. The grasshoppers sunned themselves fat and happy on the warm road and when I nailed them just right they snapped. For most of the day, my only diversion was to research where they snapped loudest. Between the head and thorax seemed to work best, at their little grasshopper necks.

I chose this Pacific-to-Atlantic route to take advantage of the wind, which everyone said *should* blow *most* days from west to east. This morning it began hard from the west but quickly swung north and tried to bump me into the ditch. Passing semis threw fierce little tornadoes across the road. By early afternoon the wind turned into my face. I hardly looked left or right, but tucked myself as tight to the frame as possible, trying to keep the white line moving underneath. For ten hours I did nothing but turn pedals, saw nothing but the line.

Which can make a person snap. Shortly before sunset a grasshopper landed on my arm. The sun banked off its gaudy blue-green wings and phosphorescent eyes. It seemed to size me up for supper. I screamed and shook it off. I threw the bike in the ditch and fell belly up in the dry brittle grass—*I can't do this I can't do this I can't do this*—the first words I'd said or even heard all day.

I sat there for probably fifteen minutes. I rocked in the wind and chanted that stupid phrase over and over. I don't know if I was praying or just losing it. Regardless, no clouds opened, no angels sang. All I could do was to get on again. I made Gildford in a half hour, driven by the hope that there'd be a cheap motel to hide in, any place out of this wind. But Gildford's stores were all boarded up. Grass grew in the streets.

The door of the Methodist church was locked. A window of the church kitchen budged, but I got it no higher than a couple inches. I can't believe this: I was actually trying to break into a church. I tucked myself into its window well and shivered. I couldn't bear the thought of tenting in this wind.

Three blocks away stood a rambler and a machine shed. A wooden sign, "The Bettenes'," thrashed against the house. The lights were on, the only ones in all of Gildford. A pair of rusted swings squeaked on the porch. Only when I heard the door's security chain fall did it occur to me I had no idea what to say. The pinch of a face that abruptly appeared in the doorway didn't help.

"I'm sorry to bother you, ma'am, but, uh, my name's Brian Newhouse and I'm from Minnesota and I'm riding my bike alone across America and I'm, uh, freezing. Do you have, or do you know of a place I could unroll my sleeping bag out of the wind for the night? Maybe your shed?"

She stuck her head out and blinked into the wind. She was probably seventy, tiny. Her hair dyed a crayon maroon.

"Where you from?" The voice sounded like the swings.

"Minnesota, ma'am." Her eyes looked me up and down twice. Then, I swear, one eye fastened on me while the other went to my bike.

"The husband's out back. In the shed." The eyes snapped back together. "You have to ask him. Go see the husband." The door shut and the chain rattled back in place. I trotted around to the shed.

I made the acquaintance of the Husband's butt before the Husband. He was bent over a small tractor, and from that angle it was his most prominent feature—wide and covered in thinning denim, the left cheek jiggling to the country station on the workbench radio.

Over his shoulder, a bulb hung straight and still on a cord. No wind back there, which would do fine. I scuffed my cleats.

"Excuse me, are you Mr. Bettene? Your wife said I'd find you out here."

"Huh?" He put a hand just above that huge left cheek and straightened up slowly. His eyes were surrounded by crows' feet, his cheeks shone red as apples.

I gave him the same story as the Wife. I glanced again at the shed's back corner. He wiped his hands on his overalls and sat on a tractor tire.

"Where you say you're from again?" I'd expected a deep bass from a body that big, but his voice was nearly as high and squeaky as the Wife's. He looked confused.

"St. Paul, Minnesota."

"Where'd you start?" He squinted.

"Seattle."

"How far you say you're going?"

"All the way across. Coast of Maine."

He worked on that one for maybe one whole minute.

"Why *on earth* for?"

"I don't know. Never ridden from Washington to Maine before, I guess."

He slapped his knee and his high laugh ricocheted against the shed's tin walls and out the door.

"Never ridden! Hoh! That's a good! Hoh boy!" He laughed until he had to wipe his eyes.

"Welcome to Gildford, son!" He stood and laid a hand on my shoulder. He leaned hard. Outside, I noticed his bowed and wobbly legs.

"Got the camper up off the pickup and on the stilts for fall already, but you're welcome to her."

The camper was perched on skinny steel posts. As he climbed the steps, the whole thing tilted steeply my way. I jumped back.

He trundled inside and the camper leaned with him. "See here? You got your cupboards over here, and your range over here case you want a cook a steak or something tonight though I don't imagine you carry ribeyes on the bike." Both he and his laugh disappeared into the camper's darkness. "And back here you got your shower, I'll hook the hose up for ya, no hot, just cold, but that'll put hair on your manhood." I peeked in as he snapped a light on.

"Your light switches are back here near the radio." He twiddled the dial through static. I stepped into the camper.

"You got your blankets up here above the cot." He stepped forward to show me. The camper heaved with him, and I lurched into the opposite corner to counter his weight. He held up a blanket. "Damn! Moths got that one." He tossed it to the floor. "Here's that good one, you can use that other to keep your two-wheeler warm tonight. Hoh!" He dropped another one to the cot, then stepped to pick the first off the floor. The camper rolled my way. I jumped to the middle and felt it sway to a stop, but this put me right up against him. The smell—my God—sweat, gas, manure, maybe some paint or some thinner, maybe a dozen other things, but together they were enough to actually knock a buzzard off a shit wagon.

"Reach down there and grab that sucker for me, will ya? Old man like me, that's a long ways."

The tour kept up for several more minutes. He'd take a step forward, I countered backward. He moved backward, I leaped forward. Elephant tango. Finally, he lumbered down the steps and I pasted myself against the opposite wall of the camper and tried to look nonchalant.

"Anything else you need, you just holler, you hear? We'll be in the house!"

"Thanks an awful lot, Mr. Bettene. You don't know how much I appreciate getting out of this wind."

He reached the grass and I moved quickly to the center, stilling the camper one last time. He stuck his hands down the sides of his overalls.

"You're plum welcome! What'd you say your name was again?"

"Newhouse. Brian Newhouse."

"Well! You're plum welcome, Brian Newhouse."

An hour or so later there was a faint rap on the door. Mrs. Bettene held a plate up to me.

"Something for you." The dark wind still ripped from the east and bullied her as she stood there. She smiled timidly and pulled a scraggly strand of maroon hair back from her face.

"You looked hungry at the door." Two beef sandwiches, two chocolate chip cookies, and a can of orange soda. Even a napkin. She let go of the plate as soon as my hand touched it and fled to the house.

Later, I heard a bellow through the wind. "Brian Newhouse! Are you home this fine evening?" Then that laugh.

"Yes, sir." He wore a thin bathrobe. The wind pasted it against his body. I threw open the door. "Would you care to join me in my palace?"

"Oh no, no, that wouldn't do, no, no, no. Wouldn't want to intrude. Just stopped by to see how you're getting on."

"You've put me up like royalty."

"That's good. We're turning in and just wanted to see that everything was fine for you. Good night then, Brian Newhouse."

"Mr. Bettene? Does the wind always blow so hard out of the east like this?"

He put his hands into his robe pockets and the large knuckles pressed against the cloth. He turned his face directly to the wind and sucked it in.

"Nah, sometimes she'll blow out of the west like this, too." He deadpanned me for a second, then his face exploded with laughter. He wobbled back to the house.

I watched him go, then walked to his shed. He had a phone out there and I wanted to tell Ma and Dad I was still alive.

She was frantic with worry again and in a rush asked about cars, what I eat, and where I sleep. It was a near-perfect repeat of our first call. Dad said little, less than usual.

"I've never seen it so dry," Ma said after she settled down. "This afternoon, it was so hot and still. Down the gravel road I thought I saw a tornado. But it was just a car billowing up dust behind it. It hung there big like a funnel cloud."

Dad's silence was nearly complete. When his fields are this dry, there's little anyone can do to draw him out.

"If I find rain, Dad, I'll send it your way," I said. He laughed a bit and said that would be most appreciated. And that was all he said.

I hung up and walked back to the camper remembering one stretch of weather years ago. Five weeks in the heart of the growing season and not a drop. The corn leaves yellowed from the tips inward. And they didn't hang curving down as usual but pointed straight up—the plant's attempt to shade itself and tip the slightest moisture, even dew, into the stalk. On the way to town each week we drove past miles and miles of erect yellow leaves. That was the quiet summer, when we kids removed our shoes and eased the screen door closed, when Dad bent over the kitchen counter radio each noon and played the forecast almost inaudibly. My only other memory of sound that summer is of the cicada's scrawling whine, always in the hottest, stillest, most insulting part of the afternoon. Dad said less and less as the dryness wore on. Eventually he didn't even turn the radio on. Mother watched him, brought Mason jars of lemonade out to him in the shop, but even she was unable to get him to say much. He was disappearing right in front of us—drawing into himself, shading himself like the corn.

When it finally ended at week five, he left us all at the supper table and went out to the porch. I went to the window and can still see him so clearly walking up and down as storm gusts pushed rain through the screen onto his face and pasted the darkening denim shirt to his chest. He hummed something slow and sweet and happy and sad. Then he sang. He belted out one word over and over again, "Hallelu." I looked over my shoulder. I wanted no one else to see him—alone and singing to the rain like a lunatic. I was afraid that somehow the kids in school might find out and laugh at him. But also I didn't want to share him. Not with Mom, not with my brother or sisters. This is the only time in my childhood when I remember wanting to put my arms around him.

At two-thirty I woke. Someone was in the camper.

The Bettenes' yard light fell on the sink and across the other cot. Without my glasses everything was fuzz. I listened hard for movement but heard only an odd sound of something like organ pipes. Then that too was gone. I switched on the camper light. No one. But there'd been a voice, I'm sure of it—that's what had awakened me.

I am absolutely sure I had heard these words: I am with you.

AUGUST 15

285 MILES

Williston, North Dakota

Most maps show Highway 2 arrowing straight across eastern Montana into North Dakota. But the road lies more like an old carpenter's ruler—the hinged wooden kind you unfold six inches at a time: ten or fifteen miles straight, a hard little jog north or south, then another straight stretch. The jog is so slight you'd never notice it in a car, but on a bike the wind strikes a new part of the body, its cold a surprise as it bristles into the ear. I plow down 2 turning my head every which way to keep its whispers out.

For three days straight I've been cranking my head like this, checking the mirror for semis, dodging dinks. The big news yesterday was a kid on a bike. I saw him come in the mirror, a tiny black figure swaying hard back and forth. From a distance, I thought it was John. I turned around elated and raced to him. But it was just a kid on a Stingray.

"I seen you go by our ranch, and wanted to know where

you was going," he panted. He was breathless and bucktoothed and probably all of eleven.

I looked across the fields and saw about three miles back a clutch of low, flat buildings, the only visible structures anywhere. They looked squashed by this endless sky.

I should've given him something, a spoke or a granola bar, anything. But I was so disappointed he wasn't John, felt so alone knowing that I was going to have to plow on again by myself. He asked a couple of awkward questions about how much the bike weighs, how far I ride. My answers were little better than yes, no, depends. I let him squirm. He toed the dirt and put his foot in the pedal again.

"Well," he said. Then turned home.

The handlebars are grooving deeper and deeper into that little valley at the base of my palm. My hands are turning numb. When I lie down at night, the fingers tingle for a few minutes. Last night it felt as if I'd stuck them in champagne. I woke with a start in the middle of the night, feeling nothing in the left one at all.

A café radio in Wolf Point said the drought stretches as far east as Illinois. I get back on 2 and pedal into this wind, and all I can hear is drought. I can hear it here and I can hear it 1,500 miles east on my parents' farm. There, the sounds of drought are the kitchen clock's second hand groaning toward the 12. The neighbor's dog. Things you don't hear in good times. The creak of the couch springs as Dad sits there biting his lip, turning inward, while Mother tries to keep him facing out.

Here it's just this damn wind.

Ma's probably going nuts. I remind myself to call them
when I reach Williston. Maybe I can get Dad out of his own
shell. Maybe he'll have some interest in what's happened to
me these last days.

The drought broke gently at the North Dakota border. A hint of mist on the back of my neck. The mist thickened
quickly and within minutes I was shivering. I pulled into the
Badland's sharp hills. Out of Montana finally. How many days
has it taken me to get across? It seems like I left John months
ago.

I locked the bike at a truckstop outside Williston. The place
was full of truckers, and the sight of me in yellow head-to-toe
Gortex made them shut up. I ordered spaghetti. Still none of
them said much. I cleaned that plate and ordered double biscuits and chicken gravy, and everybody heard. The guy in the
next booth gave me a quick eyeball. The biscuits were fresh
and hot, so I ordered another plateful, and when they were
done I asked the waitress for one more round of spaghetti. A
guy with an enormous flannel plaid gut resting against the
counter elbowed his buddy and they both gave me the once-
over. Still no one was talking. The lemon meringue pie was
also fresh—meringue will turn to flypaper if left too long—so
what the hell. The pieces were kind of small. Meringue is
mostly air anyway. The waitress brought three slices. By the
time I said, "I guess that's it," just about everyone in the place
was doing his best not to look, some better at it than others.
Flannel plaid couldn't help it, he was in full stare. I nodded at
him as I walked to the door. My cleats made too much noise
and the tinkly bell sounded like spoons dropped in an empty
wooden drawer.

"You sound like you really need a place," the Lutheran preacher said after a long sigh. "If you'd been here last year, I'd have said no problem. But the oil wells are all dry. And you've probably seen the fields, what with the drought and all. We've had too many break-ins. Last month the council said we can't let people into the church after hours."

"That's OK, thanks anyway—" I had the phone halfway back to its cradle.

"No wait. Let me finish. What we've done is set up a fund for folks like you. We've got an arrangement with a local motel. I'll call them right now and tell them you're on the way. It's on us."

"No, no." It was bad enough I'd asked him to shelter me—I could've pitched a tent somewhere—but now to pay for it . . .

"No, thanks, really I can't. I'll—"

"Hang on a second." He put me on hold. "There, too late," he said as he came back. "They're expecting you, so just get over there and have yourself a decent night's sleep. You sound like you could use one."

He gave me an address he said was ten minutes away. I should've asked him if that was in bike or car minutes. In the dark and dripping cold, west somehow became east, north turned to south, and I pedaled by one bar three times before realizing it was the same one each time. For an hour I wove through dimly lit streets dodging semis and their splash.

Finally, the Super Ace Motor Inn appeared, a single-level cinder block building, "Proudly founded in our nation's bicentennial." My room smelled like locker room socks.

I flopped on the bed and picked up the phone. In another minute Mother's voice was there and then Dad came on the shop extension.

"It's raining in North Dakota. The drought is breaking here."

"Here too," Ma said. "We got two inches last night. The weatherman says there's more on the way. Hallelujah!"

"The fields going to make it after all, Dad?"

He took a second to respond, as if he'd been listening to some other conversation.

"Have you been to church, Brian?" he asked.

"Church?"

"Uh-huh."

Anger flushed through me. Shit. I've ridden 1,200 miles, half the nation is burning up from drought—and all he asks about is church?

"No. No churches," I lied.

"Well, I suppose it's kind of hard to find one. If you get time," he said.

I thought I'd immediately fall asleep when I lay down, but a half hour later I got up and watched the drizzle turn to real rain, and the semis' splash to huge peacock plumes of mud-water. I rummaged through the nightstand for some distraction, but found only a Gideon's Bible. I pulled it out and flipped through it aimlessly. Then closed it. Reopened it. And closed it again.

I shut the light off and set the book on the stand. In a couple of minutes I reached for it again. The pebbled, fake leather cover. Its pages crisp and new. All hotel Bibles feel unused. I let it lie on my chest.

"It is the sincerest wish of the Full Gospel Businessman's Association that by placing this Holy Scripture in your hands, you will come to a fuller knowledge and acceptance of your need for Jesus Christ as Lord and Savior." My father used to stamp that inside thousands of Bibles every winter in our farmhouse mudroom, his stamp clean and bold, stark black on the bleached white paper.

Hotel Bibles. Dad had a route of all the area hotels. At times our mudroom was floor to ceiling in Bibles. They came to us 124 to a box. Dad would knife the boxes open and set a stack of fifteen or so in front of me on the deep-freeze lid. My job was the bookmark. Into every Bible two bookmarks were slid, one printed on stiff, canary yellow paper containing Dad's own personal favorite scriptures, including, "For God so loved the world, that he gave His only begotten Son" and "For if ye do not repent, ye shall be thrown into a lake of eternal fire, and ye shall gnash your teeth." The second slip was white and listed the FGBA's chapters. I'd bookmark each Bible and slide it the length of the freezer lid to Dad where he'd stamp.

The worst part of Bibleing was the paper cuts. Despite its smooth cover, the pages were little razors that invariably found the soft parts of the hand. One afternoon, I got a deep one in the web between the thumb and index finger and it bled good. I looked up at Dad. He was stamping away, the weight of his arm making the freezer hinges creak. I sucked the blood and looked around. The scene was surreal. I mean, we were literally waist deep in Bibles and I could see my breath in the backroom cold. And I was sucking blood.

"Dad, why do you do this? I mean, you don't get paid for this, do you?"

He just kept stamping. For three or four more Bibles, till he'd finished his stack. He set them into the cardboard box, then looked at me with a deliberateness adults rarely grant children.

"When I die, when each of us dies, God is going to ask, 'Why should I let you into my heaven?' I have to have something to show for myself down here." He picked up another

Bible and stamped it, a little slower than the rest. "I'll be able to tell Him, 'I tried to save souls.' That'll have to do."

He started stamping again. I wondered how many Bibles, how many boxes of Bibles, how many hotels' worth of saved souls it would take for him to get into heaven. He's worked his ass off all his life to gain God's approval. Fine. I hope he gets it.

But there's me, here, in a moldy fleabag motel that smells like wet socks, and I can't feel my own left hand, and I'm exhausted to the marrow. Can't Dad ask me about something more than church? Is that all I'm worth? Whose heaven am *I* trying to get into? Shit.

AUGUST 16

 70 MILES

Newtown, North Dakota

Dear Andrew:

When I last wrote you I was holed up in a Montana motel waiting out a storm. Today I'm in a little greasy spoon off downtown Williston, North Dakota. Not really a storm but thick drizzle. Between puffs of it I can see the bank thermometer: 48 degrees.

I've been keeping a journal, mostly a place to bitch about how cold and how wet and how windy, blah, blah, woof, woof. I understand that a trip like this is all about wet and cold and wind, but I never thought it would be this hard. I step into cafés and the weatherman on the radio says, "record low maximum temperatures today" and the farmer at the register sniffs, "she's a cold one." Every day is beginning to grind into another and the big challenge of this thing is simply to find a warm place to sleep.

Today's destination is New Town, North Dakota, population 1,335. The map I've spread on the counter tells me it's seventy miles away, and—oh—here's a treat: there's a little white box between Williston and New Town that says "No Services Next 70 Miles." Great.

Thirteen men and boys are in this place, the only female is the waitress. I am in screaming yellow rain gear; they, to a man, are in denim. I don't know if they were silent before I walked in or the sight of me stunned them, but as soon as I tingled the little door bell everyone turned. The word "staring" doesn't capture it; they, even the little boys, *put me* in this seat alone at the counter. Only when I asked the waitress for oatmeal did they start to eat and drink again.

I came out here to escape and now I don't like being a stranger; that is what I am in every café, in every grocery store, to every person I ask for a place to sleep. I miss somebody who knows me.

A father and son sit to my right. The boy, probably ten, doodles on the place mat in front of him and looks to Dad; the old man, maybe forty-five, stares at the end of his cigarette, then out the window. Not a word passes between them.

They survive on wheat and oil drilling, but oil's gone bust and drought has incinerated the fields. In the last three days across eastern Montana and western North Dakota, I've seen nothing but hundreds of miles of flat, burnt fields. Now this rain. Thousands of acres are washing down to the Missouri this second.

The dad just lit another cigarette. All these men and their boys—the only sound is a dropped fork. He just caught me looking. City kid on a bike, just passing through. Sorry. I spoon the last of the oatmeal and pay the waitress.

So. Life in western North Dakota. The rain hasn't let up but I might as well get to it. Tonight, with luck, I'll be 70 miles of No Services closer to the Atlantic and some kind preacher or farmer will put me up on a basement couch. Still looking forward to some real heat in Wisconsin.

Brian

A farm implement dealership marked Williston's final sign of civilization. When I rode past the last stack of tractor tires, the wind slapped me as if it were an open hand. I stumbled from the pedals. The wind was dead east probably thirty miles an hour, gusts upwards of forty. The map showed that Highway 1804 would plow fifty miles into it before turning southeast to New Town. I looked over my shoulder at Williston—I could still see the café back there—but stepped again into the pedals. I found the granny gear, put my head down, and pushed.

The pavement might as well have been wet sand. For the first several hundred yards I actually spoke to each leg. *OK, left, pick it up, push it over. Right, push it down, pull it up.* The front panniers caught the wind like sails, and every time the wind bumped a degree either side of east, the handlebars wrenched. A mile up the road, the wind jumped squarely northeast and nearly dumped me from the bicycle.

After a few miles I actually started to get accustomed to the work. There was no use bitching about it, and nothing to do but pedal. The real problem was the terrain. North Dakota was supposed to be flat. I think I could've taken the wind or the cold mist—but both, set against amazingly steep gulches that reminded me of clean-picked skulls, had the effect of concrete in the cleats. North Dakota was supposed to be flat.

Dad spent his teenage years near here, and he and my mother once drove my brother and me across what seemed like days of checkerboard flatness to his old village, where weeds and tall brown grasses had taken over Main Street. His old house leaned hard; the wind had just about bulldozed it over. I remember thinking that, here, in all this flatness, if I could stand tiptoe on our Buick's roof I might just see our farm down in Illinois.

Ten A.M. and more steep hills. Around me spread the colors of drought, and across the terrain came the long slow-rolling thunder of a storm still miles off. The mist thickened to cold fat drops. Suddenly, thunder belched right over head.

And then the sky opened.

The road disappeared, North Dakota disappeared. My own feet practically disappeared. I could've been standing under one of those chemistry lab emergency showers, the kind that dump a thousand gallons a second on your head to blast flesh-eating chemicals off. I didn't know what to do. Williston was twenty miles back, New Town fifty ahead. This kind of rain couldn't keep up for long. I reached for an apple in the handle-bar bag. My gloves were soaked swollen, and I couldn't peel them off or even bend my fingers around the apple. I palmed it with both hands and bit. It slipped and rolled into a race of muddy ditch water. I dropped the bike and groped for it, kneel-ing blindly down into the mud. I bit my left glove, ripped it off the hand, and found the apple yards away. That little scar in my left palm stood good and high. I ate and tossed the core into the stream. It tumbled wildly away. Water rivered down my glasses and North Dakota looked absolutely surreal.

No villages, no gas stations, no wide spots in the road, nothing. And nothing to do but get myself out of it.

A pair of headlights appeared in the mirror. They slowed to pass, then pulled even. A school bus. The doors flipped open and a man's voice called, "Get in. I'll give you a ride."

The shoulder was rutted so I kept pedaling and looked for a smooth place to stop and put my feet down. I also tried to see up the stairs what kind of person made the offer, but the rain was still too thick and the bike jiggled too hard. We continued like that for several hundred yards, the bus inches from my elbow, doors wide open.

"No thanks!" I shouted through the rain and waved at the door. He stayed for probably a half minute. A puzzled "OK" drifted down the stairs and the doors slapped shut. The bus climbed a hill and vanished. Rules of the Road are Rules of the Road. No rides.

Little spats of lightning swarmed and leaped through the clouds far ahead. As with the thunder, I assumed I had some time before they fell on me. Suddenly, though, they jumped to a mile up the road, and ten seconds didn't pass before a bolt slammed into the earth a hundred yards to my right. Then all hell broke loose. An oak slightly behind me took hit after hit until one huge bolt nailed its crotch. The roar alone nearly knocked me from the bike, but the sight—I have never been that close to lightning, never knew that it is an actual *thing*, a thickness, not just light, but a substance as big around as a telephone pole. The tree's main branch splintered, yawned away, and crashed on the road.

In the next minutes, lightning bolts landed as close as thirty or forty yards away. A picket fence of lightning. All afternoon I crawled three and four miles an hour out of one storm into another, never so alone or frightened in my entire life.

B̲y̲ evening, the rain fell as a cold drizzle, but the wind, that damn wind hadn't lost a notch. New Town finally formed in the mist as if out of an anguished dream. I looked at my hands—slightly blue, wrinkled, no feeling whatsoever in the left palm. I looked at my face in the mirror—lips bluish, cheeks hollow as the gulches. Over my shoulder, the wheel prints stretched back toward Williston. I normally leave only one print. But here were two, and they wobbled drunk-assed all over the road. I remembered that story about a man who dreamt of his footprints on the seashore. The one where he demands of God: "Look, here are my footprints in the most troubled time in my life. Where are yours, how come you didn't walk beside me?" God answers: "My child, this is when I carried you." What a stupid story. The man comes off like such a whiner. And God sounds like one big condescending shit if you ask me.

I knocked on the door of the New Town Catholic Parish House. A tubby white-haired man in a black clerical shirt answered. The white collar was sproinged halfway out of its slot.

"Sorry, council policy, can't let you sleep in the church, lots of problems with Indians and robberies." He didn't have many teeth. I thanked him and turned to go.

"Hey, just a second, were you that biker out on the highway this afternoon?"

"Yeah, I'm afraid that was me."

"Good grief, I saw you out there and wondered what in the world. Where you going anyway?" I was shivering but I answered his questions. He pulled a charred corncob pipe from his pants pocket, then filled and slowly tamped it.

"Well, it's not much," he said into the first swirl of smoke, "but I've got a back room here you're welcome to have it tonight if you like."

The room's sole decoration was a crucifix nailed to the door. But it had a bed and it was dry. I dropped my bags and puddles immediately formed under them. The priest offered me a bag of chocolate cookies and a half gallon of milk. He may have meant for me only to have a few, but I ate the entire thing and drank all but a drop of the milk. At last light, I peeled off my clothes, wrapped myself in blankets, and collapsed on the bed.

In my dream I walked a long hallway, the floor, walls, and ceiling all made of glass. I was dressed only in dry clean riding shorts and cleats. To my left, outside the glass, stood aunts and uncles; my brother at age thirteen when he knocked my front tooth out, then his face ten years later when I stood up for him at his wedding, and a third time—the faces of his two children now crowding his own; faces of the grand-fathers I never knew; my mother's face sprinkled here and there like rose petals in a bush. They were all like flowers. Even the fat uncle I hate, the one that blew cigar smoke in my face when I was a kid, there he was, a pompous flowering cactus. It was a greenhouse in reverse. They leaned forward against the glass to see me pass. They all looked so worried. They were all there except my father. I couldn't touch them or smell their aromas though I breathed deep to try. That was the most important thing: they were outside the glass and they all were fretting for me; all except Dad. I kept walking down the hallway, my cleats noisy on the glass.

AUGUST 17

 70 MILES

Minot, North Dakota

As I rode out of New Town a bank clock told me to set my watch ahead an hour. Central Time Zone. My left hand was useless, the knee scraped hard, and the cleats were as soaked this morning as when I peeled them off last night; but I was finally in the Midwest. East of New Town, the hills flattened, the burnt fields turned honey yellow with wheat and sunflowers, and a redwinged blackbird squalled at me to get the hell off his property. Home.

I've made it at least this far in one piece.

South of Minot, a thunderstorm rolled fast across the bike and though the storm was mostly noise and water, a young woman pulled her pickup over to offer a ride. She looked scared for me. "No thanks," I hollered through the rain, "I'm having fun if you can believe it." Rules of the Road. Like the bus, the pickup stayed at my elbow for the better part of a minute before driving off. If I made it through yesterday, absolutely nothing will keep me from making it on my own to the Atlantic.

Suddenly, though, the bottom bracket made a sharp grinding noise—probably grit driven in by yesterday's deluge—and I limped into Scheel's Sporting Goods downtown. The mechanic was on vacation and the manager opened his shop for me. I flushed the bracket, soaked the bearings in gas, checking everything for pits and scars, then took Duncan's mangy toothbrush and scrubbed every single ball bearing and the bracket's insides just to make sure. They all looked clean. One grain of that sand could screw this whole trip, and no way—not after yesterday, not after three weeks of beating my ass this far— would that happen. I found the mechanic's stack of fresh shop towels, dried off all the parts, and rescrubbed.

I lavished fresh grease into the bracket, put it all back together, and wheeled the bike through the store for a test ride outside. One of the checkout women, young and pretty with dark brown hair, looked at the bike and panniers, then smiled—the nicest moment in this whole burnt–prairie week.

Minot was now dressed in sunshine. My father used to tell me about Minot, and from those gloomy Depression era stories Minot has existed in my mind as little more than a dustyard for cattle slaughter. Here, though, on a Saturday afternoon in August were quiet streets of elm, lilac, and effusive gladiolas. Brick Victorians. And lawns. After Montana's endless brown and gray, sunlight on the deep green of these lawns almost hurt the eye. The bike pedaled greasy and quiet and I turned down street after street soaking in the order and the lush green.

Back at Scheel's shop, I packed my tools and grease. The checkout woman punched the clock behind me.

"Where you going?"

She was even prettier up close. Please oh please don't stammer. "Uh, across America." I busied myself with a crescent wrench.

"Wow. By yourself?"

"Yeah, if I, if I got this bottom bracket fixed right."

"What's wrong with it?"

She pulled her store jacket off, and underneath wore a pair of bright yellow jeans and a white blouse. When she pushed back her hair I looked to my tools and forgot what she'd asked. She squatted at the bike and wrinkled her forehead.

"I've got to learn about this stuff," she said. "Is this the bottom bracket?" She touched it.

"Yes."

"And this is the chain wheel, right?"

"Yes."

"And that's a spanner wrench."

"You're pretty good, you know all this stuff."

"Well, I'm learning. My fiancé and I are planning a bicycle honeymoon, and he's been teaching me."

Oh. Fiancé.

She wiped her fingers on a shop rag. "Where'd you start?"

"Seattle."

She opened wide dark brown eyes.

"Where are you and he going?"

"I think we'll ride around Lake Superior. Do you camp out?" She looked at my sleeping bag and tent.

"Lately I've been mooching off preachers, sleeping on church basement couches, that sort of—"

"Really! Brad and I are Christians. I bet he could find a place for you tonight at our church."

It was the way she said "Christians." I quickly finished packing my tools.

"Thanks anyway but—"

"Would you stay? I'm sure Brad would want to find out all he can from you about touring."

"Well, thanks but I've really—"

"Oh please. I'll make you supper!"

The next thing I knew I was standing in her shower watching North Dakota grit slide down the drain.

The bathroom was a bright violet color, filled with late sun and the flowered smells of a woman. A wooden plaque on the wall said, "For God So Loved the World that He Gave His Only Begotten Son." Outside, a tinny radio played a church service while she hummed along.

She snapped off the radio when I sat at the table.

"I just called Brad, and he says you're welcome to stay in his spare room tonight. I'll drive you over as soon as you're finished."

She set out a plate of sandwiches and we sat down. I waited for her to say something like "Why don't we pray first," but she quickly took the first bite and I breathed a sigh of relief. Nancy Craney is twenty-six, a third grade teacher who works at Scheel's during the summer. In a couple weeks, she'll move to South Carolina to attend Bible college in preparation for overseas mission work. I kept her busy with questions about Brad and Minot in hopes she wouldn't practice on me. Her answers came with such an ease that we soon talked about her dad the insurance salesman over in Fargo, mine the turkey farmer in Illinois, and laughed about what weird last names we each have. She told me about the kids she'll miss this fall, one boy in particular who has trouble with math. When she laughs her eyes nearly shut and her glasses nudge down her nose. She took her glasses off once and I had to remind myself that this woman is engaged. I tried to keep my mind on Karen in St. Paul. Through the first plate of sandwiches, then another, then a third, there was hardly a moment's silence. Jesus didn't come up once, and I felt as if I hadn't eaten or spoken since I left John.

Her car was a 1974 Olds Cutlass Supreme wagon, repainted a phosphorescent lime. The quintessential bomb. I loaded the bike in the back and she wired the door shut with a coat hanger. I felt chivalrous after such a meal, so I did something that surprised even me—I opened her door for her. She got in with an odd, pleased look on her face.

I want this for the record: I only took the ride because Brad lived *west* of her house. Which, in effect, is ground I've already ridden. If he'd lived *east* I would have pedaled. But once we got moving, oh, I wanted her to turn around and drive me all the way to Maine and right off that last dock into the Atlantic. The unfathomable luxury of the internal combustion engine! The ease! On the highway, she opened the Olds up and I stuck my head out the window.

"You'll stay for lunch tomorrow, won't you," she called through the wind.

"Ah, you've done so much for me already, Nancy. But I've got to make a wedding in St. Paul next week."

"Stay. I like talking to you." I think that's what she said anyway. She sped up and the wind messed her words. We had to be near 70—that's when old tanks like this smooth out and hum. I ducked inside. The speedometer lay on its zero post. This week, I've seen every single solitary blade of blasted prairie grass between here and the Rockies, and could've counted them if I wanted. But here, even the telephone poles ticked past too quick to count. The Olds rode like a rocket sled. She looked at my knuckles whitening on the door handle and goosed the gas a couple times; she laughed and rolled her window down to fill the car with prairie, then slowed to turn off the highway. She parked outside a large rundown house near Minot College. "There's Brad. You'll like him."

Brad leaned against a tree, a small man, his face a blend of worry and melancholy, his mustache the color of sand. I sat in the car for just a second and looked at him. One of the shortcomings of this route, I suppose, is that so many of the people I meet look so much the same, so much like me. Had I gone from south to north instead of west to east I would've cut across most of what America offers in the way of race. Straight across the north, though, like this, it's almost all smooth manila skin, the tiny nose, the earnest forehead; faces of northern Europe homogenized like cream of mushroom soup. Brad's face was remarkable only for its unremarkableness, for that sameness. His hands were stuck deep in each pocket.

"Welcome to Minot," he said, hand stretched for mine. "I'm Brad." People along this way talk like me, too. We are all these middling baritones. His grasp was weak but warm and he reached with his other to take my panniers.

My room tonight is in what could charitably be called a student dive. A house of stains and warped walls. I wheeled the bike in and laid my wet clothes from yesterday on the floor to dry. Down the hall I heard Nancy. "He's really interesting . . . lunch tomorrow . . . Ask him . . . bicycles . . ."

"We'd be pleased if you'd join us for lunch tomorrow," Brad said as he walked in my door. "Nancy says you know a lot and could teach us a thing or two."

"He's an animal," Nancy said and came in beside him. She stood slightly taller than he. "A hundred miles a day." Brad looked impressed.

"Thanks, but I really need to move on. I'll take off in the morning."

"A hundred miles a day," he said. "Seems to me you'd want

a rest after something like that. I'm getting my nursing degree across the street." He nodded toward the college. "You know, the body can only take so much."

Like a flashback all the veterans of this ride seconded him. "Six on, one off," they'd all told me. Ride as fast and as far as you want for six days, but always take at least one off. It'll catch up with you otherwise. I've just pulled seven. I thought of the wedding next Saturday. I want to be there, have Karen brag about me to her friends. I looked at my left hand and rubbed its fingers across the palm: I could barely feel a thing.

"I'm making a huge lunch tomorrow, Newhouse," Nancy said and walked from the door as if ending the discussion. "You'd be a fool to miss it. You should see him eat, Brad. I've never seen a man eat like that before. I'm going shopping. You coming, Brad?"

I had the house to myself for the next hour. Their refrigerator door held a picture of them: he with a serious Yes-we-certainly-are-going-to-be-married look, she with her fingers bunny-eared behind him. The living room was spare with only a guitar leaned into an empty corner, an exhausted mud-colored couch, and an old rocking chair. On the wall hung what must've been their formal engagement portrait. The Fine Christian Couple, he posed a head taller than she and looking into the middle distance.

I sat in the rocker, laid the guitar against my belly, and watched my left hand stumble for the chords as if it belonged to someone else. Once I found them, though, the chords were a kind of comfort. The music warmed the spot where Nancy's food lay. I rocked and sighed.

"You play guitar, too," Brad called from the kitchen when they returned.

"No, just a couple of chords, " I said and quickly set it back in its case.

"No, no. Go on, play the thing." Brad walked into the living room. "I'd like to hear you." He sat on the couch and folded his hands.

I stumbled through my whole whopping repertoire: the A chord, the E, then the C. He got bored quickly.

"So why are you riding across America alone?"

"Just something I have to do." I played the A again.

"Where did you start?"

I've answered these questions I don't know how many times now. For waitresses, gas station clerks, tall thin farmers who politely hold the grocery door open and nod at my bicycle. There are six, asked almost always in this order:

Where you from?

Where did you start?

Where you going?

How far you go each day on that thing?

Whad'ya eat?

Where you sleep?

These six do it for just about everybody. Brad, though, wanted to know about gear ratio, how to work the steepest hills, the equipment I considered essential, he even asked about spoke gauge, for crying out loud. It was rare to find someone so interested and I stopped strumming and lay the guitar on my lap. Nancy came in and sat next to him on the couch.

"Don't you get lonely out there?" she asked. "I mean, we'll have each other when we go." She put her hand on his. "But you, you're all by yourself."

She looked at me with the same odd pleased expression as when I'd closed her car door for her, as if we'd met years earlier and she's just about to recall my name. It flattered me, made me nervous. I don't remember what I told her, something about that's what I signed up for, you just have to do it. Something like that. I looked at the guitar the whole time.

"OK, so what about your rear," she said. "My butt's gonna get sore." We all laughed and I looked up and leered at her like a dirty old man.

"Leather. What you need is leather, sweetheart," I said. Brad's eyebrows shot up while she feigned a smoky come-hither look at me until she and I laughed, then Brad.

"Get yourself the most expensive leather seat you can afford. Before you put it on the bike, soak it overnight in oil, then take a rolling pin and beat the hell out of it."

It slipped out, the H word, but she didn't blink. He did. "Beat it for an hour a day. Do that for a week. Then put it on the bike and ride it. After a hundred fifty miles you've got a custom fit."

Brad seemed to have had his fill at that point, and sat back.

"How about you two?" I asked. "What are you doing after the wedding?"

"I'll finish my nursing degree at the college," Brad said, pointing out the window. "By that time Nancy'll be partly done at South Carolina Bible—"

"And then it's overseas," Nancy finished for him.

"Where?"

"Africa probably," he answered. "I'd like to do medical missionary work. The need is incredible." He paused. "You've been staying with preachers. What kind?"

"Lutherans, so far. That's how I was raised."

"How do you do that, find a place to sleep?"

"I just ride into town, look under Lutherans in the yellow pages. Practically all the preachers went to seminary in St. Paul, so for them in a small-town parish, I'm the big city they remember as a student. I'm kind of exotic. Most of them seem pleased to have the visit. Their wives usually offer to do my laundry, bake me muffins for my handlebar bag."

"Geesh, that sounds rough," Nancy said.

"Do you belong to a Lutheran church?" Brad asked.

"Well, I attend one, but I'm still shopping around for the right one."

"What do you mean, the right one?"

"You know, one that feels right." I was going to tell him about Andrew and preachers who built bicycle wheels.

"Some preach Jesus and the Bible," he said, "and others preach other stuff, whatever makes the folks in the pews feel good."

I started to grip the guitar's neck. Uh-oh. The medical missionary. Here it comes.

"See, I think a lot of Lutheran churches are just plain soft," he said. "They don't give enough Bible, or enough Jesus."

He then asked more questions, careful questions about the churches I've attended, about doctrine and sin, probing with the same thoroughness he had for bicycles. He asked them politely, unlike most who do this, and I did my stumbling Sunday school best to answer him. But you could tell he was zeroing in. And sure enough, "Why did Jesus come here? Are you a sinner?" He got down that deep and I can't or don't want to remember my answers. I could only watch my hand grasp the guitar neck while the rest of me froze up. Always this same paralysis. Except in my head where the wrong answers bounce like spilled BB's. *No, I don't want to get saved, I don't want you to want me to get saved, what is saved anyway? And would you please just leave me alone?*

I came up at Brad's "Is Jesus your Lord?" shaking my head.

Nancy touched his arm. He looked at her. You could barely see it, but she nodded toward the kitchen. He paused for a second.

"Well, breakfast'll be about eight tomorrow," she said. "We're going to church after that. We'd love it if you joined us but you're welcome to sleep in if you want. Either way, we're gonna eat big come noon." They walked into the kitchen and rattled bottles in the fridge.

I thought of my bicycle leaning against that stained bedroom wall. I could grab it and be gone in five minutes. But suddenly all the exhaustion of seven days and seven hundred miles of Montana and western North Dakota fell on me. My hand eased on the guitar neck and my thumb found the lowest string, E, and plucked it. The guitar resting against the wooden rocker made the whole chair buzz in E. I put the guitar back in its case, slipped quietly into my room, and went to bed.

AUGUST 18

Their church is a small white prefab house, the kind you see rolling down the highway in halves, one truck at a time. The Sunday school let out as we approached and kids spilled into the North Dakota sunshine greeting Brad and Nancy by name.

I decided to stay this day in Minot because a bit of feeling has returned to my left hand. I figure a day off the bike will get more of it back. And if they're going to feed me lunch, I'd better go to their church. Call it politeness. Call it an extension of last night's numbness.

We sat halfway back on the right. Reverend Mark Bendall stepped into the pulpit. He resembled Brad and so many of the others in the pews, except for his crewcut of extraordinary bristlinesss. The Air Force runs a base north of town. He must be an airman. Great. Up in the air, junior birdmen . . .

"My topic today is prayer," he began, "prayer in the time of crisis." People scribbled on notepads from the hymnal racks. "The text is from Matthew twenty-six.

"Then Jesus went with his disciples to a place called Gethsemane, and he said to them, 'Sit here while I go over there and pray.' Jesus took with him Peter and the two sons of Zebedee. Grief and anguish came over him, and he said to them, 'The sorrow in my heart is so great that it almost crushes me.' "

Bendall's voice was a high warm tenor. The way he said "crushes" struck me. I've heard this story a million times and never heard crushes. Christ crushed.

"Jesus went a little farther on, threw himself face downward on the ground, and prayed, 'My Father, if it is possible, take this cup of suffering from me. Yet not what I want but what you want.' "

Bendall closed the Bible. "Anybody here have that kind of week?" A couple nervous titters.

"I made a fascinating discovery this week. I discovered Gethsemane is the Aramaic word for oil press. Here we see Christ coming to the realization that he will die, and die painfully. The events of Holy Week that we know so well are about to unfold. And the fact of his own death is breaking in on him. He was being *pressed*, driven to pray like he'd never prayed before. In Luke's gospel it says his sweat fell like blood on the ground around him.

"When did you pray last? This morning? Last month? Remember, it pleases God to hear from you. God loves the time we share with him simply talking. We are his children."

Gag. Some of us unsaved heathen aren't his children. I started to flip aimlessly through the hymnal.

"But when life falls apart, what do you do?" His voice was gentler and as I looked up, some hurt seemed to cross his face.

"When everything is blown apart and you have nothing left, what happens?

"Couple nights ago I got a call. It was the Bjorklands. I know you've heard about it by now. Let me tell you, it is the hardest thing a pastor can do, to sit in a hospital with parents whose teenager has just had a tractor roll on him. Most of the ribs crushed. The doctors come, they go, some good news, then a setback. And you know, there was not a thing I could say to them."

He looked out the window. He looked ashamed. "There wasn't a single word I could say to them," he repeated. "Not a word to try to help them make sense of it." He looked back down at us. "So we just waited. And waited. The family was all there. Someone suggested we pray. So we sat and held hands tight and prayed."

A jet rose hissing from the base. Bendall stopped and listened to it. He looked again out the window and said more to himself than us, "When it all falls apart where do you go?" Then he reopened his Bible and read.

"He drove into my heart the arrows of his quiver. He has filled me with bitterness. He has made my teeth grind on gravel and made me cower in ashes. My soul is bereft of peace."

Then deep in hurt he looked over us and his voice came back strong.

"That was Lamentations and that was *exactly* the way it was in the hospital Thursday night. Do you get that? He has made my teeth *grind* on gravel." He shut the Bible.

"Have you faced a tremendous overwhelming pain this week? Something so big that you knew for certain God *could not* be there—in that pain, in that emptiness? That you were all alone?

"Christ in Gethsemane is getting the life pressed out of

him. He's about to be killed, and he knows it! He knows it and the only thing left to do is pray. *My soul is bereft*. Thursday night we knew that Bob wouldn't live, and we were forced to pray because there was simply nothing left to do.

"And how about you?" Bendall looked straight at me. Suddenly, I saw myself two mornings ago as lightning obliterated that oak thirty yards from my bike.

"God says call on me at those times," Bendall went on loud and, I swear to God, the man did not look at another person in that room. All these people he knew well, people who call him Pastor—he looked past all of them and straight at me, pressing me against the pew. "Call on me in that moment when you feel abandoned, when you are certain you may be crushed. I am there! I am with you even when you cannot hear me or see me. I am with you."

The room slipped away as I heard that voice in Bettene's trailer again.

"God is faithful," Bendall continued, finally looking at the rest of his congregation. The front wall of the church might as well have been a movie screen—the Williston lightning ripping across it, that school bus and the old priest who took me in. The pew back felt like stone and if it hadn't been there I might have toppled. Over and over again I heard those words that had awakened me from a dead sleep in Bettene's trailer. I am with you. And how do I say what happened next without sounding like a prayer book? A deep quiet rose into my body. It didn't come from on high or anyplace above. It began in my thighs as if flowing from below the pew, from below even the foundation of that flimsy prefab church. I don't know how to describe the feeling, other than the assurance that I am watched.

Going down the church steps, my legs buckled slightly—either from the sermon or from atrophy in unused walking muscles—and Brad caught my elbow. I grabbed the railing. It was painted black and I could feel its warmth and a few rusted paint flakes that came off in my left palm—more sensation coming back. Brad smiled and didn't say a word. He will make a very good nurse. It occurred to me then that all I've done these last three weeks is push up mountains and into wind. The muscles of grace, the ones used going downhill, are all shot. He and Nancy drove to the house. I walked back and soaked in as much of Minot's green as I could hold, feeling almost what it is like to learn to walk again—every lift of the foot, every setting of it down. Minot College's big front yard was a lake of green, and each step across it felt rare. I took off my shoes. The cool grass . . .

Nancy was at the sink when I opened the kitchen screen, already changed from her church dress into jeans and a white lace blouse. Vegetables lay on the counter and water ran from the faucet.

"Have a good walk?" She pushed her glasses up her nose with the back of her wrist.

"After all the devastated prairie I've seen this week, Minot looks like paradise. It's so green."

She picked up the vegetables and started to scrub. She looked out the window above the sink. "I love that about this place. They used to call it the Magic City. A hundred years ago when the railroad came through, they set up a tent camp a little west of here. Everybody thought that would be the town. But the railroad brass thought that a spot on the Souris River would be better, and bang, the whole town moved right here just like that. They had something like five thousand people move in practically overnight. That's why they called it the Magic City."

She shut the water off and toweled her hands. "A lot of people think Minot is the end of the earth, but we've got clean air, not much crime, a symphony, places where folks paint and exhibit their stuff. Kids graduate and move to Fargo or Minne-apolis as fast as they can, but I like it here."

"But you're going to Africa."

"Well, for a time anyway. That's the plan. Here, make your-self useful, chop these radishes for me. There's a space at the counter over there. Brad'll be back in a bit, he's getting some milk."

"When are you two getting married?"

"Next June. It should be nice that time of year. I want it outside, I want to see the prairie during the service. But Brad. He's so proper about things. He wants it inside our tiny little church. We go round and round about it. We go round about almost everything. The only thing we agree on is that we want to get married. But the cake, the reception." She laughed and unwrapped a chicken from its bag. "You ever been married?"

"I got close, twice."

She didn't say anything, and something about all that green, the church service, the safe sounds of water running in the sink—I just dumped the whole story out, everything I'd thought of telling Duncan around the fire weeks ago but didn't. How Lili and I started in high school, my annual Dear Jane letters to her and how I always came back. The first engage-ment and my cold feet. The second and hers. Then the end and how it gave way to this trip. I didn't mention Karen. That was a whole 'nother story. When I finished, the peppers lay in bite-sized heaps.

"Weddings," Nancy said. "They're a pain in the butt. I think people should elope."

I laughed and remembered the elaborate plans we'd made, twice. "You mean all I needed was a ladder?"

"Mercy me, what would the neighbors think?" She slipped into a perfect Dixie accent and fanned herself with a clump of broccoli, eyelids aflutter. "A fine upstandin' Christian woman like me, runnin' off in the middle of the night with some man? Scandalous!"

I got more vegetables to chop. She cut the chicken. And for the next half hour we moved around each other like dance partners, the ratty kitchen linoleum creaking under our feet. She adopted another accent, I think it was Julia Child blathering on about the proper way to cut beets. I gave her my Nixon imitation, which I've always thought was better than fair, and instructed her on the fine points of chicken dismemberment. When we washed dishes we pretended to be from the Bronx. When we set the table, we were a stuffy butler and maid in a British castle. Brad must've taken the long route for the milk because everything was ready and he still wasn't back. We killed time by slicing one more tomato and pepper apiece, each in our original spots by the counter.

"You know, Nancy, if you take the stem off, the green pepper looks kind of like North Dakota." For the second time, she didn't say anything. I turned to look at her.

And this picture will be etched in my mind, always. She is simply standing there, her back to the sink, framed by the sun-filled window. She holds half a tomato in her hand and the juice drips to the linoleum. For perhaps five or ten seconds there is this tableau: her smile at me, the dripping fruit, the sun behind her lighting streaks of red in her brown hair. Then she turned to the sink. For the next long minute the only sound was our slicing knives.

"Well, I think . . . I think that when Brad and I are married next June, June fourteenth, I think you should just ride your bike back here and be in our wedding."

Seconds later the screen door opened.

"It smells great in here," Brad said. "What's for lunch?" She hugged him hard. He looked surprised and kissed her cheek.

Lunch was a huge success, "huge" being the operative word. Pasta, chicken, and enough vegetables to choke a pig. We sloshed it down with milk and beer and capped it all off with warm brownies. It was excessive, and it was wonderful. They sat across the table from me, and Nancy's hand rested on his shoulder. We talked only of bicycles.

After dishes, Brad stretched and yawned. "I've got to work late tonight, you guys. I'm gonna nap. Nancy, would you call me in an hour?"

He went to his room and I looked at her. She was busy at the sink, the sun still behind her but now it silhouetted her arms and waist inside her blouse. She started to turn my way and I said, "I need to see some more of Minot, Nancy. I'll be back."

I walked for hours, knowing he'd be up and they'd be together by the time I got back. Once more across the green of Minot College, then past the railyards where Minot began a hundred years ago. Over the Souris and to the edge of the Magic City. Wheat ran to the sunset.

I'm attracted to Nancy. OK? There, I said it. She's a Christian, like Karen, yet she hasn't shut herself down as Karen has. She's still alive.

But she is not just Nancy. She is NancyandBrad.

They were climbing into the Olds when I got back. He was in his nursing whites.

"The house is all yours tonight, Brian," Brad said. "I'll be back around six tomorrow morning."

"I'll take off about six-thirty then. Have a good night." I shook his hand with both of mine, and tried to convey with that gesture all the appreciation I really felt for him. The food, his spare room. This rest. Even dragging me to his church. He climbed in and Nancy came over.

"I'm going to drop him off at work, then I'm busy at church. So, this is it."

I quickly held up my hand to shake hers. I said, "Thank you for every—"

She opened her arms and hugged me. Not the polite Lutheran kind, or the Newhouse kind, but the kind with arms wrapped all the way around. The warmth nearly made my legs buckle. My arms were frozen at my sides.

She said, close to my ear, "You remember me, all right?" and hugged me even tighter. I started to bring my arms up to hug her, but she backed away and slid inside without looking up.

The next morning's ride was through the North Dakota checkerboard I remember from childhood. All along that stretch cloudbursts rose and fell, and the broad flat land became a kind of stage for them. They looked like dancers. One trailed a gray veil miles behind her, another stood alone wrapped in a swirl of blue-gray chiffon. Many took partners, split, and joined up with new partners. Others glided from horizon to horizon unattached. A blade of light cut through one, producing a half-rainbow. A shower spattered up behind me and I pulled off my helmet. Then lifted my face to the rain.

AUGUST 19

 95 MILES

Leeds, North Dakota

Rugby, North Dakota, geographical center of North America. I'm halfway. I stopped at the post office where a package and a letter waited for me, general delivery.

The package was a shoe box from Karen. Inside, she'd packed fifteen little doodads, things like a kid's school eraser with the word *star* printed on it; a little key chain with a tiny tin globe dangling from the end; a couple of marbles. Other stuff. I pawed through it wondering why this? And what am I supposed to do with it? Carry it? Great. More weight. On the bottom of the box lay a note.

Dear Bri,

I hope you get this stuff all right. I went to the dollar store and bought it for you just because. I figured you might like something fun. The eraser is because you're a star to me. The key chain globe you can use for a map if yours get wet. The marbles are cat eyes, so you keep a sharp eye out for traffic and get home safe to me.

I hope like crazy that you're all right. I've got my entire women's group praying for you and your safety. Our women's pastor the other night, all of a sudden in the middle of our meeting, she stopped us and said she felt you needed prayer that instant. So that's what we did. Did you feel it? Has anything bad happened? Call me when you get this. I miss you so and hope you're safe. You're my hero.

Love,
Karen

AUGUST 21

205 MILES

Moorhead, Minnesota

The towns along Highway 2 click by like railroad ties—Rugby, seven miles later Pleasant Lake, another seven Knox, still another seven York—all laid down a year apart in the 1880s and named for the British men on the Great Northern's board. I wish I could say that each one was fascinating and unique but I have hardly raised my eyes from the road since Rugby. I don't know one from the other. The wind has been a terror, blowing straight into the handlebars at no less than twenty-five miles an hour. Even when I turned southeast at Devil's Lake it tacked exactly against me and kicked up a notch to nearly forty. Three days since Minot, eleven hours each, I've buried my head to duck it. And the world has shrunk to the white line at road's edge. Diversions: broken glass I wipe with a gloved hand from the tire; a squirrel, its entrails sprayed in front of it. Once, I stopped pedaling to see how long the wind took to stop the bike. Two seconds.

South of Devil's Lake somewhere I walked into a field and

threw the bicycle against a tall stack of hay bales. Sick of the wind, sick of everything. I rifled through the handlebar bag for something to eat and spilled one of Karen's damn marbles into the field. I picked it up and cocked my arm back. With the wind, Lord knows how far I could fling it. Halfway to Montana, maybe. Why the hell did she give me these anyway? I put it back.

I sat on the lee side of the bales—quiet, finally, back there—and ate some grapes. The train of wind roared around the bales. After a few minutes, I told myself to get up—I was starting to relax, to feel too good, the sun especially warm on the black Lycra covering my thighs and hips. Just a couple more minutes, though. I lay into the hay fingering Karen's marble, holding it up to the sun and watching a rainbow trapped in the cat's eye.

A sweat broke under my shorts, and I enjoyed it with half-closed eyes. The Lycra looked and felt as if someone had melted dark chocolate over my legs. I remembered the night when I rode my bicycle to Karen's office just to plant a sweaty I-rode-thirty-miles-for-this-moment kiss on her lips. I had on only cleats and these same shorts, and leaned across a stack of legal books open on her desk to kiss her. She started to pull away but I didn't let her and she slowly gave in, wrapping her hands through my hair. She leaned forward, across the desk into me. The sweat ticked onto the books.

We picked up a pizza on the way home and put it on the middle of my living room carpet. She slid a finger under the hem of these same shorts. "You have really nice legs, Bri." The pizza box got kicked aside, clothes flew everywhere, and the hair she wears up each day fell like warm rain on my face when I pulled the pins out. We pored over each other, and in the last light I noticed that one of her eyes is slightly bluer than the other. The different shades made me think of wolf eyes.

She said over and over, "I want to. But we can't." We kept rolling and groping, though, and suddenly her back arched, her fingers dug into my arms, and her body bucked. She called out, "Now, now, now." The words made no sense and at first I thought they were an invitation, the gate finally swinging open. Before I could make a move, though, a cloud crossed her face and she snatched her blouse from the floor and clutched it to her chest. She sat up and rocked back and forth praying, "I am pure. I have sinned. I am so sorry, God. I am pure."

I picked the bike off the haystack and walked it back to the road. The wind was howling now, straight over the handlebars. I crawled across deserted Fort Totten Indian Reservation and Binford's steep grassy hills. About fifteen miles outside Cooperstown I had to stop again. At a truckstop, I slumped on a counter stool while the radio played—like some bad cosmic joke—Bob Seeger's "Against the Wind." Outside, I slipped into a phone booth.

"Brian, I need to apologize to you."

"What for?"

"You know the last time we talked?"

"I remember," I said. My reflection in the Plexiglas was smiling. "Your fantasies? There was a certain waterfall—"

"Yes. That was wrong."

My face fell. "Wrong? Karen, that kept me going for about two days straight. That was gorgeous."

"It's just the flesh talking. And I shouldn't tempt you like that. It doesn't please God—"

"Karen." A hard gust nudged the booth, rattling the flimsy panes. The door shot open. I slammed it shut. I stood for a second with my hand on the door as all words left me. The fatigue, the frustration. I didn't have a thing to say to her.

Back on Highway 200 the wind was finally dying down for the evening. The last ten miles into Cooperstown were a straight shot out of the west, and the setting sun threw my shadow probably a quarter mile over the handlebars. I bent over and chased it.

Three hundred miles in three days and all of it straight into a wind that feels as if someone had aimed it at me. My legs don't look like my own anymore, swollen with muscles I never knew existed. Sometimes, pushing into the wind, I chant Karen's name over and over. Sometimes it comes out like a curse.

AUGUST 22

80 MILES

Elbow Lake, Minnesota

Highway 52 approaches Fergus Falls, Minnesota, from the northwest, cutting deep into the black soil the last mile or so before town. The ditches there rise a good ten feet above the road and form a chute that collects and drives the wind northwest. Of course, I came to Fergus the exact wrong way up the chute. The wind was probably doing 45 and as I lowered my head to the handlebars, this snippet of last night's dream popped into my head: my feet, booted in concrete, were strapped to the pedals and the speedometer read minus three.

At the edge of Fergus, a bright red dash cut across my mirror. I shoved the bike onto the shoulder, and the sports car whisked by, inches away. The gravel was soft and deep and I started to fall. I stabbed the right pedal down to power through it, but suddenly pinging snaps sounded underneath. I ripped my foot from the toe clips and stood shaking while the red dash flew around the last corner into Fergus.

Five broken spokes in the rear rim.

"Shit!" I tried to roll the bike, but the tire dug a crisp little ditch in the gravel. The rim was warped so badly it was jammed against the frame.

"Shit!" This was supposed to be a big miles day—it *had* to be if I was going to make the wedding. I wanted to pull within at least 150 miles of St. Paul by tonight, then somehow tomorrow pour it on like never before. The rim was completely shot.

"Shit!"

At the first phone, I called K. & K. Tire and Schwinn, Fergus's only bike shop.

"We're on the east side," an old voice said, " 'bout two miles from where you're standing right now. If you can get it here, we'll fix you quick."

I picked up the rear of the bike and aimed the front wheel down the sidewalk. Minutes from the phone booth, I remembered how when I flew with my bike to Seattle, the airline clerk's eyes had popped open as she watched the airport scale whip up to eighty-one pounds of bike and bags. My arm felt as if it were being drawn from its socket. All those fancy muscles that have shown up in my legs over the last weeks—fat lot of good they did me now. I had to drop the bike. For the next two hours the rear tire laid a stripe on Fergus's sidewalks as I shoved the bike, literally, from one end of town to the other.

The rear tire blew at the last hill. I yelled and ducked, sure it was a gun shot. Raising myself from the sidewalk, little kids across the street laughed and pointed. A postal carrier came up the walk and said, "She'll go faster if you pedal her."

I could just read the headline now: FERGUS FALLS POSTAL WORKER FOUND BLUDGEONED BY BICYCLE RIM.

By the time I reached K. & K., threads stuck out of the tire and the rim was mashed even harder against the frame. A silver-haired guy at the counter waved me in.

"Come on in. You're top of the list. My boy Gary's all set up in the back."

Gary leaned against the shop bench wiping tools. He was all of fourteen, fifteen tops. Fuzzy-cheeked, a few soft pink pimples on his forehead. Every shop's got one of these: a kid who needs a summer job, is basically interested in bikes, but doesn't know squat. You end up doing the work or hover around him just to make sure he doesn't screw it up. Good-bye, St. Paul. This is going to take forever.

"Whoa. You fall or what?" His voice hadn't even changed yet.

"Sort of." I leaned the bike against a tractor tire. "Got run off the road. I'm not sure how it happened."

He was a good-looking kid. Wispy white-blond hair, corn-flower blue eyes of a surprising intensity. He ran his finger against the rim and tried to push it away from the frame. It didn't budge. He pursed his lips and shoved the rim with the heel of his hand. He whistled in admiration.

We got the bike into the stand and I turned to his bench. I'd need a couple spoke wrenches, a long crescent, a pair of pliers, and a heavy wire cutter.

"You have to loosen the quick release first," I said, but he already had the wheel off and into the bench vise where he gave it a twirl.

"This is *really* bad," he whispered, his eye level with the rim. He took a felt pen from his pocket and tapped ink onto certain points.

"Should we trash it or fix it?" I wanted to get on with this.

He lifted a pair of dainty little spoke wrenches from the pegboard and gave the rim yet another spin. He grinned the smirk of teenage boys who know something you don't. His braces glinted under the shop fluorescents. Then, from a bench drawer he pulled the biggest rubber mallet I have ever seen.

"What are you going to do with that!"

"This is my persuader," he said. He gave another spin of the rim, eyeing it like a golfer would a putt, laying the mallet handle just above it. I stood back and watched, feeling a light sweat break on my back. I had seventy dollars in that rim. He cut the broken spokes out, laced in new ones, and spoke-wrenched them as tight as he could. Another spin. Still bad. Another leveling of the mallet. Then he turned to me and said, "I'm ready, but you may not want to see what I'm about to do, sir." The look on his face told me he was about to perform a cesarean without anesthesia, that it might be better if I waited outside.

"I'll watch."

He lifted the mallet high over head, then smashed the rim. "YAH!" he hollered. The rim bounced in the vise, and the new spokes sang out in pain. I flinched. He smashed it again in exactly the same spot. "Now!" A third time. "I said NOW!" He dropped the mallet and spun the wheel. It actually looked a little better. He grabbed the spoke wrench.

"Do you have to hit it so—" I said.

"C'mon sweetheart, c'mon sugar," he whispered, ignoring me. He worked the little wrench, practically kissing the spokes as he tightened them. "Little bit more now, that's it." The rim groaned. Suddenly he frowned and tossed the wrench to the bench, grabbed the mallet, hauled his arm back, and hollered.

A flurry of blows followed and he started to breathe hard and smile. He took the K. & K. shirt off, never setting the mallet down or taking his eyes from the rim.

"You piece of SHIT!" he bellowed, hammering the rim. He froze and his eyes darted to the shop door—afraid, I imagine, that Dad would come in and chew him good for swearing in front of a customer. The door stayed closed. He checked me. I looked at the rim—it was indeed straighter—then nodded at him. He started again.

"Get up. NOW!"

I sat on a tractor rim and watched. His accuracy and force were remarkable, especially for a boy, and my rim slowly, agonizingly straightened. Gary was totally in his element. "You bastard," he yelled, his voice cracking in excitement. This time he gave the door only a perfunctory check, then tossed the Persuader down. He plucked the spokes as if they were guitar strings, listening to the pitch each made. Quickly, though, he picked up the Persuader again and did his adolescent best to burn the air with profanity.

Half an hour later and the rim looked brand new. The show of my life.

"You're amazing," I said.

"You just gotta know how to finesse them a little," he said and wiped the pimples on his forehead with a shop rag. They were bright red now. "A little wrench, a little mallet, they come around." He gave me this worldly, you'll-learn-this-someday look. "It's still got a little hop at the seam. Other than that, she'll hold. Settle up with my dad out front." He tossed his beloved mallet back into the drawer with a flair, trying to be cool. Actually, he *did* look pretty cool, but at the last minute his facade broke: as I wheeled the bike out the shop door, shaking my head saying to myself, *This is incredible*, he gave me a kid's smile—all braces and pimples.

His dad charged me only seven dollars, but I gave him a ten and told him to give the rest to Gary. Then onto 52, back against the southeast wind, four hours and forty minutes after the red dash cut through my mirror.

I wish I had asked Gary, standing there with his spoke

wrench and beloved mallet, what he wants to do with his life. Maybe he doesn't know. Who does at fourteen?

"Gary," I would've told him, "rim repair. Blue sky, blank check. Go for it."

The Rim Wizard of Fergus Falls. I should've asked him.

Tonight it's a nice Lutheran church in Elbow Lake, lots of brick, not too big, twenty miles south of Fergus. From the church kitchen, I called Karen and told her that I couldn't make the wedding. St. Paul is 175 miles away, and might as well be a thousand, especially with this damned wind. I wanted so much to impress her. I told her I'd try to make it by the day after tomorrow. Save me a piece of cake. She wanted to drive out here tonight and pick me up.

"Oh, Brian," she said just before we hung up, "I got canned today."

"You what?"

"Half canned, and half quit. When my boss hired me he was all, 'Yes, we're a Christian law firm, we want to hire you because you're a good Christian attorney. We're all Christian attorneys.' A couple weeks ago I started giving him some grief about the new Mercedes he'd just bought. He even paid cash for it. And how he's trying to claw his way up the local Republican ladder. And, I probably shouldn't tell you this, but he made a move on me a few weeks ago. I let him have it with both barrels. Since then, it's like he's been trying to drive me out. Giving me three times the usual work. Jerk. So that's it. I'm out."

AUGUST 23

175 MILES

St. Paul, Minnesota

When I pulled the church door closed behind me at 6:30, the usual long sharp shadows of these prairie mornings—and the winds that rise with them—were absent. A thick sunless fog lay on the town. Cheerless, but no wind. I turned on to State Highway 55 and took advantage of it, shifting out of third gear for the first time in days. I actually sat up. What a concept—no headwind. Karen's house on the east side of the Twin Cities lay 175 miles straight southeast and if the wind held off I could make it in a day and a half. I stroked the downhills hard and shifted into fifth, then sixth—the speedometer showed double digits, numbers I haven't seen forever.

It couldn't last. A hard little shower sprang over the handlebars, followed directly by the same wind I've bucked for days. The bike slowed as if braked, the handlebars wrenched lightly back and forth. I shifted back to third. My hands on the bars have gotten good at gauging the wind by now; from the southeast, 21–22 m.p.h. I put my head down and crawled.

Then. Magic.

The rain stopped. The wind died. As if the spigots from which they both ran had been snapped off. And within minutes, from north to south, in one long arc, the overcast and fog were peeled like a blanket from a bed. I expected to see a hand up there, furling it away. A gust of wind chucked my shoulder. It swung hard behind me and seemed to grab the seat, flinging it forward. I shifted out of third again. Down a hill, fifth gear, then sixth. The wind blew stronger now. I shifted onto the big chain ring, the one I haven't touched since John and I dove out of the Rockies. The wind was chasing me now, stronger still. Raindrops dangling from telephone wires or corn leaves turned to diamonds in the sunlight. Eighth gear, tenth, the top—twelfth. Another hill. I flew up it in a second and ripped down its back at forty miles per hour. The wind kicked a notch higher. The phone wires swung on their poles like jump ropes.

I hit Barrett at a solid 35, right past SPEED LIMIT—25. I hesitantly touched the brakes. But when was the last time you saw a cop run radar on a bike? I snapped them off and sailed head down through town and back into the waving corn. Hoffman next, then Kensington, then Farwell—each a handful of miles apart and each little more than a water tower and jiggling storefronts. By late morning I flew through Glenwood, Sedan, and Brooten. The wind blasted. The towns and people began to smear; the gas station guy held his hat in the wind and became the shopper and the postman and the farmer near his shed and the next town's gas station guy, holding his hat and waving. Lowry, Paynesville, Eden Valley sped by minutes later. It was like riding the merry-go-round, everything out of control blurred and spinning around and around. It was like making love—the handlebars that feel like her hands as they lock in yours, unlock, and lock again as you speed up. And when you're through the stoplights and back in the fields you slow some, you hear the quiet again, your own breath, your beating heart. Weeds rattle in the ditch, unlatched barn doors bang far away. In the headwind you never hear these. With the wind, they are music. Late afternoon; Kimball, Annandale, Buffalo. Evening, and the Cities' western suburbs. I buy a rose from a street-corner Moonie. Cross the Mississippi into St. Paul. The streetlights are just snapping on as I knock on Karen's door with the rose behind me. When she hugs me—the warmth of her chest on mine—my legs leave and she is as much holding me up as holding me.

AUGUST 24

St. Paul, Minnesota

Karen and I stood arm in arm in the sun-filled churchyard and greeted her friends. "Look! He made it!" she called as they came up the walk. She tugged my waist. "One hundred seventy-five miles yesterday! Look how skinny he's gotten!" She wore a flowered blue dress; the sun lit her hair; her friends oohed and aahed. Two thousand miles just to stand here for these minutes—it was worth it.

Karen didn't want to miss a thing, so as we stepped into the church she said we had to sit down front. She took my hand and we slowly walked the aisle. She beamed. Some leaned and whispered to pewmates. As we neared the front I felt as if she were showing me off—the heathen she'd bagged outside the fold. I'm also her choice over these fine young men in the straight-backed pews, flashing their pasted smiles over grinding teeth as we walked by. I liked that.

She and her roommate were saved in this church. For that reason I shouldn't have been surprised when, after the vows, a small dark-haired woman got to her feet, raised a tiny fist above her head, and opened it.

"Oh, I love you," the woman moaned. Great, some wacko or an old flame of the groom's. Somebody will walk her out. Nobody turned to her though, not even the groom.

"Oh, I love you so," she muttered again.

"Who is that?" I whispered to Karen.

"That's Irma, the women's pastor here. She's a prophetess."

"My children," Irma said with her head down and eyes closed, "the Lord God says I love you so and I called you here today." She looked up and opened watery caramel eyes. "Ed, I called you out of your loneliness to be a companion to this woman. Your loneliness, the hunger of your heart, will end today."

Ann and Ed stepped back to their places as if nothing were out of the ordinary. Irma's voice started to rise.

"And Ann, I called you to this man. He will father your children, and your joy will be great in him. Your joy will be great in each other. And when your friends and family look on you they will see some of the joy of the coming marriage feast."

She began to rock back and forth in the pew a bit, eyes now closed, her body and outstretched arm ramrod straight, hand still open.

"As I blessed the wine at the marriage feast at Canaan, so I bless this bond between you, Ed, and you, Ann," she said, her voice louder still, now with a kind of pleading tone. "It is my joy to see you so. Oh so much joy. Joy you can't contain, joy that'll spill into your children. Your path here has been fraught with thorns and Satan has tried to crush you. But you are strong, strong in me, and have nothing to fear!"

Suddenly her voice shot to the rafters. "Satan, I bind this marriage. I *bind* it! You have *no* power! You are gone! I *van-*

quished you at Easter! All who would believe in me, and aaaall who would call on my name will be saved!" Around the room hands started to rise, moans of "Thank you Jesus, yes Lord, praise you God," as Irma went on wailing and rocking.

"This marriage will be a light to all men! No one shall put it asunder. Oh, the love I have for you! Oh the joy oh the joy oh the joy! Receive it now, my children. Receive it now! Oh, I love you so!"

Karen rocked, her beaming face lifted to the ceiling. *Tucka-tucka, kakata, kakata.* Behind us, a man bawled like a little boy.

Irma was smoking. "I drive Satan from this room, from this marriage, from this world! The joy the love the joy the love I have for you!"

Karen placed a hand on my leg and rocked and nodded and clucked her secret prayer.

These people. They all *get* this stuff. My father gets it. Why don't I? Why *can't* I?

OK, God, I want it. Whatever it is, whatever you call it. I want it.

I waited, every nerve on fire. After all these years of staving it off.

Irma's hand, still raised above her head, started to shake badly, as if she'd been holding an invisible cinder-block this whole time. It jerked downward, suddenly bringing with it the cries in the room. Karen placed her own in her lap. Hankies came out. Irma wept, "Oh I love you" a last time. There were a few sobs near the back. And that was it.

They felt the fire. I watched.

I kissed her good night at her bedroom door, then kissed her again. The third time her hands came behind me and pulled me toward her. Her tongue touched mine and, as usual, lit the kindling. I walked her a few steps backward toward her bed. She put a hand on my chest.

"Whoa, we have to slow down here," she said, "or we're gonna end up just like we did on your living room floor."

I looked around her room and hoped to pull a clever line from the air, something to change her mind. But my eyes landed on the black leather Bible on her nightstand.

"OK, I'll take your spare room again."

I turned and was almost out her door when she took my hand.

"I know this'll sound crazy, Brian, after what I just said, but . . . can we sleep together? I want to . . . just sleep next to you."

"You mean sleep. As in sleep."

"Right, just sleep. If it'd be hard for you, maybe we shouldn't, I don't want to tempt you, or us I mean, any more than we can handle. I know I could handle it. But if it'd be hard for you—"

"Honey, it's already hard," I said, and pressed my hips against hers.

"Not that kind." She smiled a little and moved away. "Well, maybe that kind, but more, you know, spiritually hard to sleep together."

She left to get into her nightgown. I stripped to my boxers and T-shirt and dove under the covers.

I should've known her gown would be white. Knee-length cotton. Lace just above her breasts, buttoned to her collarbone. Thin enough so her waist and hips were silhouetted through the material.

"I try to read a chapter a night before lights out," she said, and picked the Bible off the nightstand. She crawled under the covers and smoothed the pages open on her lap. "Let's see, Ephesians. Here, chapter two.

"But God's mercy is so abundant, and his love for us is so great, that while we were spiritually dead in our disobedience he brought us to life with Christ. It is by God's grace that you have been saved. In our union . . ."

I watched her read, then lay back. In a moment the flow of words faded into just another late-night sound. Her voice was soft and low. I stared at the O'Keeffe prints on the wall, tulips whose long smooth throats slid down to darkness.

". . . and makes it grow into a sacred temple dedicated to the Lord. In union with him you too are being built together with all the others into a place where God lives through his Spirit. Amen. Thank you, God."

She closed it. "I love the Word, Brian. It's life to me." She set the book on the bed and rolled onto her side, hand under her head.

"Do you ever think about me out there when you're riding?"

"I've got that pretty picture of you in the map case so I can see it during the day. Sometimes I talk to it."

"What do you say?" She hunkered into her pillow and smiled.

"Sometimes I tell it where we're going next, and how hard it is to keep pedaling all the time. I don't know. Sometimes I tell it I don't understand you, or your faith, and that I'm trying. Other times I look at it and get turned on. Lots of things."

She moved closer. "I think about you a lot, too."

She paused a second. "I love ya, Bri. I want you to know that." And she leaned across the pillow and kissed me. She slid her body almost next to mine and we lay there, hands at our sides.

"I love you too, Karen." I wanted to mean it. I wanted to

feel it. I said it in order that I might feel it. I lay my hand on her shoulder and kissed her. She pulled me to her and I smoothed her hair. She took my hand from her hair and placed it on her breast. After two thousand miles with little in my palm but the handlebar's curved steel—here was her heartbeat, the cotton soft and warm. She closed her eyes and smiled. We lay silent. A tear rose in her right eye.

"Brian, I'm really happy with you," and she kissed me with a fierceness, with her entire body. My hands slid quickly under her gown. She peeled my T-shirt off, the sheets wrapped around us, and we both struggled with the buttons of her neckline. As they fell open, she pulled me down, down to kiss her neck, her chest, the skin at the bottom of the long row of buttons.

Our thrashing inched the Bible to the bed's edge. Seconds later it slipped and landed with a sickening splash.

She didn't seem to hear it. I got off her and pulled my T-shirt from the twisted sheets.

"What's wrong?" she asked.

It lay there like roadkill, a crow with heaped black wings. I picked it up and pulled out the bent pages. I knew within minutes she'd be praying her eyes out.

"I better go to your spare room, Karen. I'm sorry. I'm really sorry."

"What," she started. Her hair was all messed up. The gown's neckline lay wide open, her chest still quickly rising and falling. She didn't get it. I put the Bible on the nightstand, picked up my clothes, and left, saying, "I'm sorry."

AUGUST 25

I called Andrew and we agreed to meet in Eau Claire tomorrow. He asked me what kind of miles I expected out of him each day across Wisconsin. I shouldn't have, but I mentioned my 175 the other day, mostly for effect. There was one . . . long . . . pause. After all, I am the one he used to haul like a lead wagon through seventeen miles of flat cornfields.

"Well, you'll have to take it easy on an old fart like me," he said eventually.

Beyond that, this day is memorable for one line. We stood at her bedroom door and kissed good night again. Only once. Nice and polite. She could've been my aunt.

"Thank you for not asking to sleep here, Brian. It's best, isn't it."

AUGUST 26

107 MILES

Eau Claire, Wisconsin

I woke to Karen pulling back the top of my sleeping bag. The sun was barely up. Without my glasses, I could only make out her gown and that it was buttoned all the way. Beyond that she was all haze. She slid in beside me, laid her head on my chest, and was asleep in a minute.

An hour later she stood at her ironing board and worked on the day's blouse. Sunlight streamed in an east window and silhouetted her body through the thin gown. I stood across the room, behind her, and watched. I walked to her and ran my hands across her neck and shoulders. She kept ironing. I felt her waist. She ironed a minute more, the board squeaking, then her arm slowed and stopped. I felt the smoothness of her stomach. She leaned her head back into my neck and sighed.

I could've picked her up and swept her into her room. But we would just replay the misery of the other night. I stepped back. Without a sound, without looking at me, she picked up the iron and finished the blouse.

She left for work and I tried to write a love note, something mushy and true that'd make her smile when she finds it tonight in her silverware drawer. But everything was so jumbled, her apartment so quiet. A clock ticked, a truck passed. Nothing came to mind that wasn't religion or my testicles, which felt swollen.

"Thank you for this weekend. It was wonderful to spend time with you. See you in September. Love, Brian."

I wrapped it in the tines of a dinner fork, then stepped into the sun on her front porch and yanked the door closed until the bolt caught.

Such a late start. It's evening now in Menominee. "Twenty-six miles to Eau Claire," says the girl behind the counter at the DQ. She stands on her toes to look at the bike. "Oh, way too far on *that*."

East of Menominee, the speedometer flirts with thirty miles an hour. The sun is down now. Light settles into the hayfields.

Then, these signs. "Road Construction Ahead." "Pavement Ends." Finally, "ROAD CLOSED. EAU CLAIRE 18 MILES."

I am standing in the middle of what is supposed to be a road. It is really just piles of wet sand. There are no yard lights, no moon. I can't see a thing and I don't know what to do. I mean, I really don't know what to do. I pull down my shorts and piss, flailing at mosquitoes with a free hand. I can't even see the stream.

My other senses open up the road in front of me. I walk the bike through sand until the pavement takes up again. If I swerve too close to the ditch, loose gravel under the tires sounds like popping corn. I smell roadkill and swerve away from a hump of mid-lane darkness. Ditch grass is a wet slap. Broken glass is a sinking feeling in the gut: quickly I lay my gloved hand on the tire, brush it clean, and hope.

Finally, a smoothly paved side road.

Two people pedal up from a farmyard light into the black of this road; one of them wears boots that hang way over the pedals; the other is frail, tiny. Their bikes creak.

Still a ways off, I call, "How far to Eau Claire?"

The squeaky pedaling stops for a long moment.

"Eleven miles?" a man says.

"Do I stay on this road?"

Silence again.

"Can if you want," he calls. "Quicker, take a right at the tavern four miles up."

Now I'm with them. Each of us a moving shadow to the other. We ride slow and, by sound, keep from bumping elbows.

"Four miles. What's it called?"

"The Buzz Inn," she answers. "There's a streetlight in front of it, the only one between here and Eau Claire."

"Thanks. Have a nice night." I pull away from them and look back. Nothing there except a timid creaking sound.

I didn't bother to ask the hotel desk what room Andrew and his family were in. I walked past a hallway and glimpsed a bike against a wall. A Colnago is like a Ferrari, and his has a paint job that reminds you of lips just made up and licked. I can safely say it is the only one in Eau Claire on this

August night, probably in all of Wisconsin. How he affords one with six kids and a preacher's salary has always eluded me.

"Annette just asked me if we should go look for you in the car," Andrew said as he opened the door. He wore only his faded blue-check boxers and his Coke-bottle glasses. "I told her you wouldn't take a ride, even if we found you, so we might as well sit tight." I wheeled my bike into his room and his wife and two little daughters hugged me.

"Haven't you thrown those boxers away yet?"

"These? They're just getting comfortable."

It was a good line and we all got a small laugh out of it except Andrew, who looked grim and tired. Rubbery ashen circles sagged under his eyes.

His girls spread their sleeping bags onto the floor. I took one bed, Andrew and Annette the other. The girls whispered and giggled for several minutes and fell quiet shortly after Andrew turned the lights out. At the edge of sleep I heard Andrew and Annette almost silently making love.

AUGUST 27

 100 MILES

Wisconsin Rapids, Wisconsin

Dawn was eighty degrees and humid. By the time we stepped into the pedals our shirts were soaked. Annette, sweat beaded over her lip, said, "I got you each a little gift." She pulled two water bottles from a bag and handed them to us. They were white and new, a black CAMPAGNOLO emblazoned down their sides. "You'll probably need an extra one today," she said, and nodded at the sun. I shook it. Ice and water sloshed inside. "I've heard Campagnolo is the best, so there you go." She looked shy, but pleased at having tried to surprise her husband. Andrew just took his and laid it into its frame. She touched his face. Tears rose in her eyes and she quickly turned to their car. The girls were waiting. She opened her door and he coasted up to her. She kissed him like she'd never see him again.

Andrew is a small man and when he crouches to his frame to duck the wind, there's little to see from behind but his legs whirling as if they were made of piano wire and pulleys. That's the usual picture anyway. This morning, up and down the sharp hills of west-central Wisconsin, he was completely out of rhythm, his legs jerky and weak. Time and again, I caught him and passed, then downshifted to slow him. He would rest behind me for maybe a quarter mile, then roar ahead, nailing the next hill without downshifting or breaking cadence. I'd say, "We don't have to go this fast," or "You're going to kill yourself." He'd slack off for five or ten minutes, but gradually turn it on again and roar around me. We kept this up for hours. Every other mile I pulled ahead and tried to draw us back. It was leapfrog, and the gap between our bikes varied wildly throughout the morning. By early afternoon his gray head began to hang, his shoulder blades jut like those of an old horse. The darkness on his face last night seemed to have deepened. I felt for him, some. On the other hand, he had it coming after bonehead stunts like not shifting for these hills.

Long swatches of time passed without a word between us. I didn't expect much talk—our old ride chat usually consisted of his sparse directives like, "Spin circles," which meant I was pushing the pedals too much; "Grab a wheel" was his offer to draft for me (he said that one a lot); "Pick up a tooth" meant use a bigger gear and haul some ass for a change—but for hours today, past deep red dairy barns and century-old farmhouses built to resemble southern mansions, he didn't say ten sentences, and hardly even looked up. I asked him about the note he'd taped to these bicycle wheels, the one asking if he could ride across Wisconsin. What had caused him to write it? He shrugged and kept pedaling.

By Wisconsin Rapids he was in no position to jump ahead of anyone. In my mirror his face showed an exhaustion I've never seen on him before. Some people at this stage look plain tired. He looked bewildered and furious. He had to walk the last hill into town. I waited for him at the top and, as I watched him climb, remembered my first race, a thirty-mile loop through the fields and woods of northern Illinois. I'd managed to hold on to the pack for the first twenty miles or so until someone made a break. Break riders win races. Several pack riders attacked, trying to haul him back in. Andrew led the attack, out of his seat thrashing his bicycle from side to side; riders trailed him like exhaust. I stood in the pedals to make the move but at that instant the strength in my legs evaporated. The sensation hit my arms, and suddenly I could barely hold myself up. Andrew caught the break rider, tucked behind him, sucked his rear wheel, and flew. The next miles were an embarrassment. As the pack pulled away I told myself to shift, come on, bootstraps time, all that horseshit, but I wobbled over the road like a drunk. Even the *really* slow riders, those whom the pack had dropped long before the break, appeared in the mirror and passed me easily. At four miles to the finish, Andrew was suddenly there with me. He'd already finished. I've never felt so embarrassed. But he was a gentleman, and all he said was, "You want a wheel?" He pulled me to the finish. I'll never forget that, that he came back.

I pulled him into Wisconsin Rapids. We ate supper, found two couches in First Lutheran's youth room, and were in our sleeping bags by ten.

Just before lights out he took off his glasses. He blinked a few times my way and rubbed his eyes. I was only fuzz to him now. It surprises me that those blue-gray eyes are so large, proportionate to his face. The thick lenses make his eyes look so small, as if you saw them down the wrong end of a telescope. When I first attended his church, I was intimidated by those glasses. I'd been able to buy off pastors I'd known before him, with churchiness or mere politeness. But Andrew and his tiny eyes seemed to really *see* me—how I stumbled into my adulthood screwing Lili over and falling repeatedly in and out of born-again religion. For some reason he still wanted me to join his church and ride bicycles with him. At this moment, glasses off and waving at a lamp to find its switch, he didn't look like a pastor anymore. He looked like any guy on the street.

He is a renowned snorer. But the minutes ticked by and the only sounds were traffic and him turning in his bag.

"Andrew? What's wrong?"

His rustling stopped and perhaps twenty minutes dragged between us. Down the hall, a phone rang.

"Somebody's dead," he said immediately. "It's almost eleven and they call the church office." His voice was bitter and flat. The phone kept ringing, punctuating his sentences. "They call no matter what time it is. I got four calls at home in the space of one morning. Like everybody in the nursing home just decided it was their time. Which was bad enough. Then some teenagers decided to go get drunk and plow their car into a tree south of town. Then there were two more to do."

The phone kept ringing.

"Eleven funerals in three weeks. I built your wheels just to stay sane. I taped that note to them in the middle of them all, when I was preaching one funeral after another and it seemed the phone rang before I got my robes off. After a while you start wondering what the hell to say. The family looks to you and you're running out of answers. I'm supposed to be the holy one. Last week I asked the council if I could take a weekend off, and they said I'd already used up my vacation. Can you imagine that? All that death and all those funerals and they basically said, go to hell. So I just left. Annette and the girls are the only ones who know. And you."

Ring.

"You have no idea how good it feels to know that isn't for me." When the phone finally stopped, his snore started almost immediately.

AUGUST 28

 80 MILES

Neenah, Wisconsin

A thunderstorm rolled over Wisconsin Rapids in the night and wrung yesterday's humidity from the air. The sun rose clean and brilliant.

On the edge of town Andrew took off again, but when I passed him and slowed, he downshifted and drafted behind me for several miles. Finally, after yesterday's mess, he took my lead.

At midmorning he pulled even. "So tell me about this Karen." He looked more himself now, the sharp, inquisitive face behind bottle-bottom glasses. I didn't know where to start. I handed him the picture from my handlebar bag; she wears the white dress that, on one of our dates a few months ago, caused a guy we met to walk into a fire hydrant.

"Hoo," he said.

"That's her graduation picture from law school. She's a lawyer."

"What flavor is she? Catholic?"

"She was born and raised Catholic, but she got saved and now she's a fundamentalist."

"A fundy? She's a fundy?" He sat up and rode no hands, looking at the picture fluttering in front of him. "Your dad will just be *thrilled*." He slapped his knee and laughed for the first time.

Late morning in Amish country. We passed black buggies with orange "slow-moving vehicle" triangles on back. We waved. The bearded men with reins in their hands would nod and the women smile slightly. Around noon I heard Andrew hum a snatch of a hymn.

He asked if we could turn in to one of the farms. It looked just like any other, the white square two-storied house and the red barn. In the front yard stood a hand-painted QUILTS sign.

"We're going to have our thirtieth wedding anniversary this weekend. I've been looking all year for the perfect thing."

The woman inside wore an ankle-length cotton dress; her kitchen smelled of sage and manure, kerosene and fresh bread. Our cleats on her bare wood floors were loud, and Andrew's orange jersey looked garish against the blank cream walls. Near the sink about shin high in the wall was a hole the size of a football. Another gaped on the opposite wall, and in the living room still another. In each case, the sheet rock had been ripped away and left ragged.

The quilts lay on her dining table. She showed us in and began lifting the corner of each, her motions slow and dutiful. When Andrew put his hand on a white one, she averted her eyes. The pattern was of snowflakes, few and far between at the border but gathering more thickly toward the center. By the middle it was a blizzard, but each flake remained distinct.

The quilt's two halves were a mirror image of each other. Andrew, awestruck, traced the stitching with his fingers. Her eyes, still on the oak floor, showed absolutely nothing.

"How much is this?"

"Dis vun vill be offered a' tree hunnerd." The consonants were thick in her mouth.

He lifted his hand and she leafed through the quilt corners again with that same burdened motion. At the bottom of the stack, when Andrew had seen them all, he asked to see the white one again. He gave it a long yearning look, then turned to her, I suppose to see if there was room for a little negotiation, but her face returned nothing.

"These are remarkable creations," he said, defeated. "Thank you. I guess I can't." We put our helmets on, thanked her again, and she showed us out, her eyes still on the floor.

"I noticed those holes in the walls, too," he said as we walked to the bikes. "She must've bought the house from a farmer who wasn't Amish. Those were where she'd ripped out the old electrical outlets."

Two children peeked around the corner of the house, each carrying a kitten. Compared to the deathly quiet and plainness inside, they looked lively with those kittens and the rich summer hills behind them. The boy wore black britches with a buttoned front flap, and the girl had a dress and bonnet identical to the woman's.

"Hi there. What's your cat's name?" Andrew asked. We rolled the bikes slowly toward them. They didn't answer and kept their eyes on their kittens for the most part, sneaking glances at our bikes. The closer we got, though, the children looked sickly, each with skin almost as white as that quilt. They had dark circles under their eyes. I pulled my camera from the handlebar bag. They ran into the house, clutching the kittens as if for dear life.

Old racer. He had to take his turn even after ninety miles, and now in a cold seeping mist. We rode fast downhill east of Weyauwega, when he tried to pass. The edge of the highway stands about an inch higher than the shoulder, and with the icy rain penetrating his bones he couldn't pull his handlebars hard enough to jump it clean. His front wheel caught and he cried out. The snapshot in my mind is of him halfway down but his face is already pained. I couldn't look longer than that. So then there's sound: flesh and metal banging asphalt, the skittering of eyeglasses.

The streetlights were just coming on as we entered Neenah. The buzzing orange light and the cold mist made Andrew's elbow look like glazed raw meat. He was lucky—no broken bones or spokes—but he was barely able to hold his head up. The phone rang as we stepped into Karen's parents' house and her mother handed it to me.

I can't remember a word of what Karen said, only the contrast between how warm her voice felt and the sight of Andrew in the corner dripping grime and blood onto the cream linoleum. She was a bath, he was roadkill.

She called again after supper. In all this riding I've forgotten that she is jobless now and has to move. She was in her living room surrounded by boxes, and I could see her pull nervously at the ends of her hair.

"I put Ann on the plane today. She's flying to Texas to be with Ed, he had to go back to work. This place feels so empty, and now you're gone, too. I just wanted to hear your voice again."

"Do you have anybody to help out?"

"Not really, everybody's got to work. I just don't know how I'm going to get all this done."

"Where are you moving to? I mean, you know where you're going?"

Long pause. "Well, my sister and her husband say I can stay there for as long as I need. And some women from church are probably going to rent a house in another month or so. But right now, I don't know. I guess not. Brian, it's scary as hell to leave here, it's been five years."

She said hell. The woman actually said hell.

I put the phone down and found Andrew in his room, he and his raw elbow clean from the shower. His wife is going to pick him up here on Friday; they'll drive back to St. Paul to visit their son. I asked him for a ride. Those little Finnish eyes grew large for a second and he didn't reply right away.

"You sure you want to? Go back?"

He stressed those last two words too much. I returned to the phone.

"Karen, could you use an extra hand packing this weekend?"

"What do you mean?"

"Well, Andrew's driving to St. Paul on Friday with his wife, and I'll come along. I'll be with you to help."

"Brian, no!"

"Why not?"

"Oh, Bri, what about your trip?"

"I didn't say I was quitting, I'm just offering to come back for the weekend. I'll catch a Greyhound back here."

"Brian, it's your bike trip. You've wanted this so much ever since I've known you. I wouldn't think of asking you to stop, for this."

"That's why I'm offering."

Pause.

"So I'll be there sometime Friday late, OK?"

I could hear the smile in her voice. "Well, OK. Are you sure?"

There is so much that I am patently unsure about—how sex and God are all botched up between us, just for starters—but not this. She could use the help and I simply want to do it. Maybe also now that she's leaving her place we can start something new. Less Jesus, and more heart and body. If we can't, then this whole mess isn't worth it. I'll give this one more go. I want it to work. I can catch a bus back here Sunday.

"I'm sure, Karen."

AUGUST 31

St. Paul. Again.

Almost all of Karen's things are in my basement after a humid afternoon's slave labor. Come Monday, she thinks she'll go to her sister's. She's in the shower now. Only a rug and a lamp and our two sleeping bags are left here in her living room. All afternoon as we emptied this room the echoes sharpened, and I was glad for work that kept my head busy. We started here months ago—among the art books and the trace of perfume from her bedroom, the scent of basil from the kitchen. Today, though, it became walls and a bulb in the ceiling. So much of what I want her to be, gone.

SEPTEMBER 1

Last night she came out of the bathroom wearing only a kimono. She asked me if I liked it. Black silk to the thigh, apple trees blossoming pink and white and cinnamon across her chest. I could barely speak.

"I saved it from the boxes," she said. "I wanted to wear it for you."

She sat cross-legged and smiled as I admired the gown, especially those trees. I tugged the kimono's belt. She turned out the light, unknotted the belt, and slid the gown off. As my eyes adjusted, moonlight fell in long blocks through the windows, and threw her hair and waist into profile. We performed our ritual, the sounds of frustration now loud against the bare walls. The room was hot and damp. Eventually, I started to laugh. Her body bristled for a second, then she laughed too. We wouldn't get anywhere. We rolled away from each other.

"Poor boy," she said. She wiped the sweat on my temple

with a finger. "Paul said in Acts that it's better for a man to take a wife than to burn."

"Do women burn?" She lay on her side, curve after curve in the moonlight. I rolled her onto her back and kissed her breast.

"You know I want to, Brian. We can't though, not now. Someday, though, maybe."

I must've stared at the ceiling for an hour, long after her breathing fell regular and slow beside me. Somewhere around three-thirty I fell asleep.

Now, Sunday morning, she was whispering in my ear. "Stay an extra day. You worked so hard yesterday. Rest today." I didn't even have my eyes open.

"I should get back." I pried myself onto an elbow. My watch read eight. She put her hand over it. The bus left for Neenah in an hour. I lay back down. It was only going to be for a minute. Her fingers stroked my forehead, then my eyelids, and made the dark even darker. Then it was noon.

This afternoon she mentioned that several people at her church were praying for my safety and how nice it'd be if I went to tonight's service with her. I wanted to beg off, but my calendar wasn't exactly booked. The air all day remained heavy and still, in need of a good thunderstorm. As we walked toward her church, the congregation's singing poured out the open doors. Inside, a tall blond man, riveted in the classic pose of eyes clamped shut and hand overhead, prayed aloud to the congregation.

"Lord, I just want to invite you here in a special way tonight. And if there's anyone who needs and is seeking a special touch from you tonight, Lord, let this be the time and let this be the place for that to happen. Yes, Lord, thank you, Jesus."

Karen slid her arm through mine as we walked up the aisle. I had the distinct feeling, again, that she was pleased to show me off, that I was a little dangerous compared to the blow-dried pew-boys, and she liked that. We sat halfway up on the left. She kept her arm in mine, her breast smooth against my skin. Huge fans rolled the hot moist air around the room. The faithful glowed.

We sang hymns from an overhead projector. Between each there were testimonials and corporate moaning. The music and waving hands began to take me back to my childhood, where I sat petrified next to Dad at Holy Roller services. At the end of one hymn, a man with a guitar stood up. He slowly picked the notes of a single chord. A few quietly sang, "Thank you, Lord. Yes, God," and other phrases. The guitarist shut off the overhead. More voices joined in. "Praise you, Jesus. Be here tonight, Lord." Hands rose. "You are my God. There is no other." More voices came along and riffed up and down that chord. "Yes, Jesus. Thank you, Jesus." The guitar grew louder and the humid air thickened with singing. "I am yours, Lord. Make me holy, Jesus." Karen started to rock and moan. "You are the holy one. Be with us, Jesus." I made up a few phrases but they fell stupid and false from my lips. Everyone around me looked to be in such glory. As if the guitar notes were a scaffold by which they could pull themselves higher, into a better version of themselves.

The pastor called over the music, "A time for deliverance. Deliverance from nightmares, temptation, fear, pain, whatever Satan is binding you with. Come." The music kept piling higher and higher and before I knew it I was standing and walking forward. I walked into the music. I did it for Dad and Karen and maybe even myself. I don't know right now.

There was a line of six or seven of us. I saw the pastor lay one hand on a woman's head and with his other chop the air over her. I was fine in the back of the line, but suddenly with one ahead of me, I exploded in sweat. I looked in a panic around me. Those who a second earlier had been in such ecstasy—now they looked silly.

What the hell am I doing here?

Then he was in front of me.

"Hello, brother. What is your need tonight? Brother? You're here for deliverance? Brother?"

I shut my eyes and blurted, "Yeah. I've been running all my life and I think it's deliverance from always thinking that one day I'll have this whole thing figured out but most of the time I'm just frightened to death of Christ. I'm sick of it. I can't figure it out, what all these people have got that I don't have."

I wanted to start crying. I felt so fucking pathetic. But with a born-again preacher in front of me, I just couldn't let myself cry. It all came out in more sweat. He was expecting someone already saved who just needed a simple spiffing up, this deliverance. He looked at me with huge brown eyes, blinked several times, and found himself.

"Brother, what's your name? All right, Brian, do you know what you're asking?"

I know exactly what this means. Get on with it before I run out.

I nodded.

"OK, then, Brian. Just pray what's on your heart." He closed his eyes and laid a small hand on my shoulder.

I couldn't get any words out. He had his head down. God, he looked serious. He opened his eyes after I didn't say anything.

"Do you need help?"

I nodded.

"That's OK," and he laughed a little, and I felt my shoulders loosen some. "It's a big thing you're about to do. I'll say a few words and you repeat them."

But then I didn't want his help. I shook his hand off my shoulder and scrunched my eyes shut.

The words weren't great and I don't even think they were what I wanted to say, but it's what came.

"God. I've been running all my life. Satan has tried to separate me from you by making me afraid and convincing me that if I wait and if I just use my brain enough, I'll figure this out. But I can't. I confess this, and ask Christ to come into my life now."

I really wanted to feel something then. Lightning in the legs, or waves of love crash inside the ribs. That always happened in the "Guideposts" testimonials. The only sensation I had was the feeling of my shirt absolutely sweat-painted to my back. I opened my eyes. The pastor beamed, literally beamed. I tried to work up a smile and I suppose I did, but it was limp. I needed air. We shook hands and I walked the length of the aisle right out the open door.

SEPTEMBER 3

Aboard the good ship Kewaunee,
somewhere in Lake Michigan

Man, I hate big boats. But it was either this six-hour ferry across the lake, or a four-day ride around its southern end. So here I sit, topside, in a swarm of Wisconsin houseflies, all of us bound for Michigan. The rail is six feet away. I made myself go look over the edge a minute ago, then kind of staggered back to this bench. The water's probably sixty feet below and I can still feel it; the south wind drives it against the hull and the ship shudders. The horizon's not moving. We could be standing still for all we know.

The lifeboats are only seven steps away.

The captain just came on the horn. We're making good time, he says. We'll be in Michigan in three hours. He seems to think we're moving.

Just as I boarded the Greyhound for Neenah, Karen handed me a New Testament. "This is the Word, Brian.

Read it. Get into it. You'll be surprised how much this will mean to you now."

I pull it from my panniers and find in John, "Whoever drinks this water will thirst again; but whoever drinks the water that I give him will never thirst again." A few times over the last two days I've felt it, *something* different sloshing around inside me but so small I can't put a name on it. And then under the hot sun I think about my lips on Karen's breast or I swear when my chain slips—maybe I've sweated it out already.

SEPTEMBER 4

122 MILES

Mt. Pleasant, Michigan

It will be the humidity, the bugs, and the rapist of central Michigan that I'll remember about this part of the trip.

Michigan has two seasons running simultaneously. At their tops, the maples begin to dribble orange glaze, early autumn; at handlebar level it is summer at its most brutal, ninety-five and a choking humidity that got me off the bike twice to gauge the tires, convinced they were half flat.

The bugs were brainless contraptions, one species in particular which didn't bite or move once it landed, but just sat. Swiping at them usually smeared them against my skin. By the time I reached Mt. Pleasant I was essentially flypaper.

I wasn't surprised, then, when a young woman looked at me and ducked quickly inside Central Michigan University's Methodist Wesley Center. She pulled the door behind her and the security chain rattled in place.

I knocked on the door and heavy footsteps approached, then the door opened a couple inches. He was probably six five and had a great bushy gray beard. The eye I could see was a soft blue.

"Yes?"

"Hello, my name is Brian Newhouse and I'm riding my bicycle across—"

"Where are you from?"

"Minnesota. St. Paul. I've never been on campus before and I was wondering—"

"How did you find the Wesley Center?"

"Well, I was just looking around. I've never been here, and I've been on my bike all day and I just pulled into Mount Pleasant and this is where I stopped. Do you know of a place where I could sleep tonight?"

He shut the door, removed the chain, and opened it only wide enough to squeeze through. He was probably fifty, and everything about him was built heavy. He walked to my bike and touched the seat, and looked at my bags covered with bugs.

"Where are you riding to?"

I tried a little aw-shucks look at my feet. "I'm going to Maine. Probably end up in Rockport, right on the coast."

"Where did you start?"

"On the other coast, not far from Seattle." This was usually where people's facade started to crack.

"How long you plan on being in Mount Pleasant?"

"Just overnight. I'll be gone first light tomorrow."

"Why do you want to stay here?"

That got me a little pissed. All I wanted was a place on the floor for six hours. I reached for my bike. "Listen, I'm sorry for asking. I'll move on."

"No, wait. Sorry for the grill job. What'd you say your name was? I'm Tom Jones, Methodist pastor here." He held out a huge hand. "We're all kind of skittish around here, especially the women. We've had four rapes this first week of classes. The police think it's someone from the outside. Women have been coming here at night to study. They say it's the safest place on campus. I try to keep it that way.

"You wouldn't be looking for a shower, would you?" He brushed a couple live ones from my shoulder. "Phys ed department's right over there. Communion will be at nine if you want to join us. We've got a room for you."

Tom lit several candles, then turned off the fluorescents and sat his heavy body down on the carpet. We totaled eight, all cross-legged in a circle. Book bags and tennis rackets leaned against the wall. A large white candle stood next to the wafers with a pitcher of wine.

"On the night in which he was betrayed, our Lord Jesus took some bread, and when he broke it, he gave thanks, saying . . ." The wafer was comically small in that huge hand.

" 'This is my body,' " and he snapped it in half. " 'Take it and eat it.' And then Jesus said this to his friends, 'As often as you do this remember me.'

"And when he had broken the bread and given it to his friends, he took the cup, thanked his father and said, 'This is my blood, shed for you and the remission of all you've done wrong. As often as you drink it, remember me.' " Tom poured the wine into little plastic cups, then sat back for a second.

Outside, an electric guitar shrieked from a dorm window. Tom smiled, rocked to his chubby knees, and picked up the wine and wafers. The window slammed shut and the music died.

"Jim, this is my body, broken for you." A skinny blond kid with a face full of acne took the wafer.

"Elizabeth, this is my blood, shed for you." She wore jersey number 88, and tossed the wine back as if it were a shot.

He knee-waddled around the group and stopped at each kid, saying nothing for a second, then his or her name. Jerry. Lisa. And then, This is my body. For you. He waited for each to finish, then waddled on.

When I was growing up, we celebrated Communion the first Sunday of each month, "whether you need it or not," the joke ran. The rite never made sense, how the bread is a body and the wine is blood, and how consuming them made any difference at all. This was just something the farmers and their wives did every four weeks. I liked its parade aspect: the procession of large square-built women leading skinny leisure-suited men who fumbled with buttons all the way up the aisle. But afterward, the remarkable thing was that when they walked back to their seats they looked so unchanged. If this had been blood they'd just drunk, not Mogen David, they should've looked ebullient or grossed out, anything but normal. Communion was just something they did.

Tonight's communion was different. Maybe it was the way Tom did it—on his knees, and that he said each name, then waited. And the fact that outside these walls lurks a rapist, and I could see that on the face of each woman as she ate and drank. For all their vagueness, the words I've known since childhood touched me. No one moaned or rolled their eyes, as in Karen's church. We ate the wafer and drank the wine in silence. Maybe it was a glimmer of faith. I don't know.

I was last in the circle, ready for him to have forgotten my name.

"Brian, this is my blood."

It was grape juice. Methodists. God love the Methodists.

He closed with a simple prayer; he named each in the circle again, something specific like a big test or trouble at home. If he mentioned me at all I thought it'd be under some kind of blanket Methodist deal.

"And for my new friend, Brian, I ask protection for him as he makes his way. Keep him safe on his blue bicycle. Let friends come into his life that surprise him with generosity."

Touched, tears welled in my eyes.

"And finally, God, I ask for healing in the mind of him who is terrorizing this community tonight. The rapist. Please heal his hatred. He is your child too."

I have been named with a rapist, practically in the same breath. Maybe Tom had some lingering doubts about me. I didn't mind.

I am hungry for what Tom fed us here. The rapist—at least in some dank, unlit corner of his heart—must feel the same.

SEPTEMBER 5

 91 MILES

Swartz Creek, Michigan

Southeastern Michigan is a fantastic bore. Table-flat, it's speckled with little farms that some other day I might call cute; but under heavy clouds, even heavier humidity, and swarms of those same damn black bugs, they barely registered. Southeastern Michigan is a place to get through, a head wind to duck, bugs to honk out of my nose.

The one lively moment of the day came south of St. Charles when a terrier yapped out of his farmyard after me. That bushy mustache and fierce, ankle-high bark—he made me smile for the first time today. Just when he reached my right pedal he stopped, whipped to the left side, and chased again. I cheered him on back there. Valiant dog! Then a little tinkle caught my ear from the right. A glance over that shoulder and a sleek black Doberman was rising like a cruise missile out of the ditch, aimed right for my leg, his only noise the clink of his tag. All I remember at this point is throwing the gear levers to the top, then chancing a quick look back at his teeth and tongue near my calf. I remember slowing down about a mile later but the rest is a breathless blank.

The only other thing that sticks out today is a sign painted the color of blood on a garage in St. Louis, Michigan: "God, Guns and Guts made America GREAT! Let's keep all three!"

The ride is shifting now. Today I pedaled to get it over with. Andrew is behind; Karen is behind; the Atlantic is still way too far away to think about. So I just pedaled. I didn't talk to anybody.

Late afternoon, I stopped to rest in an old cemetery. I wheeled the bike through the weeds and gravestones and leaned it against a tall pointed pillar, grayed with lichen. Ruth Bartlett, 1817–1890. The base was cracked and the stone leaned north at just the right angle for a tired back to rest against. Her children's stones were scattered around her. I saw none for a husband.

My grandparents and great-grandparents are all buried a half mile north of our Illinois farm, and the hilltop cemetery is the sole lovely spot in the township. Oak and ash trees and immense lilac bushes encircle it, then the fields and wood lots tumble down to Monsen's dairy and, just beyond, our house. As a teenager, I often finished my bicycle rides at sunset walking up the grassy hill to find great-grandfather's grave. I'd sit on the stone and look south.

Our barn, which looked so dusty and faded in noon sun, would glow red as a drop of fresh blood. Once or twice I heard our bell call out over the fields, Ma hoping I was nearby. Two rings then the echo off Monsen's barn. Supper.

I had little clue about what I wanted to do with my life, and I always came to the cemetery to try to figure it out. The farm was probably not going to be it. I had a little awareness that it would be college and Lord knows what after that, but not a farm life.

Once, I brought Lili there and we spent an hour or so walking, hands clasped behind our backs among the stones, reading the names aloud, and marveling that most of the stones
were for children who lived only a year: on our stone alone
were Christina, 1869–70, and Anna, 1871–72, and one listed
only as Infant, June 6, 1878. These names faced south, watching the farm. The names of their sad parents faced the sunset.
On the north was a short poem, part of it lost to a lichen which
filled in the chiseled letters.

> *All those who die in the Lord*
> *. . . are only asleep.*
> *Therefore, do not weep . . .*

I remember the last bit of summer sun slanting just so across
the stone's face, and how Lili read the letters cloaked by the
shadows, and when the sun had gone down she read the stone
as if it were Braille. I can still see her fingers moving gently.

> *. . . gone before . . . trusting the Lord . . .*

I think of the hurt I caused her and I would take our ten years
back if I could and wish we'd never met. Her kindnesses come
to me at all the wrong moments these days. She never thought
my affection for the old cemetery odd. Someone else might
have laughed or been creeped out. Karen would probably start
praying aloud right there. Still, I only brought Lili there once.
This was my refuge. Every other time I came alone and simply
watched the light leave the land. Perched on my great-
grandfather's stone I received an implacable sense of belong-
ing to a place, of home.

SEPTEMBER 6

98 MILES

Port Huron, Michigan

Lord, I have never seen it rain like last night: nine inches in two hours the radio said, and the lightning thwacked the wall of my borrowed bedroom in nearly continuous blasts. The road east of Flint was swamped this morning and I plowed right into it, leaving cars literally in my wake. I wished the storm would've cleared this awful humidity but it only thickened it.

The storm gave rise to today's memorable line, captured during lunch in El's Diner. A fleshy elderly woman with bright blond hair came from behind the counter and tossed her plastic El pin down the counter till it hit the pie plate. "I'm going on break, Stevie, get me my coffee." She squeezed herself into the booth in front of me. Stevie, beautifully tall and probably sixteen, straining under an armload of dirty dishes, said "Right away, El," and rolled her eyes to the ceiling.

El lit a cigarette and two more women entered, rumbled over to her booth, and packed themselves breast and belly into their seats. The two lit up and they all looked like triplets. The El Convention. El the First held court.

"Shit, did she rain last night. Never saw her come like that. How much o' that shit we get anyhow? Basement flooded, sump pump broke, and that lazy old man never got his fat ass off the—and I *told* him basement's gonna flood and we're gonna drown and what's he gonna do? Just sat there. First thing this morning, I turn on thirteen to see what the hell, and they got a picture of a nigger floatin' his car, it's a Volkswagen, floatin' it right down the street."

Then, this beauty: "Is that legal, for a nigger to float his Volkswagen down the street?"

Big laughs and clouds of cigarette smoke chugged up from the Els as they worked on that one.

Tonight I spent with parents of a former colleague. Their house is only yards from Lake Huron and after dinner I watched the sky, soaked gray with humidity, melt into the lake. Freighters called way out there. Ninety-two degrees now at 11:00. I'm tired, and getting tired of this trip. I think back on the altar call. John. Headwinds. The little milestones. None seem to matter tonight. And another thousand miles of humidity to plow into until the Atlantic. Even the big goal of wetting the front tire seems pointless. Karen will still be a dilemma, Lili and our ten messed years will still tie up my heart. And I'm saved—yippee. Most of the time I don't feel one damn bit different.

It's all waiting for me back home. More or less the same as when I left. Great.

SEPTEMBER 9

 220 MILES

Niagara Falls, Ontario

I haven't written these last three days because they've all been so much the same: hot, humid, and flat. No experiences to note, just riding. Actually, more like waiting than riding. My own inwardness and this oppressive weather form a kind of glass-walled room in which I sit until the Atlantic. The room rolls on, the ditch glides by, there is little else to tell. This is drudgery. A job only to be done with.

The days are exhausting and dispiriting, the nights punctuated by fantastic storms. I've slept in a tin shed, a church basement, and a born-again preacher's back bedroom, while each night the sky tries to shake the chokehold of this humidity. I lie awake scared. Between storms, there are dreams.

One in particular stays with me. I was the captain of a spaceship and had just come through a horrible battle. Nearly all the crew members were dead and everything was scorched. I could even smell singed hair.

There is a passage of time, days or years, and the ship arrives home. There is no land here, no trees or buildings, simply more dark space, yet I know it to be home. I walk to a huge pair of wooden doors. As I grab their handles I see my arms are festering with wounds.

Inside, suddenly there is light. *Blue sky everywhere.* There are no walls or windows but I am inside a defined place. Window frames appear and hang in midair; they frame sections of the sky like paintings. The air is delicious and cold, and, having breathed smoke so long, I suck it in. As I walk, my shoes click against a glass floor. Below is only more sky.

A figure appears far off. It is a beautiful straight-backed throne. Steps lead up to it. A man sits there. I never see his face but I know he is my father. This is his palace. I walk toward him.

Rich, warm air begins to pour in through the window frames. As I walk the fabric of my torn uniform begins to thin. Eventually it peels and flutters away. Another part of me floats above to watch. There I am, walking on sky toward the end of this hall. And now time reverses itself and I see me below growing shorter and younger. The arms and legs that seconds earlier had been covered with sores are clean now, the skin boyishly white. The stride shortens. The hair thins. I am a toddler now. I reach the steps to the throne and without pausing crawl up them into the man's lap.

Instantly, I the adult am back in the body of this child. I grab the folds of cloth at his breast and bury my face in them. Then the battle scenes and lightning storms come back to me and with a man's voice I cry for my stupid mistakes. I weep and weep and push my face toward his heart. Then I feel his right hand, huge and warm, rest on my shoulder while his left softly cradles my back. I see both hands for just a moment; the skin is cracked. I lie back and, finally, breathe slow and calm.

All day today, I rode with the image of those hands, especially the cracked skin of the index finger. Dad always used the side of that finger, like a rag, to wipe snot or diesel fuel away. As he drove the tractor, the sun would bake the skin until it split. Sometimes the cracks would bleed. I looked at my own hands on the handlebars, shaped square as his but city soft. I remember how he used to like them for backrubs in the spring and fall, when he'd spent days half cranked back looking at the plow or planter behind the tractor. At night he'd ask me to rub his back, and I'd sit kitty-corner on the edge of his bed with him spreadeagled face down. The smell of Ivory soap, the sweaty places he'd missed washing, the small knotted old ropes under the warm, rubbery skin. He used to love my hands. "You have strong hands for a boy. You should become a chiropractor."

Now I look at them on the bars. The left one is nearly numb again.

Somewhere east of Niagara I put a quarter in a truckstop pay phone. Something about that dream; I wanted to hear if he was still the man who had said nice things once about my hands. Pathetic, but I wanted it.

"Are you eating enough? Is your bike holding up? Have any cars tried to—you know—have they come close?" Ma worried.

Dad is still just a presence on the extension, lending those dry little chuckles and little else to the conversation.

"Oh, the sweet corn's boiling over. Bill, you talk," and the phone clunks down.

"Well. Not much to tell really. Got three quarters of an inch last night. Your brother's farm missed it completely. He needs it worse than we do. Other than that."

"Now I'm back." It's Mom. "Whew, we have got sweet

corn. Your Dad's just been going great guns in the garden and mercy, so much to freeze. Now where were we? Oh, yes, Tuesday night we had the whole family over and they all asked about you and we all said wouldn't it be great if you were here."

Ma goes on, then me, then her and me again, but it all fades to this picture of Dad on their bed, his shirt off, his tan deep up to the elbow, his white hair wet from finger combing. He lays back on the bedspread, the phone crooked in his neck, his dark cracked fingers laced over his white belly as he enjoys the sounds and smells from Ma's kitchen.

But what is he thinking? I really wonder what he thinks of me.

SEPTEMBER 10

 100 MILES

Rochester, New York

I was sucking down my third milkshake of the morning at the Tasty Freez. Overhead, the green tin awning wasn't so much shade as an oven roof. Rings of melted ice cream slowly baked on the tabletops. A voice came from behind and rolled fast toward me.

"I said, where you going!"

At first, I thought it was Malibu Lars—the blond hair, the fair skin tanned deep, the mirror shades. He skidded to a stop. It was a dirt bike, though, with fat knobby tires. Too clunky and *way* too déclassé for Lars.

"Didn'cha hear me back there?"

"Sorry, I didn't."

"Man, I yelled from the road. Saw your bikes and bags and shit and yelled where you going and you just sat there. What are you eatin'?" His voice was strained and high and he talked like a chipmunk.

"Mint chocolate chip. Flavor of the month."

He rolled a red bandanna off his head, sucked some sweat from its folds, then draped it over the handlebars. He took his glasses off and I noticed the skin around his eyes was a deep red. The eyes themselves were so bloodshot you couldn't tell their true color.

"Flavor of the month, you say," and he dug in his shorts pocket. "Let's try this shit."

He put his shake away in gulps, then grabbed his forehead and rocked.

"Ice cream headache! God, I hate them!" The burn around his eyes flushed brighter.

He squinted at me. "My name's Mark. You goin' to Rochester? Show you a shortcut." He slowed his rocking. He had a long jagged scar on the chin.

We got to the road and he bolted off. Tires that knobby and fat weren't supposed to roll so fast. But—I can go faster than you, my Dad can beat up your Dad—we had to get this out of the way. I caught him in about a quarter of a mile and blew by.

"Damn that hog! She goes good," he yelled up to me. He rocked back and forth. He smiled and jerked the handlebars hard, everything about him tight and wired.

"I was sick."

"What with?"

"Well, it wasn't really sick, more like what you might call wounded."

"Wounded?"

"Well, more like what you might call shot myself in the leg."

He sat up and rode no hands; his knees pumped like pistons. He worked way too hard. We rode past a bank thermometer that read ninety-six.

"Pretty incredible, eh? Shot myself right in the leg."

"When did you get out of the Marines?"

"Last year."

"Did you *want* to go to the Gulf?"

"Hell yes! I'd just as soon some ayrab shoot me, and get a purple heart stuck to my chest, then me nail myself."

"You stay in the corps long?"

"Nah. My CO and me had what you might call a disagreement and he booted me, said it was the booze, but I still have a chance to get the discharge changed if my lawyer ever gets off his butt."

"What do you do now?"

"Not much. Couple days a week I'm at Hall's Jewelry. You've heard of it, it's the biggest one in Roch. I design jewelry. I made my own earring. See? Like it? I could make you one. Other than that I ride my bike back and forth from Niagara and wait for my lawyer, the asshole. My brother lives in Roch. I hang out with him, work, try not to drink, I go to an A.A. meeting if I can. I go back to Niagara."

"Don't you drive?"

"Nah, that's the other thing he's supposed to be working on, getting my license back. Me and a buddy also had a little disagreement one night and I put my beater into the trunk of his Grand Am. That was pretty much it for the license." He laughed and put his hands back onto the bars and stared down the road. Dark gray-green clouds were forming on the horizon.

He sat up again and rode no hands. In that strained voice he yelled, "It's rancid out here!"

"You don't mind getting wet, do you?" I nodded at the clouds.

"Look at that. We might make it though, we're almost at the shortcut."

A mile or so later we turned onto an asphalt bike path wide

enough for us to ride abreast of each other. Running northeast gave us a fantastic view of the clouds, which looked like roiled-up water at a ship's bow. The wind turned and shoved us suddenly from behind. We shifted up and started to fly as lightning began to flicker. The clouds took on a yellow cast. After a minute he nodded at them and said, "Technicolor, eh?"

After that, the wind *really* kicked in. We picked up a few more gears and got flat to pull probably five miles without a word, the trees noisily bowing our way. Then it started to rain. As the first drops slicked our skin, I noticed two long ragged scars on Mark's bicep, and another on his calf.

At a clump of trees close to the path Mark hollered, "Watch out for these, they bite," and he slowed. Tree roots pushed up underneath the pavement and buckled the asphalt. I tried to copy the way he stood, thighs clamped to the seat. He tossed his bike nimbly around the bumps, but I hit them and the bike bucked and I nearly fell off twice.

"Heads up!" he hollered again. "Rug rats." Ahead were a half dozen boys on bikes, probably on their way home from school, bright day packs bulging. One in the back suddenly flew into the air and crumpled onto the pavement. His bike fell on his legs. The other boys didn't see him and continued. Mark charged at the boy, slapping his bike through another set of root bumps. I picked my way and by the time I got there the boy was up. He sucked in half breaths to keep from crying, the knees of his jeans scraped open and bloody. The rain came faster now, the drops hard and cool. At his feet lay his bike, the front wheel out of its slots and jammed diagonally in the forks.

In a smooth, almost balletic motion Mark flipped the bike onto its seat. He pulled the front wheel but it didn't budge. He pulled again, then held the front forks like a bow and the wheel like a bow string and gave it everything he could. No luck, and the kid whimpered. His friends were now on their way back for him. Their yells got lost in the wind, and the rain picked up a notch. Mark stood on the handlebars and grabbed the wheel with both hands and closed his eyes. More scars stood out on Mark's straining arms, one long one on his left forearm and two shorter ones near the right shoulder. When the tire finally gave, the boy reached for it. He simply touched it, as if to see that it was still good. He nodded, then Mark spun the tire, remarkably still true, into the fork slots and tightened the quick release. With the reverse seamless motion he flipped the bike upright. He squatted at the boy's knee and wiped the blood and grit away with his thumb. The boy gasped and made fists. Mark got his face right down there, looked at the knee, then stood. "There you go, kid."

The other kids pulled in. The boy kicked a piece of buckled asphalt. "Ah, my stupid wheel just fell out. I was trying to pop a wheelie over these things. Thanks, mister." He rode off with his friends.

Mark looked after them. *I wish I'd had the camera ready. This man, all wire and scars, standing there with rain dripping from his nose, fists on his hips.*

"No problem at all."

Rain. *Almost* solid water. Lightning close by. And oh the air—lightning-scoured, rinsed with cold clean buckets of water. The humidity is gone. I can breathe again. The hair on my legs stands straight out of flesh covered in goose bumps and the grime runs into my socks and I'm out of the saddle shifting finally all the way to the top and our backs are sails and we roar over the waves laughing, lightning in our spines.

At the Alcoholics Anonymous meeting house, guys chain-smoked and played cards. I waited in the doorway while Mark made the rounds. No one seemed glad to see him except two grizzled men at the coffee urn. At least they shook his hand. Mark asked for a woman named Susan and they each raised their eyebrows but, no, didn't know where she was.

At the Perkins, while the waitress laid out our plates, a slim young woman in a peach blouse came behind Mark, put her hands over his eyes, and said, "Guess who?" He smiled, stretching the scar on his chin tight.

"Well, let's see." He slid one hand up her arm. "Kinda hairy. Bob. Is that you, you old fart?"

She rolled her eyes and I was struck at how sad they looked even when she smiled. They were a dark olive color. She bent close to his ear and murmured, "Try again, or I'll break your nose off."

His hand shuttled up and down the arm. It *was* hairy, and exotically dark against his own sunburnt arm. I put her at about my age.

"OK, OK. Well, come to think of it, it's a pretty skinny arm you got here. Hmm. It's. It's. Piss, I can't remember. Got to start drinking again."

She bit his ear, leaving marks. "Move over, you're buying me supper."

Mark stood to let her in and stayed up while she settled herself. I was struck by how courtly and old-world the gesture was for such a coarse, blunt man. I was also struck by her long dark legs and white cut-offs.

"Hi, I'm Susan," she said, holding out her hand. "When did you get in town?"

"Word gets around fast. Only, what, an hour ago?" Mark said.

A coffeepot came and she poured for him, he for her. They

immediately began to chew over people at the meeting house and the steps of the A.A. program. They sat close and she frequently touched his shoulder. I tried to look interested in the place mat—the forest maze printed with a little fuzzy brown bear at the START and a big parent bear looking confused at the FINISH. I whipped Mopsy through it in about ten seconds, then found alternate routes for her by knocking down a tree here, a bush there. When Susan looked at Mark, I watched her for a few seconds, those sad pretty eyes. He didn't return her touches. When she looked at me I made sure my eyes were again on the maze, taking Mama Bear through it now, a little nervously, to Mopsy. Susan's hair was black but with strands of lighter brown underneath. High, Native American cheekbones like Karen. I brought Mopsy and Mama Bear into the maze's middle. Her blouse was unbuttoned one button further than Karen would and her breasts strained against the peach cloth. I put Mopsy and Mama Bear back in their corners.

Plates clattered onto the bears. Mark's steak was black.

"Ah, just the way I like it."

"So, where you from?" Susan asked me. Suddenly my cheeks were warm.

"Minnesota. St. Paul."

"Noooo kidding."

"You been there?"

"Yeah, last year for a little." Immediately, she looked even sadder. "Ten billion lakes."

"Where? St. Paul?" As soon as I said it, she looked trapped and turned to Mark as if for help. He shrugged.

She took a long drink of water. "Well, kind of out in the country. You ever hear of Hazelden?" I said yes but wasn't sure, somewhere north of the city maybe. "I was there for a month last summer. My parents didn't know what to do with me by then and they'd heard Hazelden was the best so they packed me off to Minnesota."

"Man, could she drink!" Mark interrupted. He leaned toward me, mouth full of charred, crunchy steak. "Put *me* under the table!" He looked at her. "Man, could you drink! Oswego, you remember?"

That sadness on her face suddenly broke and a beautiful alto laugh tumbled from her. She leaned her head on his shoulder.

"She could *drink*!" Mark said and pointed his steak knife at her.

"Yeah, and I could sniff glue and swallow bucketfulls of pills and thanks to Daddy's money I could get coke whenever I wanted." She sat up. "When he found out, Daddy got pissed." She stuck an index finger in the air. "Off to treatment!" Mark burped.

"They sent me to all the places around here. A week or so, sometimes three, but it never took. It was always worse when I got out." All the light in her face left again. She was no less beautiful sad. Mark set his knife and fork down and took a long pull on his water. He looked to the other side of the Perkins.

"I was doing Mom's rubbing alcohol after a while, trying to get off on her hair spray, anything. They didn't know what to do, so, like I said, Daddy'd heard about this place in Minnesota so they shipped me."

"Did it work?"

"Damn right it worked," Mark said. He threw an arm around her shoulder, squeezed hard, and looked proud. "She's so dry now she's a fire hazard."

"Yeah, well, I had to."

"I gotta pee," Mark said. "I heard this next part before anyway." He left.

"Mark and his bladder," she said. "That's the only reason I

used to drink him under, he's forever pissing it away. World's tiniest bladder for a guy."

"Why did Hazelden work when all the others didn't?"

She ran her hand through her hair. "It's in the middle of goddamn nowhere. Lakes and more lakes. No place to sneak out and get anything. It was the first resident treatment I got, too. I mean I was *there,* basically locked in for four weeks." She stared at her water glass. "I was away from my drinking friends, too, for that whole time. So, it was the whole thing, the solitude, the program, the break with folks here. Even Mark. That's why he had to pee just now. He doesn't like that part."

She suddenly looked accusatory and angry. "Why am I telling you this? I don't know you."

"I don't know, other than that I asked." It seemed impossible at that moment to guess her age. The lines on her face and those sad eyes—maybe she was older than me. Her face softened the next minute as she looked at her glass again.

"Anyway, Mark was still drinking then and he was pissed that I was getting help. I came back and kicked him everyday until he went to A.A., now he's doing pretty good. What about you, you in A.A.?"

"No. I met Mark between here and Niagara this morning and he kind of took me under his wing this afternoon."

"He's like that. He's a crazy. He's mean when he wants to be, but he took care of me a lot last year, too. He's kind of the brother I never had. So where you riding?"

"The Atlantic."

"Don't let him shit you, Susan," Mark said as he crash-landed back in the booth. "He's just riding around the block." He picked at the last ashes of his steak. "Found him riding in circles outside the Perkins just before you came."

On the way to his brother's house afterward, Mark didn't

say a thing for several minutes. Which struck me as odd—he'd hardly shut up the whole day.

"Guess how old she is, Brian," he said eventually.

"I don't know. I was wondering myself. Maybe thirty?"

We stopped at a traffic light and Mark said, "She's only seventeen. Check it out. Sevennn-teeen. And she didn't tell you half of what her old man did to her."

We finished the evening with MTV. I haven't seen television in weeks and all those tanned bodies, the color and the speed of those images. I stared until my eyes dried. It bored Mark. He yammered on the phone to one friend after another. Around midnight he picked up the remote and snapped it off. The lamp far across his brother's living room threw an odd sideways light on him.

"That's it," he said. "Foam the runways, I'm comin' in." He opened the hide-a-bed and took his shirt off. The lamplight made his scars stand high and white.

"How'd you get them?" I asked. He looked at me, and I touched my arm and chin.

"It's a long story." He flapped his sleeping bag open and laid it on the bed.

He shut off the light. In the darkness, I heard him smooth the bag out and climb in. I didn't get up. After a few minutes he began talking. His voice startled me at first. I thought it was somebody else—he sounded warmer, slower, so different from that strangled chipmunk rasp I'd heard all day. I could just make out his silhouette on the bed, hands behind his head.

"When I was in the corps, I only wanted one thing. Out. Out bad. But my old man had been a sergeant in Korea, and that's pretty much what was expected of me. Be a leatherneck. All the Marines did was teach me how to stay drunk."

He lay quiet for a minute and I heard the furnace turn on, probably the first time since last winter. It smelled of diesel and an old stale closet that'd been closed for years. The warm air felt good and reminded me it is nearly fall now.

"You know Klinger on Mash," he asked. "How he wore dresses all the time just to make his CO think he was nuts to get the discharge? I tried to drink my way out. But they'd throw me in the can, and I'd dry out, and they'd see through it. So I upped the ante. I got knives. I started cutting myself up, make them think I was suicidal."

He paused for a second and rustled noisily in his sleeping bag, and I think he said, "Who knows." He turned again and his silhouette touched his chin. "So these are what you'd call the fruits of my labor." He tucked his hands inside the sleeping bag.

"When I shot myself in the leg, they got the picture. They gave me enough stitches to get out the door, and I was an ex-Marine exactly five hours and thirteen minutes later."

He turned over in his bag, and put his back to me. I went to my room, turned out the light and got undressed. That poor bastard. All that blood, just to get out. Just to say no to his old man. I stretched out in my own sleeping bag and stared at the ceiling for probably a half hour, hearing Mark's voices, the one so fast and tight, all nerves and scars. And the other, submissive and weary, *that's pretty much what was expected of me* . . .

I should have no beef with my father. He never pushed me into anything. Well, maybe Jesus, but that beats the Marines any day. Dad was either in the field, or in the shop killing turkeys, but he never shoved me into doing either. Poor Mark. I fingered the scar in my left palm, and thought of the ones on his arms. And that one on his chin—it lies about a quarter inch from his carotid. Good grief.

SEPTEMBER 12

 150 MILES

Holland Patent, New York

It's fall now. How complete and sudden the transition. Two days ago I rode shirtless. Now, the Adirondack maples are dredged in orange and lemon. I wear a sweater and a jacket. This morning, in the gorgeous brittle air, I even put on the mittens.

The stones of this fence feel good against my back. They're smooth and warm. Under me is ditch grass, crisp from a couple nights of frost. Across the road, a woman leans storm windows against her garage and washes them with soapy clockwise sweeps; one by one the panes emerge bright as mirrors.

I can feel the Atlantic and the end coming, probably no more than a week away now. The change of season signals it.

And now I don't know that I want it to come.

A guy at a truck stop just gave me some peaches for free. He said, "Your money's no good here," and filled a small paper bag. With these warm stones against my back I eat and let the juice run down my arm. I remember John's poem.

I gather wood.
I build fires.
Oh what happiness.
Oh what joy.

I had another Dad dream last night. No Jungian imagery. He simply stands in the farmhouse door and opens his arms as he sees me ride up to him. He wears that ratty rust-red sweatshirt, the one with weld holes in the front. His face so relieved, proud. That's all.

SEPTEMBER 14

150 MILES

Middlebury, Vermont

"D ad! Hello from Vermont!"

"Brian! What day is it? Is this Saturday? You usually call on Saturdays."

"No, Thursday. I'm just about through with the trip, though. I wanted to tell you that."

"Huh, how do you like that."

Pause.

"What's going on there?"

"Let's see, not much. Your mother is gone to Circle tonight. I've got MacNeil-Lehrer on and she should be back in about a half hour. How about yourself?"

"I'm in this little college town, Middlebury, it seems to be parents' weekend or something. Lots of students walking around with their folks."

"You say you're almost done?"

"Yeah, only a few more days."

"Huh, well."

"How do the crops look?" I ask. "Need any rain?"

"We could stand some, I guess. Got a couple inches last weekend. Your brother needs it worse still."

"I hope he gets it."

"Yep."

"Yeah, well." Then a long stretch of phone hiss.

"Your mother will be back in just a bit, if you want to call again."

"Nah, that's OK. Just say hi to her. I'll call again when I reach the Atlantic."

"Be sure to. I'm sure she'd like to know when you've made it."

The sidewalk seemed to surge underneath me, then drop.

"So long, Brian."

I slammed the phone into its cradle and stepped from the booth.

"Mother wants to know when I'm finished, Mother will be proud. Shit! Could you care less?"

I began to walk fast. Through central Middlebury, through clusters of college students, many stepping wide out of my way. I was still furious a mile later near the town's edge. At the last houses I walked past a park bench. The sun was nearly down.

Across the road one silver maple caught the setting sun. The sun shifted behind a cloud for a moment, then came back in an absolute blast of autumn glory. The tree flared like a struck match.

I've crossed most the North American continent alone on a bicycle and only now do I see why. I have damn near killed myself just so he'd say a decent word about me, so he'd notice me. Give me actual words. Not Ma, him. I see you. You're good. Anything. Just once. What a fool I've been.

SEPTEMBER 17

225 MILES

Richmond, Maine

Tomorrow, the Atlantic. I only needed one last place to stay. Richmond looked as if Norman Rockwell had designed it, right down to its whitewashed steeples and village green. I found a Methodist church and ducked my head into the pastor's study. "Sure, no problem, use the couch in the youth room." I thanked him and said I'd be back. I'd seen a school on the outskirts of town and I needed a shower.

I leaned my bike against the wall outside the principal's office and found a janitor. "Help yourself, the shower's in the locker room," he hollered over his vacuum. I pulled the pannier containing my toiletries off the bike, including a clean T-shirt, shorts, and shoes. Nobody around in beautiful Rockwellville. I left the bike unlocked for the first time.

I was rinsing the suds out my hair and suddenly stopped. A niggling little voice inside my head spoke plain as day. *My bike is gone.* Shampoo slid into my eye. I rinsed it and shrugged the voice off. I haven't a psychic bone in my body and, besides, a theft in this town?

At the mirror combing my hair, there it was again. *My bike's been stolen.*

I stepped out the school door. Only my helmet and gloves lay where I'd leaned the bike.

I stepped back inside and closed the door, my hand on the handle already shaking. I stood there for a few seconds.

I will walk through the door again and it will be there. This is just a dream. I will now wake up.

I ran the entire perimeter of the building, hoping some kid had just played a trick and hid it around the corner. I turned to the schoolyard and ripped at the tall weeds along the fence. I ran into the building. I ran out. I ran back in. Then out again into the weeds.

Finally, I located another janitor. He jumped when I tapped his shoulder. "I need your help," I yelled over his vacuum. "I've been riding my bicycle all the way across America and I have one more day to ride and I was taking a shower a couple of minutes ago and left my bike and all my stuff outside and NOW IT'S GONE and I've looked everywhere around the building and can't find it at all CAN YOU HELP ME?" He ran to the principal's office and called the police.

The officer picked me up in the schoolyard and we blew, lights and sirens, eighty miles an hour down a little road west of town. The cruiser was old and the shocks were mushy as oatmeal; each little hill we flew over pulled my guts lower and lower. The headlights reflected beer cans in the ditch grass and several times I grabbed the dashboard ready to shout "There it is!" After miles of countryside we gave up and slowly returned, no lights or sirens this time.

We stopped at Richmond's watering holes. I stayed

slumped in the car and watched the officer ask questions and jerk his thumb at me as he talked to parking-lot locals.

"Kevin! I should of known it was that asshole," the officer snapped as he slammed his door and switched the siren on. We headed to the trailer court where Kevin lived. "Kevin is the school bully," he said, "always in trouble with us and the principal." He laid every one of Richmond's ills on Kevin, from missing bikes and broken arms on the playground to rotten eggs heaved at church windows. Kevin was Satan himself, come up to harass Richmond.

"Damn him anyway. You ride across the whole goddamn country, and Kevin screws it up for the entire state of Maine. If we catch him tonight, you and I will personally string him up and beat the piss out of him."

It was a nice bit of hyperbole. "I'd be glad to."

"First, though," he went on, "we'll drag him behind the cruiser here, soften him up." I thought he was kidding, but the way he patted the seat, the way he stared down the road—he actually looked serious.

At the trailer court, he shut the siren off and turned the cruiser's hand beam on Kevin's home. A Dumpster outside overflowed with garbage; a couple of beat-up tricycles rusted in the weeds nearby. We drove at a snail's pace looking through the rest of the court, the light sweeping back and forth as if from a lighthouse.

So the day ends not at the church, but here at the preacher's house. The officer knows the preacher and his wife and assured me they'd help. They quickly offered a spare bed and their phone to call home and have money wired. I don't even know if I thanked them. I came into this bedroom, sat on the floor, and just stared at my hands.

SEPTEMBER 18

45 MILES

Rockport, Maine

Early this morning the Reverend stopped in my room and offered a lifeboat—his daughter's bike. Emily just turned twelve and they got her a shiny new Huffy for her birthday.

"It's not much," he said, "but you're welcome to use it to get to the coast. You've got about forty, forty-five miles. It'll get you there. The whole town feels awful about this." He's called a rally at the school for me tomorrow afternoon, he's even called the papers. His wife made a huge, guilty breakfast.

I walked to the convenience store where the wired money was due, bought a bottle of juice, and waited outside. If Kevin rode by I'd kick his pimply face into pudding right there on the asphalt. A half hour passed. An hour. The wire came and I cashed the check and returned to my post.

It was almost noon when I gave it up. I trudged back to the preacher's house and found Emily's Huffy in the garage. The bike was just out of the box, the tires still black and clean. The seat was positioned perfectly for a twelve-year-old girl.

I could call it, here. When the officer dropped me off last night he'd said, "Hell, if you want to say you made it to the coast, east of Richmond one mile is where the Kennebec River empties. That's saltwater from there on out." He had this hopeful look. "See what I'm telling you, son? That's ocean water. You made it."

I jacked up Emily's seat and left Richmond, knees banging the handlebars. The forty-five miles were uneventful and sad. A fine haze laid across the sky and dimmed the sun, just as riding this girl's bike dimmed the joy of finishing. My own blue bicycle and all the equipment, the journals, all those inanimate companions that never meant much along the way—now I missed them all.

At the last curve. I couldn't see the ocean yet but I could see the sky above it and, finally, no more hills. As stupid as this sounds, the moment was a shock. I've grown so used to this life, to the hills and the flats, to the sheer simplicity, it feels like it will go on forever.

You're done now, it's over, go home.

The Atlantic finally came into view, blue and clear as a spring dawn. For a moment I stopped pedaling, then all down the last gentle little hill I rode the brakes hard. I saw a landing where I could wet the front wheel—complete the grand dream—but at the last second I turned out onto a pier. I walked the Huffy the length of the gray boards, and at the end, dropped the kickstand, sat, and simply watched the harbor. A few minutes before sunset, a heavily laden fishing trawler motored out of the harbor. I watched its swaying mast lights all the way to the horizon.

SEPTEMBER 20

The farm

His body felt hard when I hugged him. I noticed for the first time that the top of his head comes only up to my ear now. He is growing shorter after the heart attack. He opens his arms no wider than his elbows clenched to his ribs allow. Behind my ear he said, "Just like a bad penny, come back home."

The words landed like a fist in my gut. I tried to fake a smile; maybe I'd misheard him.

Ma ran to the door, singing out my name. The air was still a little socked out of me from his words and when she threw her arms around me, her tears cool against my cheek, I could barely breathe.

"Let me look at you! Bill, look at how skinny he is. Come on, let's fatten you up. Oh, let me look at you."

The pretty flowered tablecloth, smells of garden beans and squash on the stove, a roast. The kitchen, same as ever. I pulled my usual chair to the table.

"The kitchen smells great."

"Oh, just the usual things, you know. Father's garden was great this year, wasn't it, Father?"

"Did all right," he said, seating himself.

On the settee arm Dad's wooden cabinet Phillips radio played a preacher in full rant about secular humanism. On the counter near the sink, Mom's digital radio played *All Things Considered*. Each one up loud enough to be heard but not to compete outright with the other. She turned hers off and came to the table with plates of food.

"Oh, it's so good to have you home," she said. "You must've been so hungry out there. The beans got a little too done, and I'm sick about the gravy but—"

"Let's say grace so we can eat," Dad said and smiled at all the food. Heads bowed.

"God is great, God is good," he started.

His radio stayed on.

"We will thank Him for this food. . . ."

I looked at the radio and wondered if we couldn't shut the damn thing off. The preacher practically screamed about evil this and evil that and humanism the other, and all I could think of was that there was some pissed-off army ant trying to find its way out the speaker holes while we prayed.

"By His hand we all are fed. . . ."

I noticed Dad has marked the radio's face with little black felt-tip dashes so he can find his favorite religious stations easily.

". . . give us, oh Lord, our daily bread. Amen."

"All right, then, start at the beginning. Tell us everything. Your bike, it's still stolen? Father, start the potatoes at Brian. You know how he eats potatoes."

John Runmann, the winds of North Dakota, the Michigan

storms, bike theft —I've read somewhere, interest is the sur-
est expression of love. Ma asked about everything. The bruise
of Dad's words at the door faded. I didn't tell them about the
altar call on September 1. I couldn't stand it if all he and I
could talk about is Jesus. We who've hardly ever talked about
anything.

Dad worked on his roast beef, studiously cutting the pieces,
then scooping a little orange Jell-O onto this one, some slaw
onto that one. Sometimes he turned to me, but then shifted
his weight and eyes to the radio behind him. I could've just
returned from a ride to the mailbox.

Supper's done and the dishes are all put away. Ma
chuckles at *The Tonight Show* while Dad sits alone in the dark
kitchen. The radio at his elbow now plays a hymn. I step out
the back door into the immense prairie night, the air sharp
and cold. From the backyard I can see the neighbor's corn
dryer a quarter mile away, the blue flame baking the grain before shipment. After a few minutes the flame cycles back and
cools to a dull copper color. Then it roars blue again. Then
copper, the color of a bad penny.

I remember nights like this decades ago, standing in this
exact spot, watching his tractor lights crawl across the cornfields. The whole township was a chorus of tractor engines
those nights, and his little Oliver was the tenor, wavery, halting
as he'd stop to unclog an auger or pick up a rock. He was
always out here in the fields. Or driving Bibles around the
countryside. Is that what a father is? Always driving away?

The flame cycles up azure, then down to rust. I walk across
the frosted grass to the door. The house is dark. In the kitchen,
the little corner radio is still on. I run hot water from the tap

to warm my hands and turn it on fast and loud and hope he'll say something. The radio snaps off. I hear him stand.

" 'Night, Brian."

"Good night, Dad."

"Sleep good."

"You too."

SEPTEMBER 25

After the expanse of days on the road, after all that sky over the handlebars, normal life feels tiny and odd. Everything seems fragmented. Like little snapshots.

Driving back to Minnesota on I-94, a road sign says, St. Paul—250 miles. Instinctively I think that'll take two, two and a half days. It takes four and a half hours. Imagine, four and a half hours.

SEPTEMBER 28

St. Paul

Back at work.

"Hi, Brian! How was your vacation?"

I smile, say something pleasant. Inside, the word vacation echoes in my head—that was a vacation?

"Gee, that sounds so fun, riding your bike all day. Tell me about it sometime, OK?"

I'd love to. It's all I want to talk about.

"Got to run now."

This conversation was repeated maybe a dozen times today. No one, not a single person, asked and really seemed to want to listen. By the end of today, I began to gauge my response by the face, easy as a traffic light to read.

"Hi, Brian! How was your vacation?" He didn't even look up from his terminal.

"Great. Thanks."

"That's good. Say, can we trade shifts next week? I've got this appointment."

"Sure. No problem."

And I die a little inside each time.

OCTOBER 1

At first it felt good to rest from riding. But now, in bed here, my legs feel as if they're plugged into a light socket. They feel as if they could kick the wall out. They're ready for another hundred miles.

Autumn is closing in colder and colder.

OCTOBER 5

She was fat, really fat, and her cart of white bread and doughnuts and Coke took up way too much aisle. That and her rear. I tried to go left and she went left, then right as she went right. She whipped around and, with each chin wobbling, gave me a look that plain as day said, What the hell's your problem anyway?

I want to get around you, lady. I want out of here. I am not like you. I don't come here like everybody else. I am special. I have ridden my bike across the country. Alone. I want somebody, anybody, to know what I've done—gone and ridden across the whole damn continent by myself. I am not like you.

OCTOBER 7

The church choir director has asked me to sing a solo recital next month. "Anything you want," he said. It'll be in the church parlor on a Sunday afternoon. This is the best thing to happen since coming back. I plowed through stacks of music tonight, French songs, German, English, singing loud in my living room as if I were rediscovering my own voice, gone for months.

OCTOBER 13

"Brian, do you think a woman should keep her last name when she gets married?"

"I think she should do whatever she wants to. She might want to ask her fiancé's opinion, though."

"I think when women get married, they should always take the man's name. It's biblical. The man being her covering and all."

"Her covering?"

"You know, the protection, sort of, the thing that lets her be her real self. Protected by a godly man, the woman can blossom."

"What?"

"Finding herself by giving herself to her husband. The man doesn't take over his wife but he sacrifices himself for her because of his love for her. Like Christ died for the church. Don't you want that kind of a relationship if we were to get—well, you know, married? God wants you to be my covering."

"What if a couple wants an even relationship? Fifty-fifty, or as near to it as possible? That's the way I think it should be."

"It's in the Bible. The man should lead. I'd like you to lead us more. In our relationship, I mean. Lead us in prayer and in our growing in the Lord, now that you're saved."

"Is it OK for you to lead, too?"

"But it's in the Bible!"

The last few weeks has been filled with conversations like that. Oh, and this, too:

"When are you going to make an honest woman of her?" Dad asked me on the phone.

"What's that supposed to mean?"

"Well, how long have you known her, six, seven months?"

"Yeah, so?"

"She seems to love you. Why don't you marry her?"

"What if I'm not ready?"

"When is a person ever ready? Your mother and I didn't know when we were ready, we just up and got married. That was forty-some years ago."

"I don't know if it'd work."

"A marriage is strongest, Brian, when the couple shares faith in the Lord Jesus Christ. You two share that faith, don't you?"

"I go to her church."

"She seems to have a strong faith in Christ. You could learn that, maybe get that a bit from her."

Why couldn't I, why *didn't* I, tell him that that faith of hers is becoming a steel band around my throat? I start to babble a defense to him, but it comes out wimpy and scared and I sound pathetic even to myself.

OCTOBER 31

All month my legs have burned as I get into bed, but each week a little less. Now tonight they're completely quiet. I rub my hands on my thighs and feel how they've thinned to less than what they were before the ride.

I think of old men when they first bring them into a nursing home, and how they'll sometimes have to be tied to their beds at night to keep them from escaping. These are the ones who holler all day for long-dead wives or for children who never visit to get them *the hell out of here*. The sound of rattling bedrails is as much a part of the place as nurses being paged over the intercom. For weeks some of these new ones will clang on. Then one day you come back and they're just lying there quiet as can be, staring placidly at the exit signs outside their doors.

NOVEMBER 5

Practicing my songs for the recital. Such music. But my piano accompanist says, "Can you sing any louder?"

Sometimes it's hard to even take a deep breath. The notes feel like fishbones in my throat. The bones are Karen, they're Dad, they're the overcast autumn days falling upon me. I can't open my throat. I can't sing.

NOVEMBER 8

A short dream. I lie on an operating table. A man in a long white coat grabs my throat. He shoves my Adam's apple like the doctor used to during grade-school physicals. He digs into the vocal chords. "I'm sorry, but we'll have to take these out."

NOVEMBER 10

Karen was washing dishes after supper at my place. I was drying. The only light on was the small oven bulb. The kitchen was warm and dark, and the furnace was cranked up against a cold north wind. She broke a light sweat and opened her blouse one button lower than usual. She pulled the fabric out to blow down her chest.

"You need any help with that?" I asked.

She gave me a look I haven't seen in months. She wrapped her arms around me. My blood started to warm and rise. We French-kissed and her hands pulled on my back, and I reached to her next lower button.

And suddenly everything from my neck down was cut off from me. In an instant I felt nothing for her. Nothing sexual, nothing emotional, nothing. She could've been my sister, she could've been a stranger. Just like that, the relationship was through.

I backed away with a peck on her cheek. She blinked in surprise, then said, "Thank you for your control. See, you're strong when I'm weak. You *can* lead us."

NOVEMBER 12

Recital, St. Paul

I sang some French and German songs that I have loved since college. I wanted to do so well. The audience leaned in as if they were all a little hard of hearing. Most looked courteous, hopeful. Others looked bored. The music seemed to evaporate right after leaving my lips.

They called me back for the mandatory Minnesota encore, an act of politeness. I didn't deserve one and they knew it, you could tell by the applause. Since I hadn't prepared an encore, I left my accompanist in the wings and went out alone to sing the only song I can always pull out of my hat.

> *Sweet chance, that led my steps abroad,*
> *Beyond the town, where wildflowers grow.*
> *A rainbow and a cuckoo,*
> *Lord, how rich and great the times are now!*

For just a second I wasn't the passive, frightened introvert whose life was so messed up. For just a second I stood in a

Montana campsite and John sat at a picnic table strewn with empty Coors cans. For just a second I was capable and strong. For just a second I let it rip.

>*Know, all ye sheep and cows, that keep on staring*
>*That I stand so long in grass that's wet from heavy rain,*
>*A rainbow, and a cuckoo's song*
>*May never come together again,*
>*May never come this side the tomb.*

Karen beamed in the front row. I was her hero. Dad looked damn perplexed there in the second row. What I was to him at that moment, I have no idea. But the applause hit me like a wave and I felt suddenly, utterly, embarrassed. Offstage, my pianist elbowed me.

"They want another, listen to them clap," she said.

I stepped in the door, nodded red-faced, then fled up the stairs three at a time.

At the reception afterward friends said wonderful words to me. I can't remember a single one of them. These from Dad are the only ones I recall:

"You should've sung something I could understand. Something, like, from *Fiddler on the Roof.*"

Later, as four bustly church ladies tried to one-up each other with compliments, he leaned into my ear, almost whispering.

"Don't get a big head."

Dear Andrew: November 14

You're my pastor, remember? I don't know what to do. I don't know who to tell. I've barely slept the last three nights and I'll cut straight to it here: I am a mistake to my own father.

I've been trying to get him to say something decent to me. Everything I've ever done, every recital I gave or career jump or this or that, it's all been a waste. He says nothing. My bike trip? That was supposed to *really* do the trick. I mean, an entire continent! It bombed.

Lately, I've had problems thinking straight. It's like I can read his thoughts. And I wish he would just come out with what I hear in my head—what a huge disappointment I am to him. My mind goes in and out of these fogs. In the clear times I see how Karen plays into the mess and how our relationship is little more than me trying to reach some state of holiness *through* her just to be acceptable in *his* eyes. But then the fog closes in again and I hear his voice say stuff like "Whatever you do, you're not acceptable." I really wish he would just come out with it.

In this fog, I have to blame somebody. Sometimes it's me: I'm worthless. But more and more it's all Dad's fault. I am a kid and he screwed up. He didn't love me. And so, I can't love Karen. And before her, I couldn't love Lili. I can't love anybody. I don't feel a thing for anyone. The only thing I feel is an assurance that I am bad and wrong.

Andrew, put this in a sermon if you want: Parents, bless your children. For heaven's sake, bless them.

Brian

NOVEMBER 29

This afternoon I came as close as I ever have to real madness. The sky was heavily overcast. It felt like a coffin lid slamming down on the house. I tried to read. I tried to cook. I tried to sleep. Only sleep took, but when I woke the clouds had come into the house to lie over me. I tried to breathe but they pressed on my chest. I tried to rise from the bed but they piled on deeper and deeper and threatened to push me into the ground. I ran across the street into the park. The clouds rolled toward me. I had to race from them. I heard them coming, sounding like an avalanche. The whole sky was falling. The long bare-armed trees waved and laughed at me and pointed to the sky and screeched, *November is falling, the frozen gray is falling, Chicken Little is falling, can't tell his Chicken Little friends that it's all falling, can't even cry to himself that everything is falling.*

I heard it. I had to race from it. I ran and ran and ran. And woke kneeling in the dirt next to the house. Snow woke me.

Flakes landing softly on the back of my neck. Beside me lay a bag of spring crocus bulbs that I only vaguely remember buying. I was planting crocuses, saying, "These will keep the sky up." Several bulbs were already in their holes. I'd been digging with my bare hands.

I looked up into the sky. The cinder-block gray stood safely above me. Flakes landed on my cheeks. They felt like tears.

The snow turned the dirt to mud. I was shaking from the cold but scraped the mud from my fingers and kept planting. When the bag was nearly empty I scraped my hands clean one last time and saw the puckered white scar in the left palm. And in an instant I was ten again, back on the farm, kneeling and crying in November mud.

It was the year of the corn blight, when kernels on the ear turned to gray-black mush and farm after farm went belly-up. That fall, Dad bought a truckload of clay tiling pipe to help the fields drain better and avoid future blight. He plowed a ditch down the middle of the field, then scavenged a rusted eaves trough from a shed roof and wired it to the back of the Oliver's seat. He asked me to help lay the tile. One early November afternoon, the sky overcast and the air raw with winter coming, we drove out to the ditch where he put the tractor in its lowest gear, the throttle barely off the peg. He set a section of tile at the top of the eaves trough behind him. It rattled down to me, walking behind. I picked it off and placed it in the ditch at my feet.

We worked all afternoon in the cold. I grabbed a tile, stooped, dropped it next to the preceding one, straightened, and grabbed a tile again. At dusk he turned the spotlights on. Its light was clean, with sharp edges. Frost started to sparkle at my feet. The soil got slippery. Mud began to cling to my gloves and soak through, so I stuffed them in my pockets. The clay pipe landed like bricks of ice in my hands, but we were almost done.

Just before the end of the field, he slid another one down. I reached for it, missed, slipped in the mud, and started to fall. I shot my left hand out and caught it palm down on a ragged corner of the trough. The tractor crawled forward, pulling my hand with it while my body stayed behind. In a fraction of a second the palm was ripped clean open.

The brakes squealed as soon as I screamed. I clamped my hand between my thighs and fell back into the corn leaves. Before I could let out another good one, Dad swung off the tractor and landed flat-footed in front of me. The look on his face. He grabbed my hand hard and pushed it palm up into the light. The gash was long and a brown puddle was forming, dripping onto the white of my wrist. He hacked up something deep from his throat, spat it to the ground, then wiped his mouth with his sleeve.

"Gotta get the germs out quick," he hollered over the engine.

He put his mouth right on it. He sucked the blood, then spat, spraying the leaves with wet crimson. He sucked and spat again. He put his tongue right into it, I could feel it under the flap of skin. He worked it up and down, sucked and spat. My father's tongue inside me, washing. I blushed and pulled back a bit. He sucked one good long last one, spat, and wiped his mouth with his sleeve.

"OK, put it here," he said, lifting my right arm up and sliding the hand into my armpit. Just before he placed it there, though, I saw it—the diagonal rip, garishly clean in the tractor lights, then the blood suddenly darkening the skin flap. "I think you're gonna live," he said, and smiled. He'd missed some blood on his chin.

He lifted me into the cab, sat himself down, pulled me between his legs, and laid one arm across my chest, the other on the steering wheel. The tractor lurched over rows of corn stubble before finding the smooth lane leading home. He shifted into road gear and I leaned back into his chest. The neighbor's corn dryer flame shone copper in the distance. I lifted my arm and saw the large darkening blotch in the cloth, and I could smell my father's sweat, the muddy cloth, and the blood. He laid his hand on my arm and pressed it down. The corn dryer flame flared blue, flopped on its side, and everything went black.

All the crocus bulbs lay in their holes. I covered them and pounded the earth firm with my fists. I scraped mud from the scar one last time. How white it was. I held the palm open and let snow fall on it. Snow covered my head and shoulders. Kneeling there in the mud—for the first time in months, maybe years—I let myself weep.

I remember his tongue inside my hand. The warmth in the bitter cold.

Dear Brian: December 1

I got your letter last week and received a letter from your father the same day. He and I have been trading letters all this fall. He is clearly searching for something he has never found. He confides in me and I am privileged that he does so. That you both do. His was a three-page letter, part of which was about you.

. . . sometimes I think you know my son better than I do. That's not easy to admit. Perhaps you encourage him more than I do. I may be copying my father who was by no means close to either me or my brother. But

that's no excuse. You have a great open heart that loves so much, so easily, and I understand why my son loves you dearly, and I join him. You probably see the man that he is, whereas I still see the boy. . . .

You both want the same thing, I think, and that is to know each other; to be with each other, yet in a way that honors each of you as individuals.

Without your permission, I sent him a copy of your letter to me. It so rattled him that he called me and said he had to see me right away.

We met two days later in the hospital cafeteria; people in the congregation here have had a spate of operations lately, and this was the first time I could squeeze in to meet him. We spent an hour and a half together. Over and over again, he asked what he was doing that was hurtful to you. He sees his intentions but not their impact on others. I challenged him to accept you as a different person, with a different view of life and with different gifts, and he with his, both God-given and precious. I think of my own sons and believe that in many cases it is harder for the father than for the son to do this.

He is on a spiritual search, and working so hard to gain the love of God that has already been given to him through grace. I sense so deeply about him that he wants something he hasn't found yet.

I expect you'll be hearing from him.

Andrew

DECEMBER 6

St. Paul

"Hello?"

"Brian, this is Dad."

"Uh, hi. What time is it?"

"About nine. Did I wake you up?"

"Not really. I was just lying here. I sleep in on Saturdays."

"Well, that's good."

"How are things?"

"Brian, I'm sitting here just bashed, not able to figure out what I've done to hurt you. And why you haven't been able to say these things to me."

"Uh."

I thought of lying. I could barely think through the grogginess of sleep. My first thought was to say something like "No problem, don't worry about it."

But when will we ever speak if not now?

"This is hard, Dad. I don't want to hit you with a bunch of

stuff, but there are some things. And we never talk about stuff like this."

"Like what?"

"Like, I don't know, a lot of things."

"Like what!"

"Like, I don't know. Like, after my recital. You didn't have one good thing to say. You just told me I should've done something from *Fiddler on the Roof*. I worked hard on those songs. They meant a lot to me, and to have you tell me, first thing afterward, about what I should've done . . . That's a small issue, but that's the kind of thing that comes first to mind. Other stuff, I don't know . . . I've just started thinking more and more about it since then, trying to remember a time when you *have* said something good about me, or *to* me. I really don't remember a time. There's been a lot of great stuff way back, and each time you say nothing or just tell me not to get a big head."

"Well, now, wait a minute," he said. "Sometimes I just don't know what to say, especially with a lot of others around who are saying nice things. So I say that to, well, just to have something to say. I'm just trying to be smart, I guess. But it doesn't mean that I don't think well of what you've done. Don't you know that?"

"I honestly don't know what to think."

"Brian"—his tone was softer—"that's just me trying to think of something clever to say."

"Well, Dad, I put all these clever things that you say together and place them up against hardly ever a good word and what do I have? Can you figure that out?"

There was a sniffle from the other end of the line, followed by a long silence. Then he was crying.

"I just don't ever want you to doubt my love for you."

I let his tears come, then subside. Probably a half minute passed.

"Is there anything," he said, "anything left that you have to say to me?"

Again I thought to lie. Maybe that'd been enough. But I'm never going to get another chance.

"There is another thing. It's my bike trip, this seems symbolic of the whole deal. I didn't realize it, really, at the time, but it came to me near the end. I remember I was only a few days from the coast and I called to tell you that I was almost done. I remember you said 'Make sure to call when you make it. Your mother will want to know that.' I was so hurt. It was like you didn't give a damn that I was out here doing this meaningful journey. It was then that I realized I was doing it for just that reason, to try to get you to say something, I don't know, something like you were proud of me. And when I came home, you didn't say a thing except that I was like a bad penny. That's been the biggest hurt of all."

Again came a wave of tears. Through them he stammered, "I just assumed you knew how terribly proud of you I was. I just thought you knew."

"How can I know? I can't read minds. Sometimes I need to hear the words. The plain words. That's all. When I get something else about how I shouldn't think too well of myself, that I'm bad—what am I supposed to think you think of me?"

Now I was crying.

"Do you know what that feels like to know your own father thinks you're a mistake?" I don't know if I meant it, but out it came anyway. Now I was yelling. "That he screwed up by having you? That he would just as soon wash his hands of you? Do you know?" Now we were both crying. I don't know for how long. Crying over the damn phone.

"Do you know how alike we are, Brian?"

"What do you mean?" I barked.

"You are just the same when you are twenty as when you are forty as when you are seventy, like me. My father, I can only recall him saying one good thing about me his whole life."

"You're kidding."

"It was after my first season raising turkeys here on the farm, I remember it was Thanksgiving time, business was finally going, and I had a sack of money to take up to the bank. I asked him to deposit it for me. He picked up the bag, I can still see him holding that bag. He kind of bounced it up and down, feeling how heavy it was, I guess. Then he said, 'You finally made it. You're doing all right.' That was it, the only time. I've never told that to anyone."

His voice started to wobble again. "That was all there was between him and me, so I thought the same with my kids. Do you know how alike you and I are?"

I could just see it. My father measured, literally, by the weight of dollars in his father's hand.

"That's just the way my father was, though. He was a good man."

"Dad, if you don't mind my saying so, that's bullshit. I can't imagine that if your father were to come back to you today, right now, and tell you how proud he was of you, how he thought you did a decent job raising four kids, how you kept a good farm — I can't imagine that those words wouldn't fall like water on a dry plant."

He lost it. For nearly a minute, there was nothing but unabashed sobbing. He wasn't Dad anymore. He was just one big untended scab suddenly scraped open. Eventually, he caught his breath and blew his nose. I was glad he hadn't launched into another heart attack.

"I guess that is something I thought was long gone."

"You never told that to anyone?"

"No," he said. "It just didn't seem important. My father was a good man. That's about all there is to tell."

"If you ever want to say more about it—"

"That's about all there is. Do you have anything else to say?"

There was no thought of lying now. I looked, really looked, but that was all. And all I needed to hear.

Dear Brian,   December 8

Well, the tests are finally done and the wise old men of the University of Washington are going to let me pass another semester. I'm at home with Mom now in Seattle and everything seems to be at a standstill, for the first time in months, so I thought I'd take pen in hand. A shitload of stuff has gone on and all fall I wanted to write you but never found the time.

I'll start with what happened after you took off from St. Mary, Montana. I turned north and ran into two lovelies at the Canadian border. Yvette and Monique were from France and they're in this little red MG convertible. They start talking to me. Before I know it they're inviting me up to their uncle's cabin in the mountains. The uncle is gone, so we spend the whole next day in his hot tub. The custom in France is topless. Would I object? They wanted me to come to Paris, but I took off the next day. This really happened, I swear.

Anyway, I came across this old guy on a single speed beater plastered in flower decals. He was heading to the Rainbow Convention, or the Rainbow People's Convention, something, I don't know . . . and he asked me if I wanted to come along. He kept saying "it's a real happening man . . . stretch your horizons man," so I thought what the hell.

They were up in this meadow in the mountains in Indian tee-pees and half the folks were naked. There was one guy there in an old school bus, with this big Rainbow painted on the side, and I'm not shitting you he must've had 65 or 70 bicycles stuffed inside and hanging off it. Said he just picks them out of Dumpsters or in garage sales, fixes them up and gives them away to whoever wants them. He even lives in the bus.

Lots of pot. LOTS of pot.

They were singing and dancing all night long. They offered me beans and rice and some nasty juice, some sort of papaya concoction or something. I was almost out of supplies so I took it.

I split before daylight. I wanted to make this one mountain pass that day, the last big one before I got to the flats, then on toward Seattle and Mom. It started to snow. The higher I got the faster snow fell. The rangers said they were going to close the pass. I started to feel queasy in the gut. I thought it might be altitude sickness. But I was up only about 5,500 feet. Then I remembered that juice and glop I'd eaten. I really started to feel sick. By the time I reached the top I felt kind of delirious, and I thought I was hearing snowflakes sizzle on my forehead. The rangers came by and closed the pass just after I started down the slope. There were times when I could barely see in front of me. I don't know if it was the blizzard or my head. I rode the brakes the whole way and tried not to pass out. My gut hurt so bad. I made it to this hotel at the bottom. I couldn't even hold myself up on the handlebars by then. I spent three days there. One of those days, the first one I think, is pretty much lost on me. I don't remember anything except waking up at 4:00, looking at my watch and not knowing whether it was day or night, then waking up again and the sheets were soaked and the watch still said 4:00, or it said it again, and I'd slept the whole day. Or night.

I finally made it home, but I must've still been a little delirious because I told my girlfriend about the hot tub. One thing led to another and she left a little after that.

This happened about the same time that my mother was getting together with somebody she's met through her church. He's nice. You look at him and you think his name is probably something like Ralph and sure enough, it is. He's a plumber and he's Mom's age and he treats her like gold. So last week, the day after Thanksgiving, I got a stepfather.

It's no small thing yours truly passed this semester. Next semester is the last, though, and that's the real reason I wanted to write. I graduate in June, then I'm going to ride the Canadian Rockies again. I want you to come. They're gorgeous, and the highways there are a lot wider than in the U.S. Rockies; they've all got a special lane off to the right just for bikers. We've *got* to do this, cross the Continental Divide a bunch of times back and forth. Let me know. I really want you to come.

Merry Christmas to you and to your girlfriend, too. Was her name Corinna? I hope you two are doing better than me and mine did. I imagine you are.

John

Dear John,   December 12

I just asked the boss for the time off from work. She said I won't get two months this time, more along the lines of two weeks like everybody else. But that's better than nothing, so just tell me when and where, and I'm there.

It seems you and I are leading kind of parallel lives. Maybe not exactly parallel but close. In terms of Karen, this fall, I've been trying to be—I don't really know what to call it—Christian Man or something. Once in a while I can do it but more and more the only thing I do is screw us both over with the effort. So now I get to break up with her. I almost envy you: a pair of topless French babes would make this a lot easier.

I'm glad you like your stepfather. When we rode last summer, I didn't ever really tell you how sorry I felt that you lost yours like you did. That must have been an un-believable shock, to watch him hit the floor like that. My own father and I have just turned a corner and I don't know what's ahead. It's a long story, and I'm sure you'll hear it all next summer. For now, I'm due home for Christmas and Dad and I may continue an important conversation or—more likely—never mention it again.

At any rate, I'm coming to the Rockies next summer. I'll need to buy a new bicycle and bags. Mine stayed in Maine. Yes, I made it to the Atlantic but that's a whole other story.

                                                    Brian

Dear Karen: December 13

I have been lying to you. This is the lie: that I love you and what we're doing together.

The whole thing. Your church. My "faith." The way we screw around with sex and Jesus.

It is all false. And if it isn't, then the mask I wear is.

I can justify it any number of ways I want but what it comes to is a lie.

The only thing left for me to do is to say how sorry I am and walk away.

Good-bye.
Brian

The phone rang at eleven o'clock the next night.

"Brian, this is Karen. I just want you to know you're making a big mistake. It really isn't even you that's making the mistake. It's Satan."

"Karen, no—"

"No, listen to me. You're wrong. Satan sees two Christians like us together and he feels our power. He can't stand that. He is the king of destruction and the father of all lies, and so he has to tear it apart. He loves to kill and that's what he's doing to you. To us. He's killing us. Are you going to let him?"

"Karen. That's the whole point. I told you, I've been the one who's lying. Not Satan. *Me.* Now I'm trying to be honest, and you think it's Satan. That's the whole point. I don't get the way you see God, or the way you see Satan. We can't go on. Don't you get it?"

The line was quiet for a while. Then she sniffled.

"Brian, don't leave," she said, barely above a whisper. "I'll pray for you. Give it some time, will you?"

"Please, whatever you do, don't pray for me. I'll just feel like a worse piece of shit than I already do. You've been praying all this time, and it hasn't taken. God will just tell you this is a big mistake. And maybe it is, for all I know. But I'm going nuts and it's just not working. Please, don't pray for me."

Neither of us said anything, and right then I should've hung up.

"Isn't Jesus your Lord and savior anymore?"

"I don't know. All I know is that you don't have a lock on Jesus. Nobody does. You think he's yours and you've got him all figured out, but you don't. You can't."

"Oh, Brian, Satan has you so hard in his grip."

"Karen, I'm sorry. I'm really sorry I've treated you wrongly and made you think I believe the same way you do. But I don't. So, this is it."

"Wait, can't we pray together? Over the phone, right now?"

"No. Please, no."

"So, then he's won. Satan's got you."

"Karen, good-bye."

Dear Mr. B. Newhouse: December 15

I am pleased to return to you these items, recovered from your bicycle which our records indicate was stolen on the night of Sept. 18 from the Richmond Jr.-Sr. High. On December 10 we discovered a garbage bag on the front steps of the station. It contained the items which we herewith enclose: your notebooks, camera, and saddlebags.

Attached to this garbage bag was a note which read "We didn't steal his bike, but we know who did. You'll get the bike back."

We will keep you apprised.

Village of Richmond
Police Dept.

Dear Mr. Newhouse: December 18

We are pleased to inform you that we have recovered
your bicycle, which our records indicate was stolen on
the night of Sept. 18 from the Richmond Jr.-Sr. High. It
was dismantled and delivered in garbage bags to the station steps last night. It appears to be complete. There
was a note attached to your handlebars which said
"Found." The case has been closed. We are pleased to
have been of service to you. You will receive the stolen
goods shortly.

    Merry Christmas!

Village of Richmond
Police Dept.

DECEMBER 21

The package from Maine arrived special delivery. The return address on the box was the preacher's house. The wheels were carefully taped to the bike frame, wadded newspapers protecting all the joints, and he'd even carved a block of wood to snug up the front forks. Taped to the handlebars was a card signed by the preacher and the police chief and dozens of school kids asking me to please come back to Richmond someday.

CHRISTMAS EVE

The farm

The station was wrapped in a blanket of flurries when my bus pulled in. I got out and pulled my bags from the hatch and turned toward the big Buick across the lot. Mother always comes along on the bus run, but tonight only Dad materialized out of the snow. I opened my arms to hug him. His elbows stayed clamped to his sides, only his forearms opened. We thumped backs.

"The snow's pretty heavy," I said. He pulled his seed-corn hat bill down and I couldn't see his face.

"Yes, quite heavy."

For the first ten miles home, snow streamed thick as swallows over the windshield and our conversation was mostly, I can't see a thing, I can't either. Then he turned onto a long stretch of east-west road and the snow blew with the car, and we could see fine. The conversation died. He turned the heater up a notch. A minute later he turned it down. In the dashboard light he looked frightened.

The entire family was crammed into Mother's kitchen when we arrived—a circus of nieces and nephews, brothers-in-law jawing about the Bears and the Packers, and sisters laying out a spread of sugar cookies they'd been working on since Labor Day—and Mother, as usual, had it choreographed down to the second. There was lefse fresh out of the oven, rubbery gray oysters rolling in the hot milk broth. She is amazing, all the balls she can keep in the air at once. Dad, surprisingly, stayed with us in the kitchen. He usually greets people and takes coats, then retreats to his favorite chair until it's time for him to carve the turkey or ham. Tonight he parked himself at the crowded kitchen table. Within seconds a granddaughter crawled into his lap with a picture book for him to read aloud.

The pastor called and asked in a panicked voice if I could sing "something, anything" at the midnight service because the choir director just called in with strep. I told him I would sing but I didn't know what.

As the family trooped in, Dad said, "I'd like to read us the New Testament. So we remember what this is all for." He thumbed open the frayed leather book near his plate.

"This is from Matthew, chapter two, verse eighteen. 'Now the birth of Jesus Christ took place in this way. When his mother Mary had been betrothed to Joseph . . .' "

He reads every Christmas Eve. Tonight I listened more to the voice than to the words. It's thinning as he ages, but it is still beautiful and musical. The grandchildren stayed with him for a few sentences, looking cherubic, then wheedled around to watch the tree lights and the presents. My brother's face is so hard to describe because, like my father's, his cheeks and forehead are tight from outdoor labor. I watched him look at Dad. He has that particular Norwegian way of showing the deepest attention and admiration by showing nothing. Mother smiled at me, then at Dad. She knew everything, of course, and will never mention it. She smiled at us both again.

Dad's head was tilted to the left like Reagan used to do. As the Gospel story drew on and Joseph "knew not Mary" until Jesus was born, I closed my eyes and saw Dad in that same position across nearly thirty years of memories. Someday I will reach over and shut the Bible on him. I won't slap it shut or yank it. I'll just lay a hand on it and lift it from his hands.

It's been long enough. We should talk now before we're gone. I hope I'll say something like, Let's put it away and just sit here and talk. He'll look up and be utterly shocked. Talk about what? he'll say.

Herod sent his soldiers to slaughter the innocents. The in-laws now stared at their Christmas plates, the best china. Mother laid a dish towel over the soup tureen to keep it hot. When Herod died, Jesus returned from Egypt and dwelt in a city called Nazareth, at which point Dad laid the book by his dessert plate and the meal began.

The pastor pumped my hand at the door and asked me what I was going to sing. I glanced through the bulletin; all the old carols were already taken by the congregation. I told him to just call it Special Music.

Our family filled a pew. The lights dimmed while the candles were lit. The congregation sang "Hark, the Herald" and "O Little Town of Bethlehem" while I flipped nervously through the hymnal. I couldn't find one I liked. The pastor called the children to join him on the altar steps for a children's sermon. I walked up the stairs in back to the balcony, still thumbing the hymnal.

"What are you hoping for this Christmas?" he asked the

children. Nervous titters. "A bike, a sled?" Then, "Do you know who God sent at Christmas time?" A little girl crowed, "Santa!" The congregation roared. The pastor tried to go on, but the girl kept calling "Santa" at random intervals. The pastor tried to talk but got laughing so hard that he had to stop.

I walked to the balcony railing and right then the perfect song dropped into my brain. The pastor, red-faced, waved for the ushers to come forward and collect the offering. The kids trotted noisily back to their pews, the little girl looking triumphant. The organ played and coins clinked into the plates, and Karen came to mind. The ushers handed the pastor the plates. He said a few words about special music and nodded in my direction. I hurried Karen out of my head. I stalled a few seconds by sliding the hymnal into a pew rack, then took a deep breath.

> *Some children see Him lily white,*
> *The Baby Jesus born this night,*
> *Some children see Him lily white,*
> *With tresses soft and fair.*
>
> *Some children see Him bronzed and brown,*
> *The Lord of heaven to earth come down;*
> *Some children see Him bronzed and brown,*
> *With dark and heavy hair.*
>
> *Some children see Him almond eyed,*
> *This Saviour whom we kneel beside,*
> *Some children see Him almond eyed,*
> *With skin of yellow hue.*
>
> *Some children see Him dark as they,*
> *Sweet Mary's Son to whom we pray;*
> *Some children see Him dark as they,*
> *And ah! they love Him too!*

The children in each different place
Will see the Baby Jesus' face
Like theirs, but bright with heavenly grace,
And filled with holy light.

O lay aside each earthly thing,
And with thy heart as offering,
Come worship now the Infant King,
'Tis love that's born tonight.

It's supposed to be a lullaby. I tried to sing it like that, but in the fifth verse Karen swung back into my head. It galls me what she asked of me. It galls me how I bought it for so long. That verse says it all: I see Jesus as I see him, you see him as you see him; let's not beat each other up over who's blind. The lines of that verse got louder and increasingly bitter. I even sang them over again, full-voiced, as if directly to Dad, as if to Karen.

The children in each different place
Will see the Baby Jesus' face
Like theirs, but bright with heavenly grace,
And filled with holy light.

They felt like a declaration, like bile spilling. I let a long stretch of silence settle in the church before the last verse, and tried to sing it sweetly again. When I finished, the only sounds were the tick and knock of the radiators.

After the service, family friends slapped my back and said the song was real pretty. Dad smiled but stood off at a distance, then put his coat on and got the car warmed up.

CHRISTMAS DAY

The whole family returned to the farmhouse for Swedish tea ring and cookies and presents and a fire in the fireplace and enough Christmas to stuff us until next year. When they'd all gone, Dad asked me if I'd follow him out to the back room.

"In the event your mother and I should, you know, die, we want you to know where some things are around here. Your brother is the executor of our estate but you should know, too."

He opened the closet where the tall gray filing cabinet stands. The death tour. It seemed odd—I mean Christmas Day and all. But you never know with Dad; this was his way of confiding trust, I guess. I liked it.

"Up here are all the old tax records," he said and opened the top drawer. "The years are all laid out." He flipped through a row of manila envelopes, one for each year back to 1965. "Behind them are the receipts for tractors and machinery.

"The second drawer is mostly manuals. If the stove breaks or a gear goes on the auger, you can pretty much find the right book in here.

"Down here in the bottom is all the paperwork." He pulled the drawer all the way out. It smelled of an old library. More thick manila envelopes, their edges worn thin or frayed. "The deeds to this farm, and the land out in North Dakota. This book has all the phone numbers to call, the bank, the tenants, the lawyer, and the accountant."

From the back of the drawer he lifted a shallow black wooden box and set it on the floor, then thumbed through more envelopes.

"What's that?"

"That?" he said, "An old flute." He stuck his arm deep in the drawer to pull out more envelopes.

"A flute. You don't play flute."

"Your grandfather did."

"He had a flute?"

"When he was a kid, he got it for school. I've always kept it."

"Do you play it?"

He withdrew his arm and looked down at the box. "I've tried to blow through it a time or two but I'm no flute player."

"Can I see it?"

The box was dusty and chipped at the edges. The tiny silver lock was broken open. A wizened old rubber band held the lid shut and when Dad slid a thumb under it, it snapped. He opened the box and smells of time rose out of it. The instrument lay in three pieces. It was black wood, its finger holes worn smooth and shiny, its silver keys tarnished. The cork sleeves were cracked. I tried to fit the pieces together but the cork crumbled and jammed. I looked down each barrel for a name or date.

"When did he play it?"

"He and Mother used to sit down at the piano some nights when I was small."

"Was he good?"

He laughed. "I suppose he was. It was a long time ago. I don't really remember."

I laid the pieces back in the box and rubbed the smooth black wood. I pressed the keys down; some clicked easily, others stuck. Grandfather—dead six years before I was born; large-eared, white-haired, imposing in the Polaroids—was suddenly a person. For years, all I've known of him was that he was a lawyer, a pretty hard-assed one at that, and more recently that he'd said almost nothing in the way of approval to his son. But he played the flute. He made music. He might as well have sat up in his coffin.

"I can't picture it, Dad. I mean, a lawyer, yes, but not a flute player."

"Well, he was both."

"What did he sound like?"

"I was little back then. It was just something he did. Then, after a while, he stopped."

"Why?"

"He just stopped. Why in the world are you so interested?"

I turned the pieces end over end and still couldn't find a maker's name or any date. "Can I take it and get it fixed? It's in rough shape and I know a good shop in St. Paul. They could recork it and unstick these keys. Maybe see if a person could play it again."

He laughed. "But what for?"

"I don't know. Grandfather played the flute. We should keep it in decent shape." I was floundering. I couldn't put my finger on what this thing suddenly meant to me.

"It seems like a silly idea to me but if you really want to, go
ahead. It's not doing anybody any good in that drawer."

The fields were impossible to look at on the way to
the Greyhound station. Fresh snow and the noon sun threw a
blinding glare into the Buick. Dad drove with one hand on the
wheel while the other shaded his eyes. The box lay between us
on the seat.

"Do you remember any particular songs he played?"

"I don't. I remember now that he said he used to play in
the town band, but he quit when my brother and I came along.
Then, like I said, it was just with Mother some nights when he
had time. Then he stopped altogether. For most of his life, far
as I know, it's sat in that box. I really don't understand why
you're so interested."

I opened the box. "I can't imagine a man that hard, playing
a flute. I mean, a flute? It just doesn't fit with the picture I've
got of him."

"He wasn't that hard. He was a good man."

Dad's eyes were barely slits in the bright light. I wanted to
say something like, Come on, the man said only one decent
thing in his whole life to you; I wanted to pick open the scab
again.

"It's just a flute," Dad said.

We neared town. Light blazed into the car. He laid both
hands on the wheel and squinted hard.

He said, "You know your singing the other night?"

"At church?"

"Yes. Well, you sing real fine. I wish I could do as well. Your
mother and I are real proud of you, you know."

He leaned forward and gripped the wheel as if landing a

plane in a stiff cross wind. I felt my cheeks warm and could only look at my lap.

"Thanks. Thanks. That means a lot."

"Well. You should know, is all."

We hugged good-bye at the bus station. It was slightly longer than usual. His elbows weren't clamped so hard to his ribs. Then he pulled the brim of his hat down low to shade his eyes and drove off.

MARCH 16

The repairman wasn't able to fix the lock, or locate a date or maker's name anywhere, but two weeks later the flute was recorked and its keys shone like mirrors. For most of the winter, I blew and blew through the thing but could only get the sound of my own breath out of it.

I've offered to return the flute to Dad, but he says, "No, you keep it. It seems to mean more to you than me." It lies on my piano now and sometimes when I'm practicing my singing I stop and open the battered black box and press a few keys down. I've asked Dad to tell me more about his father, but he only tells me benign or faintly complimentary stories of the old man. This instrument says more to me. It says Dad didn't pull his fathering skills out of thin air. It says my craving a good word from him is identical to his own craving; and the desire we each feel stems back to Grandfather's grandfather and to *his* father and to all the men who left their sons to be raised by their wives. Blame lies with all of them. And with none of them. It was what they knew to do.

The flute is now an heirloom. I've declared it so. An unintended gift from a grandfather I never knew, through the father who most days seems similarly unknowable. My children, if hell ever freezes over and I meet a woman compatible enough to create them with, will get it. And they will never have to wonder, never have to practically kill themselves to find out, if their old man loved them.

The crocus bulbs I planted in desperation last November are pushing aside the snow on this warm March day. Spring starts next week.

MAY 31

MEMORIAL DAY

The farm

Up on the hilltop cemetery above the farm. Every year on this day our whole family meets to tend the tall white pillar. We clip the grass, plant a few geraniums, try to wiggle the pillar to judge how long till it falls out. It barely budges. The nieces and nephews play leapfrog on the shorter tombstones. The mothers get after them, the fathers say, "Oh, let them be."

An hour before, at the lunch table, Dad and I had gotten into a "discussion" about the Holy Spirit. Was the Spirit a real spirit, like a wind (which is my opinion); or was it more like a person (Dad's, plainly explained to me with several helpful biblical references)? It started out fine but got louder and more emphatic until we had to go to neutral corners. He thinks I'll burn in hell. I think he's crazy.

But now the Memorial Day duty is done and it's time to go. Only Mother, he, and I are left. We stand near our cars—they will drive a mile to the farm, and I, five hours to Minnesota. Mom's putting the tools into their trunk.

"Corn looks good, doesn't it?" Dad says.

I say, "I thought it was supposed to be knee high by the Fourth of July? It's already almost that."

He laughs a little and looks proudly down the hill. Then he drapes his arm across my shoulder. He chats for a minute about this and that, corn mostly, and I don't know whether I want him to take his arm away right now or leave it resting warm across my shoulder forever. He kisses my neck, once, very quickly, and with a casual wave gets into the car, not looking back.

EPILOGUE

JULY 28

The farm

"And the spaceship was all burnt to bits, but somehow we made it home. I walked along this incredible hall. It was wild, there was no building there, just this beautiful sky, yet I knew it was home."

I was in my parents' home. One year after the trip. High humid summer had settled in Illinois and the cicadas were singing at midday. Their screen porch sat in the middle of that lovely heat, swamped in green and scented faintly by the neighbor's pigs. My bicycle and bags were packed in the car. I'd stopped at the farm to say good-bye; that night I was driving to O'Hare, and flying to meet John in Vancouver. From there, he and I would dive headfirst into the Rockies.

Lunch was done and we leaned on elbows at the table. Somehow we'd gotten onto memorable dreams. Theirs had all been about trains, a thunderstorm, seeing my grandmother again, the normal weirdnesses of dreams; but mine was about a spaceship and a man who grows into a child.

267

"At the end of the sky hallway was a chair on some steps and as I walked toward it I began to grow younger. All the wounds on my arms and legs began to heal. The uniform just fluttered away and by the time I reached the steps I was a toddler. I looked up and you were in the throne."

Dad had had his gaze across Flander's beans and up the long hill to their house. But now he turned and gave me his whole face.

"You were sitting there and I climbed up into your lap. You took me in your arms. And all of a sudden I was an adult, but still in this child's body, and I started to cry and cry."

His eyes were so wide—gray-blue, the color of old glacier ice.

"I sat in your lap and cried for I don't know how long. It felt so good, Dad. Such a release. And you didn't say anything, which was fine, but just held me until I stopped. It was the most vivid dream I've ever had."

My cornfield family. They just sat there. And the cicadas sang on.

"Well, that was sure something," Ma said, and straightened her napkin. Tears filled her eyes, and my sister's. Dad blinked at me, then sniffed. Ma began to clear dishes and my sister practically jumped up to help. Normally Dad does them—the only farmer I know who always does all the dishes, every meal—but he stared up to Flander's farm again until the table was empty and he and I were alone. A pig feeder clunked. His elbows were on the table still, his chin in his hands.

"I suppose that means you've wanted something special from me," he said after several minutes. "Something that you feel you've missed somehow. Something I haven't given you." His shoulders sagged. He looked at his hands.

What was I supposed to say? Yeah, you're right, you were a rotten father and you screwed me up? That wasn't right. Neither was No, you were great, no problem. At that moment I wasn't sure what it meant myself. And Dad is not one with whom you brainstorm about dream interpretation.

"I don't know," I said. "All I know is it felt so good to cry in your lap like that. Tell you everything that'd gone wrong and that I'd done wrong. And how it all hurt. Other than that, I honestly don't know."

We said nothing until it was plainly time for two men from an Illinois farm not to sit in silence anymore. He walked out to the shop.

Hours later, the women and I sat at the kitchen table. The sun was on full steam and we passed lemonade around. We talked the talk at which my family excels, pleasant and factual and none too important. Summer banter. And suddenly Dad was at the kitchen counter. Sweat dripped from him, and his face was flushed and worried.

"What's wrong, Bill?" Mother said.

"Me? Oh, nothing." He gave a little laugh and looked embarrassed. He stepped to the sink and said, "Getting hot out there." He washed then bent down to his cupped hand under the faucet and took a long drink. Our chat at the table started up again.

Hands dried, he returned to the counter, only this time he looked plainly frightened. My father, always invincible, now afraid. He blurted, right at me:

"It hasn't been all bad, has it? I mean, not *all* of it, has it?"

How quiet the kitchen fell. It was embarrassing, spectators; but in a family that never speaks its heart—now was as good a time as any.

"No it wasn't at all. There were lots of good times too, Dad.

I remember the canoe rides we took. You played tag with us and things like that. And if we hadn't had times like that and if you'd been abusive or mean, which you weren't, I'd be in therapy for the rest of my life. I guess I just wanted more, that's all. But thank God we had those other times. And that makes all the difference to me. You gave me what you could."

"Yes. Well." He looked at the counter, lost for a second. "Mother," he raised his eyes, "where are those pictures from that canoe trip? You know the one, that Christmas picture we sent out that year."

In the photo, his two sons squat next to that old turquoise tub, the autumn sun low in our faces, the brown river behind us. I look so happy. This is my favorite of all.

Years of pictures got spread onto the kitchen table. There I am with braces; there with the black-and-blue welt in the middle of my forehead from having fallen on my way to the photographer's; there's Mother just out of high school, a dead ringer for Vivian Leigh, posed looking back over her shoulder; and Dad, my favorite of him, buck naked and twenty, the devil in his eye, holding a big catalpa leaf waist high on a summer's day as hot as this one. We wallowed in these, our family history, the richness of it, the variety, stories piled one on top of the other.

Hours later, I sat on the couch going over the last of the pictures, stalling before the long drive to O'Hare. Dad plunked heavily onto the couch right next to me. He wiped at the garden dirt on his knees, still looking genuinely scared.

"Was it all bad?" he asked.

I looked at all the photos on my lap, the years spread out like movie scenes—the good and bad, but more than anything the good—then set them down and laid my hand on his leg.

"There were some very . . . very . . . good . . . times."

They seemed to sink in, both the words and the touch.

But packing the car, minutes later, he couldn't look at me. I went back and forth through the garage to get our bags and Dad got busy with a broom; now was the time the garage floor needed sweeping. A very thorough sweeping. He pushed little piles of dirt to the door, then gave them a good heave-ho into the yard. He stamped the broom twice and pushed smaller piles of dirt behind him in exactly measured jerks. Another stamp of the broom, then the last bits. He didn't miss a speck.

Normally, a few misty eyes are a part of our farmyard good-byes. But today, my sister's and mother's eyes filled up and spilled over. We all knew. Though none of us most likely will ever speak of what happened this afternoon again. We all knew.

A hug for Mom, one for my sister, too. Dad had stayed busy with the broom, but now he stood a few feet from the others and gripped the handle in front of him so hard his knuckles whitened. He looked like the farmer in Grant Wood's *American Gothic,* except Dad held that broom handle right in front of his nose.

"Good-bye, Dad."

I raised my arms to hug him and his arms opened too, hesitantly at first, but wider as I moved into him. Our cheeks met and I heard the dry crack of the broom as it fell onto the driveway gravel. His arms were wrapped all the way around me. He was shaking. Tears and the stubble of his cheek rubbed against my own. We didn't let go.

"Thank you," he said. "Oh, thank you."

The sun lay on the horizon as I parked the car and walked up the hill to the white pillar to trace once again our family's names. Neri, Christina, Infant, every year those scratches get more blurred. Our barn back down the hill glowed again in the rich green like a drop of blood. I felt the generations wave back and forth at each other—those of us on this hill and those down there on our farm—waving as tall corn waves in a summer wind. The sun edged below the horizon, the green deepened, and I walked back down the hill to begin.